AN OXFORD MURDER

A Golden Age Mystery

G.G. VANDAGRIFF

For my daughter
Elizabeth Faith Vandagriff Bailey
Who shares my love of Golden Age Mysteries

Chapter One

Summer, 1934

Until Catherine saw the lifeless hand flung out from beneath the pew, she had thought she was on a fool's errand. After all, who expects to find a dead body in the new chapel after an Oxford sherry party?

For half a minute, she simply stared as though she were observing a bizarre photograph: Short, thick hand. A bit of a rash—eczema? Unvarnished, clipped fingernails. Dead still. Yes. It might be Professor Agatha Chenowith's hand.

Biting her lip, she bent over and shone her torch under the bench. Bulging, sightless eyes stared out at her. Catherine dropped the torch and emitted a high, thin scream that sounded like nothing on earth as it echoed through the chapel. She couldn't seem to stop.

Tears were streaming down her face when Dr. Harry reached her side. His eyes followed Catherine's pointing finger, and he recoiled.

"That's torn it," he said. "Steady on. You're going to be all right. It's not every day someone discovers something so gruesome."

* * *

As Catherine sat in the Somerville College porter's lodge downing endless cups of tea, she looked back and wondered how an innocent invitation to Dr. Sarah Sargent's retirement party could have heralded a murder.

She and Dot had thought it would be a bit of fun to motor up to Oxford for a high summer weekend—a chance to see Anne and Margery and perhaps go for a punt on the Cherwell. And, of course, they would attend the summer choral service at Christ Church Cathedral.

Instead, she was in the thick of a murder investigation with the arrogant Dr. Harry Bascombe, her bête noire. And Rafe was due home from Africa in a few days. But then, these things were only trivial concerns. Poor Dr. Chenowith was dead.

Two Weeks Earlier

When her maid brought her the post, Catherine was seated at the desk in the sitting room of her Mayfair flat trying to coax forth a new poem. Her muse was not cooperating, and she had spent the last few minutes staring at her photo of Rafe—the high cheek boned face with the full, sensuous mouth and heavy-lidded eyes.

Now she turned it face down hiding her hapless composition underneath it. Her maid was a little too interested in her poetic efforts and inclined to offer suggestions.

"The usual, miss, but there are two I thought might be interesting. I put them on top."

"Thank you, Cherry," she said, taking the envelopes from the salver.

The two items were of interest—a white square that looked to be an invitation and a letter from her publishers. Heart thumping, Catherine opened the letter first.

Dear Miss Tregowyn:

We are happy to inform you that we will be pleased to publish your latest book of poems entitled Harvesting the Light . . .

Reading through the rest of the letter only cursorily, Catherine tried to still her shaking hands. So, the first book had not been a fluke! She was, in actual fact, a real poet, not a passing phenomenon. A thing so rare, she still marveled at it.

She leaped to her feet and performed an impromptu dance step in front of the hearth. What news! She must ring Dot.

First, she forced herself to investigate the other item—an invitation to a farewell dinner for Dr. Sarah Sargent, her former tutor and academic advisor at Somerville College, Oxford.

She came back down to earth. Oxford meant Dr. Harry Bascombe—the fly in her personal ointment. He would surely be at the dinner for his colleague as they were close associates. He taught modern British poetry at Christ Church.

Catherine was greatly indebted to her former tutor and would be happy to celebrate this event with her, but Dr. Harry with his Douglas Fairbanks mustache and piratical aura was another matter. His weighty review of her work could be summed up in one damaging, haunting word—*derivative*. The criticism had cut deeply.

But what had she expected from him? She knew how he scorned her.

She checked her datebook, hoping for a conflicting engagement, but she was free that evening. Her palms grew damp. What would she wear? Did she own anything that didn't make her appear a frivolous debutante?

She took a deep breath. Perhaps there was time to order something new. Something more sophisticated to give her confidence.

Catherine rang her dressmaker and made an appointment for the following morning. Then she called Dot.

"Did you get an invitation to the dinner for Dr. Sargent?"

"I did. Sounds smashing. Shall we motor up together?"

"By all means," said Catherine. "Care to come to Madame Devereaux's with me tomorrow? For some reason, I feel I have to have a new gown."

Dot laughed. "He wouldn't happen to have a mustache, would he?"

"Dr. Harry has nothing to do with it," she protested. "I got notification from my publisher today. They've offered me a new contract. I'm going to celebrate with a new frock so I look smashing and unassailable."

"Congratulations! Spiffing! But wouldn't a glass of wine be less expensive?"

* * *

Her friend expanded on her theme the next day as they took a cab to Madame Devereaux's.

"Jolly good news about the poetry," she said. "I'll be certain to mention it in Dr. Harry's hearing at the dinner. But, Cat, why do you care so much what he thinks?"

"He still prefers to think of me as a spoiled rich girl of no account."

"That's his loss. You crushed his ego. The worst thing a woman, particularly a scholarly woman, can do to a man. You bested him at his own game, and everybody knows it. I'm sure Christ Church College wasn't too pleased that you published such a revealing new biography about a poet Dr. Harry considers to be his own private property and unearthed inferences he overlooked." She laughed. "Not that I would deny you any excuse for a new frock," she continued. "You should look triumphant and on the rise."

Dot herself was a shortish redhead with a curvier figure than was presently in vogue and envied Catherine's long, lean look. But being five foot, seven inches in a world where most women were five foot five or under made her feel that she was of Amazonian proportions, and Catherine disliked her height intensely. Except when she was at her dressmaker's.

Madame Devereaux made much of her, seating them with demi-tasse cups of coffee and an assortment of pastries. "Mademoiselle Catherine, I have designed a new gown in black that would suit you perfectly. It will bring the gentlemen to their knees."

When the mannequin glided out to show the new creation, it took Catherine's breath away. Backless to the waist, except for a high Mandarin collar encircling the neck, it was fitted to the knees and flared out from there. The shoulders were bare.

"Oh! I couldn't possibly wear that to an *Oxford* function," Catherine said with regret. "Perhaps I did not properly explain myself, Madame. I need something *tres sérieux*."

The little woman showed a pout. "It will be a great loss." She beckoned to the next mannequin who modeled a closely fitted black silk gown with a square neck and a gathered voile overlay that made her appear as though she were moving through a cloud. Both elegant and serious.

"That is perfect!" said Catherine and Dot together. "And you can have it ready by a week from Thursday? I shall be leaving that Friday morning."

"*Mais oui.* And you have the sable fur? The one with the high collar that so matches your hair? This you must wear with the dress."

"Of course," Catherine agreed.

The two friends headed for luncheon at the Savoy.

Over Dover sole fillets Dot said, "Somerville won't seem the same after Dr. Sargent leaves."

"She really is too young to retire," said Catherine.

"They will be after you again, now that there are such big shoes to fill."

"I'm sure Dr. Sargent's replacement has already been selected. Besides, I don't want to hide myself away at Oxford, tempting as that sometimes seems. I prefer London or even Cornwall."

"Why is that? I thought you loved university life."

"Every little academic incident is blown up into huge proportions. A single paragraph or even a word can cause a tectonic shift."

"Yes, I see what you mean," said Dot. "But every position has the potential to be that way. My advertising firm can be a very small and exceedingly mean little world sometimes."

"Give me my little chaps in the East End any day," said Catherine. "They are just as they seem to be and proud of it." She lifted her wine glass, "Here's hoping everything at Somerville will be and will remain friendly."

"And non-tectonic," said Dot. "Now, we have given enough of our attention to Dr. Harry today. Tell me how you are feeling about Rafe's homecoming."

Catherine's stomach clenched like a fist.

"I don't know," she said.

"Has William written anything about how he is doing?" Dot asked, referring to Catherine's brother.

"William says he is in terrific form. But who knows if it will last?" asked Catherine.

* * *

When the two women set out in Dot's motor for the City of Dreaming Spires, a fine mizzle cleared up nicely during the drive. The fickle summer sun shone. How would Rafe feel about the misty English weather after the heat of Kenya?

"Perhaps, if the weather holds, we shall be able to go punting on the Cherwell," said Dot.

"Admirable plan. Let's just get settled in our digs and swing by Blackwell's first."

"If I let you inside that bookstore, you won't be out before we have to dress for dinner!"

Catherine chuckled. "I cannot come to Oxford without going to Blackwell's. Given the choice, I would far rather miss the dinner."

The initial prospect of Oxford as they crested the last hill and looked out over the valley always thrilled Catherine. Today it was clear, and no mist shrouded the much-loved spires, but the sight was still fantastical. It always amazed her from this vantage point how lacy and whimsical stone towers could appear.

Plus, there was that elusive atmosphere that came with the knowledge that learning had been going on in this spot since the thirteenth century. Oxford had a soul that inspired dreams and discoveries, launched great intellects and served as the seat of both rational and heated debate.

They negotiated the busy streets, dodging motors, omnibuses, and bicycles, finally arriving at Somerville. The porter (new since their day) handed them keys to their rooms. There was also a note from Dr. Sargent inviting them to sherry in the Senior Commons Room at seven o'clock before they would all travel together to The Mitre for dinner.

Catherine and Dot had rooms near one another in their old dormitory and were happy to see their favorite scout, Jennie. The woman must be in her sixties now, Catherine surmised, but though her hair had gone white, she was vigorous as ever.

"That happy I am to see you girls," said Jennie with her big smile. "I'll be your scout, of course. Couldn't give that job to anyone else. There's tea being served now in the Senior Commons Room if that suits you."

"A cup of tea sounds perfect," said Catherine. After removing her hat and washing her hands, she looked in the mirror to smooth her freshly waved dark brown hair. Her large brown eyes looked back at her out of a heart-shaped face. She would do. Joining Dot, she went downstairs.

The first person to greet them was Anne Tomlinson, another Old Girl with platinum hair that she wore a la Jean Harlow. It was hard to remember she was the mother of twins and that her name was now Stuart.

"Cat! Dot! I was hoping you would be here!" Catherine's heart warmed at the greeting from her friend.

"Anne!" exclaimed Dot. "How are your twins? And how do you manage to appear so glam?"

Their friend tittered. "I have a marvelous hairdresser. And the twins are never still. They managed to cover me in marmalade just as I was leaving. I had to change every stitch!"

Margery Ackerman, now Lady Margery Wallinghouse, walked over to them, teacup in hand. She practically jingled with gold bangles and chains about her neck. "My dears!" she said. "So happy to see you."

In fact, Catherine was somewhat surprised by Margery's presence.

"You are looking splendid," said Catherine. Leaning closer, she whispered, "It is magnanimous of you to come."

Margery wrinkled her short nose. "One can't hold onto a grudge forever," she said.

"Dr. Chenowith will be happy to see you, I'm sure," Catherine said in a normal tone. She was one of the few who knew that the acerbic don's public criticism of Margery's work had cost her a publishing contract.

"I'm actually hoping she won't be here—that she'll be hobnobbing with Virginia Woolf et al. this weekend."

At that moment, Dr. Sargent, the guest of honor, virtually flew into the room, her black gown billowing behind her. "Oh! Tomlinson! Ackerman! Tregowyn and Nichols! So good of all of you to come! It's lovely to see the Old Girls together again. Tutoring you women was my greatest joy!"

"We are protesting," said Dot. "We are going to block the entrance of The Mitre with our bodies. None of us thinks you are old enough to retire."

The don laughed. "Nichols, still up to mischief, I see. You shall pour me out a cup of tea."

"Two sugars?" Dot asked.

"You remembered! Yes."

Catherine asked, "Who else have you invited?"

"Well, tonight there will be my corresponding dons from some of the men's colleges, the Warden and the Dean, of course."

"No other Old Girls?" Catherine asked, puzzled.

"I didn't wish to be exclusive. I couldn't invite some from a class and not all, so I simply chose all my girls from one year, and your year was my favorite."

"Well now," said Anne. "Isn't that lovely."

"Some other Somerville dons will be joining us, of course. I think it is going to be a good group, all in all. We'll certainly fill the private room at The Mitre."

Catherine smiled at her tutor. "It sounds like a stimulating evening for certain."

The women began to chatter and catch up on one another's lives. Catherine told Dr. Sargent about her new poetry publication.

"My dear, I shall be certain to announce it this evening. I am so pleased. We shall drink to its success."

* * *

Dot and Catherine spent the rest of the afternoon walking through Oxford, enjoying memories. The sun on the Cotswold stone of the colleges threw everything into a glowing golden light. Catherine inhaled the indefinable sweetish scent she always associated with the city. They enjoyed the display of purple and red summer flowers and listened to all the college chapel bells ringing in the hours.

Of course, they did visit the labyrinthian Blackwell's bookstore where Catherine checked to see whether Dr. Harry Bascombe had any new publications. He did have one about a minor Victorian poet which she purchased to keep abreast of his scholarship.

Dr. Harry was one of that rare breed of men found in colleges who seemed to care little for material things and lived for their work. Before their falling out, she had admired him tremendously and felt honored that he took an interest in her work on the Victorian female poets.

If she were honest with herself, she knew that it irked him that she, who had wealth to spare and only an undergraduate education, should have made such an academic coup with her first book, *Life of Edith Penwyth*. As with many things in scholastic life, a bit of luck had been involved. She had grown up a stone's throw from the reclusive Penwyth's cottage and had known the old lady when she was a girl. The poet's sister had been only too glad to hand over all her papers and journals to a woman poet she knew as well as she did Catherine, instead of the irritating men who constantly besieged her.

She didn't blame Dr. Harry for his feelings, really. She just wished he could get over them. Surely an undergraduate's publication coup couldn't truly have been a setback for his career at Christ Church?

Stopping by the Music Room on Holywell Street, she and Cat bought tickets to hear a selection of Chopin etudes being performed there on Saturday evening. As a student, she had fairly haunted the place.

The sun felt good on their backs, as they retraced their steps back to Somerville. When they passed the Ashmolean Museum, they spent their last free half-hour enjoying an exhibit of Egyptian antiquities.

As she lay on her bed before she had to rouse herself and bathe, Catherine could not help but feel a worm of anxiety in her middle about the evening ahead. Had she known what they were really facing, this dread would have paled by comparison.

Chapter Two

The evening started well enough. The male dons had arrived for their sherry before Catherine came down to the Senior Commons Room. Dr. Wesley Williams of Balliol College, one of her favorite professors, was enlightening everyone in his circle about a new discovery. In Iceland, a pre-Christian Teutonic document had been found that added to the mighty legend of Wotan, the supreme god of ancient lore. She joined his circle and was happy to see that he hadn't aged in the last three years. Slim and fair, his blue eyes still held their lively gleam as he talked about the conference he would attend in Germany next month. He would be able to examine the newly discovered document at that time.

The Somerville Dean, Dr. Andrews, a scholar of early pre-Christian writings, was very interested. "I hear there are some new things being discovered in northern Norway, as well," she said.

"Yes." Dr. Williams preened himself. "That is actually my Balliol team. They have managed to track down a source of oral Teutonic legends that are still being passed down there. Something like Fairy Tales."

Catherine shivered. "I always hated German Fairy Tales. They were so brutal."

"They are of ancient derivation, as I'm sure you know. Justice was untempered by mercy in those days," said Professor Williams.

He began to expound. As Catherine listened, the back of her neck prickled, telling her that someone was watching her. Catherine turned and casually walked to another conversation group. Dr. Harry Bascombe had arrived, resplendent in evening dress, and was studying her. He always looked as though he should have a golden earring, and never more so than when she caught him observing her.

She smiled a bit in his direction, and he walked to her side. "I understand congratulations are due you," he said. "Another book of poetry."

Catherine felt herself blush, and she became automatically tongue-tied. "Yes."

"I hope these aren't so wholly imitative as your last offering." He gave her a wry smile.

Anger rescued her. "I am aware that anything I write would fail to please you."

"You are fortunate, indeed, that the public doesn't share my prejudice. I understand your first volume did very well."

"It did, as a matter of fact. And Professor Charleston of Cambridge gave it a glowing review. Perhaps you saw it."

He looked her up and down and smiled. All he was missing was a gold incisor. "That's a smashing frock. You look very well this evening."

"I would thank you," she said, "but I don't imagine you meant it."

She turned to join Dot in another group when he took hold of her arm. "Must we quarrel?"

"Yes," she said. "I'm afraid we must."

Dot was conversing with Dr. Agatha Chenowith who would have been pretty but for protruding teeth. She was a small woman with blonde hair she refused to cut, wearing it in a coronet about her head. The college celebrity, she was exceedingly difficult to please. She had taught Catherine much of what she knew about modern poetry. It was she who knew Virginia Woolf and was associated with her exclusive Bohemian Bloomsbury set. Dr.

Chenowith had published three successful volumes of modern verse.

She smiled brightly at the sight of Catherine. "Miss Tregowyn! Congratulations on a splendid book of poetry. I enjoyed it greatly. Well executed."

Catherine, who had been holding her breath, was greatly relieved. Sometimes, as now, the woman who wrote the poetry seemed wholly disconnected to Catherine Tregowyn of her daily life. "Your praise means a lot to me," she said. "Thank you."

"Would you care to do a reading?" she asked. "I should like you to come to my group in Bloomsbury as my guest. We do readings on Wednesdays."

The invitation overwhelmed Catherine. Though she had taken classes in it, the oral interpretation of poetry was not her strong suit. But perhaps she could arrange some private sessions with Dr. Sargent. She needed to make an effort with her new book coming out.

"That would be splendid. Thank you very much. I am honored that you would invite me."

"A talent such as yours should be shared."

A sudden wave of sympathy for her friend Margery Ackerman swept over her. What that woman wouldn't give to hear those words from Dr. Chenowith! Her review of Margery's poetry had been scathing, and the withdrawal of the contract by the publisher had been a terrible blow. Margery's new husband, Sir Herbert Wallinghouse, had even initiated a lawsuit.

The small, neat Dr. Stephenson of Merton approached her, and she knew what he was going to ask.

"Oh, Dr. Stephenson, I am so sorry! I haven't read your proofs yet!" The man had given her an advance readers copy of his new book of Victorian poetry. He was something of a legend at Oxford having penned the iconic undergraduate text *The Art of Poetry,* and he was just now publishing his own verse for the first time. He had asked Catherine to do a review for him.

The little man smiled. "I still have a week or so before the reviews need to be in. Do you think you'll have time before then?"

"I'll make time," she said. "I promise. I am very flattered that you would ask me to do it."

The man gave a smooth bow of his well-barbered head and then moved off to speak to Dr. Chenowith. Catherine concentrated on imprinting his request on her brain. It wouldn't do to forget.

Then Anne Tomlinson came up to talk about Catherine's new poetry collection, and she thought no more about her promise that evening.

* * *

Cabs were organized to carry the group to The Mitre on the High Street. She climbed into one of several awaiting on Little Clarendon Street by the South Entrance to the College. Catherine rode with Dr. Sargent, Dot, and the Somerville Warden, Dr. Phillips. She would much rather have walked. The evening was mild; the sun still hovering above the horizon. It was L'Heure Bleu, one of her favorite times of the day at Oxford. The colleges still retained a bit of their detail while being silhouetted against the western sky.

When they reached The Mitre, Catherine and Dot allowed their tutor and the college dignitaries to proceed ahead of them and ascended afterward.

To her relief, place cards had been laid out, so she was able to avoid sitting with Dr. Harry. Her place was between Dr. Stephenson, who would undoubtedly use the time to talk about his new book, and Dr. Phillips, the Warden of Somerville.

People were somewhat late straggling in, but after they were all seated, Dean Andrews suggested they open the champagne bottles that were out on the tables. Once it was poured, the dean said, "Tonight we salute the outstanding contributions made to Somerville College and scholarship everywhere by Dr. Sarah Mary

Sargent. We wish her well in her retirement, though the college will not cease to miss her."

"Hear, hear," the guests chorused before sipping the champagne.

The servers placed beef consommé before the diners, and the meal began. Catherine was surprised that Dr. Stephenson was not the ebullient man of the sherry party. Instead of talking about his own book, he wished to talk about the *Life* she had written of Edith Penwyth.

He asked, "Wasn't there some sort of mystery you uncovered?"

"Yes. Penwyth had a lover; only I never figured out who he was. She only referred to him as 'S.' It's a rotten shame actually, for he sent her some poetry that was quite good. I gave some of his poems to Dr. Chenowith, hoping with her expertise on the Victorians that she could reason out who he might be. But neither of us had any luck."

He nodded his face quite solemn. "Interesting. I hadn't remembered the details exactly. The book enjoyed healthy sales, as I recall."

"Yes. It was just luck, really. The Penwyths have been neighbors of ours for centuries. Edith Penwyth's elderly sister was willing to give me all of her papers as well as her journals."

"And she couldn't help you solve the mystery?"

"No. Her memory was pretty much gone, and then she died shortly afterward. She was very old."

"Hmm," said Dr. Stephenson.

At that point, Catherine turned to speak to the Warden on her other side about her plans for the rest of the Long Vacation they were enjoying until the beginning of Michaelmas Term in September. Dr. Phillips was going to Scotland with her eldest daughter to visit her husband's ancestral home on Loch Lomond.

Catherine confessed she had no plans as her brother was coming home from abroad and she wanted to spend time with him. In actuality, she knew she would see little of William. It was Rafe, his traveling companion, that she was longing to see.

When she spoke again to Dr. Stephenson, it was to thank him for his *Art of Poetry* which had helped her significantly in her efforts to compose in the medium.

"I wish I could take credit for your excellent work," he said. "Your first book of poems was marvelous. The Impressionistic technique was especially well-executed in your use of dark and light."

"Thank you so much. I was much inspired by Monet's studies."

"That was clear."

On her other side, Dr. Phillips asked about her work, but before she could reply, Dr. Sargent rose and held up her champagne glass.

"Tonight, I also wish to pay tribute to the achievement of one of my students, Miss Catherine Tregowyn who has brought acclaim to Somerville with her excellent verse and her insightful work about the reclusive Victorian poet, Edith Penwyth. Her publisher has just accepted a second book of poetry! To Miss Tregowyn!"

"Hear, hear!" the room chorused. Even Dr. Harry toasted her.

She thanked everyone and proposed a toast to Dr. Sargent and Dr. Chenowith for their coaching and instruction. It was only then that the group realized that Dr. Chenowith was not present. Murmurs began to circulate about the room.

"How very odd!"

"Do you think she was taken ill?"

"Which cab did she come in?"

Eventually, the main course of guinea hens was brought in, and the talk died down a bit, but Catherine could tell that Dr. Phillips on her left was still concerned.

"Agatha is not strong. I sincerely hope she didn't try to walk the distance."

Catherine said, "When I spoke to her tonight in the Senior Commons, she didn't mention anything about not coming. And she seemed to be in good health."

"She is devoted to Sarah. I can't believe she would miss this.

Excuse me. I'll just ring through to the College to make certain there is nothing amiss."

The warden was gone for some time. Several people around the table congratulated Catherine, and her conversation was general. No one else seemed terribly worried about the missing don.

When Dr. Phillips finally returned, the main course had been removed, and they were enjoying Stilton and biscuits.

"Mr. Hobbs, our porter, is going to organize the scouts to search for Agatha. I'm afraid she may have come over ill."

Brandy was served after all the plates were removed, but Catherine was too aware of Dr. Phillip's concerns to enjoy it.

"Perhaps I could go back to the College with you and help you to search," she said to the warden.

"That would be most appreciated. Let me just explain the situation to Dr. Sargent and the dean."

Dr. Harry was seated next to the dean and must have overheard Dr. Phillips conversation with her, for he immediately got to his feet and offered to help search. Catherine told Dot she would see her later, and the three of them left The Mitre immediately, hailing a cab on the High Street.

"What do you think can have happened?" Dr. Harry asked the warden.

"I haven't a clue. That's what worries me."

The cab negotiated the traffic, turning onto Longwall Street and then again onto Holywell. Somerville was the westernmost college at Oxford, and it took a good twenty minutes to reach their destination. When they arrived at the Woodstock Road entrance to the College, Dr. Harry paid the cabbie while the warden went to the lodge to question Hobbs about the search. Catherine followed her.

Hobbs was a short man with a round red face and a head of thick gray hair. "She's not in any of the dormitories, according to the scouts. They've just started to search the Hall."

"The chapel seems likely since it's right by the Little Clarendon Street exit," said Catherine. "I'll go there."

"Except for the library, most of the other public buildings and classrooms are kept locked at this time of night," said Dr. Phillips. "I'll need your keys, Mr. Hobbs. Mine are in my office."

Catherine was annoyed that Dr. Harry insisted on accompanying her to the chapel.

"I have a bad feeling about this," he told her, putting his hand in the small of her back as they walked away from the light of the lodge. "Watch your step. Those lovely shoes aren't terribly practical, and it's black as pitch out here."

It was only a five-minute walk to the new chapel. Catherine pushed open the door into the building.

"This is a bit unnerving," she said.

"Don't worry," he said. "I'm here."

Ignoring his comment, she switched on the torch Hobbs had leant her.

"My thumbs are prickling," said Dr. Harry.

"It's 'pricking,'" she said irritably. "But don't bring Macbeth into it, for heaven's sake."

The newly built chapel was small compared to other college chapels. It consisted of a long white nave with a small stained-glass window at the end. Enclosed benches lined the walls. From here, everything appeared to be in order.

Catherine said, "You take the right side."

* * *

Her discovery of the body of Agatha Chenowith left Catherine numb, shaken, and terribly cold. Her legs had seized up, and she couldn't move from where she crouched on the floor.

Eventually, she realized that this was a police matter, and one of them had to go ring them. She didn't want to be the one left with the body. "Would you mind helping me up?" she asked, gritting her teeth.

Dr. Harry got up and, neatly stepping over her, slid one arm around her back and another under her knees, and set her on her

feet. "Sorry. Beastly thing to find. It looks like she's been strangled."

Anxious to be gone out of the terrible place, she said, "I'll go
for the police if you don't mind staying with her." Her knees were
wobbling.

He patted her on the back. "You do that."

CHAPTER THREE

Catherine managed to get to the porter's lodge, where she rang the police.

"This is Miss Tregowyn calling from the east porter's lodge at Somerville College, she said. "I need to report a murder."

Terse questions followed along with a promise that the authorities would be dispatched as soon as possible. She wasn't to touch anything.

When she was finished, Hobbs took pity on her and brewed a cup of strong tea on his gas ring, added plenty of sugar and insisted she drink it while she waited.

As she was sipping her beverage, Dr. Phillips returned. She looked from Hobbs to

Catherine where she sat sipping tea, and said with obvious indignation, "I don't suppose you found anything in the chapel?"

Catherine took a deep breath. "I did, as a matter of fact. It would be a good thing if you sat down, Dr. Phillips."

The warden's eyes rounded, and she sank into one of Hobbs's folding chairs. "What is it?"

"I'm sorry to have to tell you this, but Dr. Chenowith is . . . Well. . . she's dead."

The warden's face froze and drained of color. "Dead?"

Catherine wanted to reach for the woman's hand or give some

gesture of comfort, but on second thought, she realized that might appear intrusive to the doughty warden. "She appears to have been strangled, but that's for the police to decide."

The woman was clutching her hands tightly together and looking into space. Catherine couldn't tell if she heard her or not.

Hobb's said, "They'll be here soon, ma'am. Never fear."

"Dr. Bascombe is waiting by the body in the chapel," Catherine added. She couldn't hold herself back any longer. Getting up, she walked over and knelt in front of Dr. Phillips looking up into her face. She laid a hand over the warden's bunched ones. "I'm sorry. It's a shock. I know she was your friend."

"I can't take it in. I was afraid she had been taken ill or something, but not . . . Never this," said Dr. Phillips. "Of course, there were those silly death threats. I thought they were from students simply larking about."

Hobbs poured another cup of tea.

When he handed it to her, Dr. Phillips' hand shook, so the cup rattled in the saucer. "Who would want to kill Agatha?"

Catherine hadn't even gotten to that spot in her thinking. She still couldn't get beyond the sight of the body.

Then they heard the klaxon, and suddenly the police were upon them. They strode into the porter's lodge, and, at that moment, everything changed. It was no longer a personal tragedy. It was someone's job.

"Detective Chief Inspector Marsh of Oxford CID," a handsome, dark man in a trench coat said. This is Inspector Davies. "Would you mind telling me which one of you is Miss Tregowyn?"

Catherine stood. "I am. It was I who found the body. I can take you there now if you like."

"Ready when you are," said the policeman.

"It's in the new chapel," said Catherine.

Dr. Phillips accompanied her and the small troop of police, four in all, who made their way behind them to the college chapel.

Dr. Harry greeted them with obvious relief. "Good show," he said. "You're here." He extended a hand to Detective Chief

Inspector Marsh. "Dr. Harry Bascombe. Fellow of Christ Church. I was with Miss Tregowyn when she discovered the body."

"Perhaps you could tell me how you two happened to be in the chapel enclosure this time of night," said Marsh.

"We were looking for Dr. Chenowith," said Catherine. "She had gone missing from a college event between cocktails and dinner."

The warden took over and explained the details of the party and her concerns.

"So, you left the Senior Commons Room at eight o'clock for the Mitre, but Dr. Chenowith never made an appearance?" Marsh asked.

"That's correct," said Dr. Phillips. "But it wasn't immediately evident that she was missing. There were quite a few of us."

"Please give Inspector Davies a list of the attendees, if you would be so good. We can adjourn somewhere else while I finish my questions and leave my men here to do the forensic work."

"Perhaps, under the circumstances, it would be best if we met in the Reading Room at the Hall," said the warden. "I will ring the dean to see if she has returned from The Mitre yet, although I can't imagine that she did not hear your arrival. Miss Tregowyn, perhaps you will show the police and Dr. Bascombe to the Reading Room."

* * *

The dean arrived as Dr. Harry was being questioned in the corner of the Reading Room that was quite large as it was used for public receptions. Catherine went to Dr. Andrews immediately.

"I'm so sorry, Dean."

"Who on earth would want to murder Agatha?" she asked softly, her chin wobbling a bit.

"I don't know," said Catherine. "However, this policeman seems the sort that will find out."

"I hope so. It makes me feel our girls and our faculty are quite unsafe. And how could something like this happen in the new chapel of all places?"

"Maybe someone was in there who shouldn't have been. A tramp or something. Maybe she caught him there," said Catherine.

The dean thought this over. "How was the poor woman killed? Do they know?"

Catherine answered, "Not for certain."

At that moment, the Detective Chief Inspector interrupted. He asked to speak to Catherine.

The questions were routine until he asked, "How well did you know Dr. Chenowith?"

"Actually she was one of my tutors when I was here as a student."

"Did you have a personal relationship with her?"

"What exactly do you mean?"

"Did she mentor you or anything like that?"

"I suppose one could say that. I am a fledgling poet. She critiqued some of my verse for me when I was here. But I didn't know her on a personal basis. I know very little about her, except that she is a significant modern English poet. She belongs to the Bloomsbury group if you've ever heard of that."

"What did she think of your poetry?"

Catherine frowned. "I don't see what that has to do with anything."

"She didn't like it, then?" Marsh raised an eyebrow.

Raising her chin, she decided to take the bait. "As a matter of fact, she gave my poetry excellent reviews."

The policeman looked at her as though he were trying to see inside her mind. "Tell me, what is your relationship with Dr. Bascombe?"

He threw her off her stride. "Excuse me?"

"Dr. Bascombe. Your relationship."

"There is nothing beyond a professional one. Not even that, really. He doesn't like me much."

"Now, why is that?" For some reason, the man smiled.

Catherine knew it for a dangerous smile. He was playing some sort of game with her.

"He's the sort of man who lives for his work. He doesn't perceive me as being that dedicated, and yet I have won some accolades. It makes him angry."

"I think you are mistaken in him. He sang your praises to me."

"What?"

"You heard me."

Catherine considered this surprising information and then drew herself up. "What possible bearing has this on Dr. Chenowith's murder?"

"A surprising percentage of the time the murderer turns out to be the person who discovers the body. It's part of the plan. Could it be that you and Dr. Bascombe were slightly inebriated following cocktails, and Dr. Chenowith caught you canoodling in the chapel on your way to The Mitre?"

Catherine felt anger flush through her. "Absolutely not! And even if it were true, why would we kill her?"

"It wouldn't do Dr. Bascombe's reputation any good, would it? What if she was a man-hater and she made threats?"

Alarms flashed. "How did you know Dr. Chenowith was a man-hater?"

He pounced. "Ah! So she was! It is often the case with these academic types."

Catherine stood up. "You are baiting me. Your theory is absurd. There is someone really dangerous out there who *did* kill Dr. Chenowith. It's your job to find him."

The Detective Chief Inspector's face hardened. "I don't need you to tell me how to do my job, Miss Tregowyn."

Turning on her heel, she walked away, her arms stiff at her side. It was obvious to her that she was going to have to look into this matter herself. She had overestimated the intelligence of the police. Canoodling, indeed!

To her surprise, Dr. Harry was still in the room, speaking with the dean.

"Excuse me, Dr. Bascombe. May I speak to you for a moment?"

Eyebrows raised, he looked her in the eye. "Shall we take a walk? Perhaps you would like to change your frock?"

"This will do," she said, pulling her fur coat closed in the front.

They left the hall and began to walk the path around the quad. "Did you realize the policeman thinks Dr. Chenowith caught us—he said *canoodling*—in the chapel and threatened you with exposure, so you or I killed her?"

"You're having me on."

"Absolutely not. Apparently, you gave Marsh the idea that you liked me. And a large percentage of murders are committed by the people who supposedly find the body."

"And so he jumped to a wholly unwarranted conclusion? Before interviewing anyone else?" Dr. Harry was even more incensed than she had been. "I never heard such tripe."

"There's nothing else for it, Professor. I think it may be up to us to prove our innocence. Are you game enough to find the real murderer?"

"As in the best type of detective fiction? Sorry. Don't mean to sound casual. Count me in."

"I'm glad you agree." Catherine felt a small surge of triumph.

"Of course, I do. Marsh's supposition is patently ridiculous. And an insult to you."

They walked for a moment in silence. As sometimes happened in Oxford, a nightingale trilled. The sound brought Catherine back to reality. Had she lost her mind? Chasing a murderer with Dr. Harry?

He said, "For starters why don't we pool our resources on the victim. The dean just told me Chenowith had been receiving anonymous threats on her life."

"Threats? Like letters cut from the newspapers and pasted on?"

"Exactly. She didn't take them seriously, apparently. What do you know about her?"

In for a penny, in for a pound.

"I was her student, not her colleague like you are. I only know

the obvious. She traveled in exalted company. Virginia Woolf &
Co. She had a sterling reputation as a poet. She has won numer-
ous awards and was an asset to the college."

"Did students like her?" he asked.

"She was very hard to please. Her standards were very high
when it came to poetry. She could put you on the pathway to success or dead-end you. It was sometimes frightful because poetry
is such a subjective thing. My friend lost a publishing contract
because Dr. Chenowith sent a bad review to them."

"Ah-ha! Now we're getting somewhere! Who is your friend?
Was she there tonight perhaps?"

Golly! I should have thought before I sacrificed poor Margery.

"You would probably find out before long. It's well-known
here. The former Margery Ackerman, now Lady Margery
Wallinghouse. Her husband is *the* Sir Herbert Wallinghouse,
Baronet. Heaps of money. He made a stink I can tell you. But
the publishers wouldn't budge, and neither would Dr. Chenowith.
Now Margery's poetry will never be published. It's like the poor
woman is cursed."

"Is her stuff any good?" asked Dr. Harry.

"I don't know if you would like it or not. It's a bit old-fashioned. Sort of mid-Victorian. But that sort of thing sells better
than the more modern stuff. People like it. It's more accessible."

"Hmm. Well then. There's a motive. Revenge."

"I won't believe it of Margery. But that won't stop the police.
What do you know of Dr. Chenowith?" asked Catherine.

"She's not fond of my sex, that much I know. Could be she
was crossed in love at an early age; I've never heard. I don't feel
myself that she is anything beyond a mediocre poet."

"You're not serious! Mrs. Woolf admires her!"

"I haven't got much time for her, either."

Catherine stood still and put her hands on her hips. "Who *do*
you like?"

"I prefer Rupert Brooke and the war poets. There's meat there.
Not the ramblings of an unbalanced mind."

"Is that what you think my poetry is, as well?"

"We have strayed from the subject at hand."

Catherine gathered herself together. He was right. But she knew one day she wanted to know what he found lacking in her verse.

"Do you know if either Dr. Stephenson or Dr. Williams had an animus against her for any reason?" she asked.

"Dr. Williams is not interested in anything modern. They got together over subjects like linguistics and the origins of English verse. He quite respects her scholarship. How are your feet doing in those shoes?"

As a matter of fact, Catherine's feet were coming out in blisters, she was sure. But she said nothing about them. Instead, she asked, "What were her common interests with Dr. Stephenson?"

"I don't know. He was more Dr. Sargent's colleague. I assume that's why he was at the dinner. He's an expert on the Victorians. And, as you undoubtedly know, he published the definitive undergraduate text on studying poetry. I don't know that Stephenson and Chenowith had that much to do with one another."

"I'll look into that," she said. "I must read the advance reader copy of his latest book. He dropped it off some time ago." Catherine shivered. "It's getting very late. Why don't we resume this tomorrow?"

"Ah! Your feet are hurting you!"

"Maybe a little," she admitted. "But I can't seem to get warm. I've been cold ever since I found Dr. Chenowith."

To her discomfort, Dr. Harry put an arm around her shoulders. "Well, then. Let's get you to your dormitory. Where is it?"

"This is the door, as a matter of fact."

"How convenient."

She held out her gloved hand. "Good evening."

He shook her hand. "Don't stay up all night fretting. Where and when should we meet tomorrow?"

"Let's have a pub lunch. That's the most convenient thing."

"All right. The Bird and the Baby."

"Lovely," she said. "Noon. Goodnight, Dr. Bascombe."

Chapter Four

Jennie and Dot were still awake and waiting in Catherine's room.

"Miss Tregowyn! We heard about the terrible doings," said Jenny. "The p'lice have been here. I had to show them your room! Is it true that Dr. Chenowith is dead? I mean, how was she done in?"

"Yes," said Dot. "Do tell!"

"It is terrible. It happened down in the new chapel. I don't really . . . The police have searched my room, you say?"

"Yes. They were here ever so long. But whatever it was they were after, they didn't find it."

"How about you, Dot? Did you see anything?"

"No. They searched my room, too. They went away empty-handed."

"Of course, they did. We've got nothing to hide. I didn't murder the poor woman, but I'm going to find out who did."

"Are you, now?" said Jennie.

"Why do you want to do that?" asked Dot. "You're no Miss Marple, Cat."

"I'm a suspect with no faith in these policemen. Dr. Bascombe and I are working together, though I can't like the man."

"He's ever so handsome, miss. Reminds me of Douglas Fairbanks at the pictures."

"A suspect!" said Dot. "Is the copper serious?"

"I found the body. That makes me a suspect in his book."

"You'll ask me for any help you need, miss?" said the aging scout. "I have a passkey for all the rooms."

"I would never ask you for such a thing, Jennie!"

"Never say never. Might come in handy, it might."

"Well, thank you. Now, off to bed with you, Jennie. I know you've got to be up with the birds."

With that, the scout left them.

"There's something you're not telling me," said Dot. "Why are you investigating this with a man you don't like?"

"The Detective Chief Inspector has a wild theory. He thinks Dr. Chenowith found us 'canoodling' in the new chapel and threatened Dr. Harry with exposure or something. It's absurd."

"It's the only thing that's happened tonight that's funny," said Dot.

Catherine took off her frock, put on her dressing-gown, and gathered her bath things. She was determined to get warm.

"I'm for a hot bath, Dot. How about if we talk about this in the morning? I've been freezing ever since I found that awful thing."

"Understandable. I'll see you tomorrow," promised Dot. "I hope you can sleep."

Going down the hall to the bathroom, Catherine wondered if the police had searched any of the other Old Girls' rooms. She would have to remember to ask Jennie tomorrow.

She ran the water as hot as she could get it and submerged herself up to her chin in the Victorian tub. Finally, she started to relax and get warm. Lovely. She had dozed off when her chin slipped below the waterline jolting her awake. Feeling like a very old woman, she slowly climbed out of the tub and rubbed herself dry. She put on her silk pajamas and her dressing gown, gathered her sponge bag and towel, and went back to her room. Catherine got in bed and slept far more soundly than she expected to.

Jennie awakened her at 8:30. "You're going to miss breakfast, miss, if you don't get up!"

"I don't want breakfast," Catherine moaned. "Please leave me be."

The scout left the room, and Catherine tried to go back to sleep. However, the image of the dead Dr. Chenowith was haunting her now.

In twenty minutes, she had dressed in her white linen suit with a navy blue polka-dot shirt. She breezed into the breakfast room for a cup of coffee and a bun just as they were closing down. Taking the items upstairs, she passed Dot's door. No one answered. Her friend had always been an early riser. She was already off somewhere.

Sitting at the desk in her own room, she made a list of things to do that day.

Catherine had two fixed appointments which she noted by their times in her diary. 12:00—meet Dr. Harry at pub. 8:00—concert at the music room with Dot. Chewing the end of the pencil, she thought about where she should start with her inquiries.

The dean. Surely, she would be the person who knew Dr. Chenowith best among the small crowd who had been there last night. Catherine didn't know for certain that the attacker was among last night's group, but it was clearly the best place to start. Closing her diary, she went down the hall to the telephone, rang the exchange, and asked for the dean's office.

After making an appointment for ten o'clock, she went back to her room and packed her belongings. Maybe the dean would allow her to stay on here for the time she was involved in her investigations, but it was best to be prepared.

She drank her cold coffee and ate her bun, all the while thinking about Dr. Chenowith. She *was* quite well-known as a man-hater. When Catherine had been an undergraduate, it was rumored that her heart had been broken, and she had never gotten over it. She had refused to take men into account ever since. Catherine wondered if she needed to look into that ancient history. It couldn't hurt. But she couldn't quite picture herself asking the dean about it. Maybe Dr. Sargent would know. She needed to talk to her former tutor anyway.

She rang up Dr. Sargent's office and found she wouldn't be in for the rest of the day. Maybe Catherine should visit her at her cottage. She had a little place west of the University. Surely Dr. Harry had a motor?

Looking at her watch, she noted that she had better hurry if she was to be on time for the dean.

* * *

Dean Andrews' office was as neat and tidy as the dean herself. She had ordered tea and the tray sat on the edge of her desk.

"How do you take your tea, Miss Tregowyn?"

"Milk and sugar," said Catherine. "Thank you."

As the dean was pouring out, Catherine reacquainted herself with the content of her walls. There were all her certificates of expertise in early Christian writings and her diplomas from Somerville. And a picture of the Warden—Dr. Phillips. But mostly she remembered the photographs. The dean was a great traveler. There were photos of her in Egypt, riding on a camel with the pyramids in the background, pictures of her before the Taj Mahal, several somewhere in the South Seas, and one of the Brandenburg Gate in Berlin.

Who took the pictures? Catherine found herself wondering. Did she travel alone or with a companion?

"Now, my dear, how can I help you?"

Catherine said, "I am looking into the murder. The Detective Chief Inspector seems to fancy me as a suspect. It's ludicrous, of course, but I don't feel I can leave things up to the police. There are probably things I am in the position to find out that he won't be able to."

The dean looked as though she doubted her hearing. "Are you certain you haven't been reading too many detective novels?"

"I'm not sure at all. But Dr. Bascombe and I . . ."

"Dr. Bascombe! He is helping you?"

"Yes. We have both come under suspicion, you see."

"You're right. It is ludicrous. I will help you, too, of course. What would you like to know?"

"I don't know much about Dr. Chenowith except as one of my tutors. I know she was a celebrated poet, that she was involved with the Bloomsbury set, and . . . well, that's about all. The police are going to take her life apart. She will have no secrets in the end. Have you talked to them, yet?"

"They just interviewed me last night about the dinner and where I was, that sort of thing. They asked me nothing about poor Agatha, except did I know that she had received death threats. Which I didn't. Who would send such a thing?"

"Possibly the murderer. If they don't find him immediately, they will start digging. Can you tell me anything about what they will find?"

"She was quite a careful woman," said the dean. "Careful in her speech and her behavior. Agatha didn't talk about herself. I have no idea, for example, where she went during the weekends or the Long Vacations. She only lived in her rooms here at Somerville without separate lodgings like most of us have."

"So she was secretive?" asked Catherine.

"No. I would stick with my original adjective—careful, or maybe private. One didn't have the feeling that she was keeping secrets, just that she kept herself to herself. I don't know if that's the way she was with her Bloomsbury friends, though."

"Hmm." Catherine had hoped the dean would be more help.

"There was that business with Margery Ackerman, of course," the dean said. "But I expect you know all about that."

"Probably not as much as you do."

"Lady Margery had already received a publishing contract. She asked Agatha to review the poetry for some material to put on her back cover. I believe she asked Dr. Sargent, as well."

"I see."

"Well, I've never actually understood what her objections were.

I thought the poems quite good, myself. But, instead of sending her very unfavorable review to Lady Margery, she sent it to the publisher, who wasted no time in revoking her contract. Her husband, the baronet, was incensed. He sued the publisher. He sued Agatha. All to no purpose, of course. It only made his wife look rather pathetic. Now she will never get a contract from anyone."

"The whole thing was most unfortunate. I don't think Margery has recovered from it," said Catherine.

"But she wouldn't murder Agatha over it, would she?"

"No, of course not." Catherine wished she were as positive as she sounded. She had wondered last night what on earth had possessed her friend to come to the dinner where Dr. Chenowith would be.

"You know, now that I reflect on it, I do believe something was bothering Agatha," said the dean. "She wasn't her usual self."

Catherine's pulse quickened. "Could the death threats have accounted for it, do you think?"

"If she took them seriously, perhaps that was it. She was very short-tempered of late. I did ask her if anything was vexing her, and she turned on *me* for a moment. Most unlike her. And there was an incident in the last term where she actually made one of her students cry."

"Did you ever talk to the student?"

"No. Most likely, I should have. But I wouldn't want anyone to think I was going behind my faculty's back."

"And, pardon me, but you never asked Dr. Chenowith about it either?"

"I did. That was the time she got on her high horse with me. She quickly backed down, however, and said she would handle it."

"Perhaps I should have a word with the student. I wouldn't confront her directly about it. Just talk about Dr. Chenowith and see if she volunteers anything. Would you mind?"

"You must be careful not to undermine the discipline of the college. That is my only concern."

Catherine kept her reaction to herself. Making a student cry was discipline? She hadn't suspected the dean of such a Victorian attitude.

"I'll be circumspect, Dr. Andrews." Taking out her diary, she asked, "What is her name? And can you give me the names of some of her chums?"

"On second thought, I would rather you didn't follow that line of inquiry," the dean said, her forehead furrowing. "It is likely to lead to rumors among the students."

"You don't think murder is going to lead to rumors? I'd be willing to bet it is the only topic at luncheon."

The dean's chin came up, and she looked displeased. "Well, I won't have you adding to it."

Catherine didn't know what to make of the drop in atmospheric temperature. "Very well, Dean. Thank you so much for your time. By the way, have I your permission to stay on here for a few days while I look into this?"

"Very well. I'll get word to the scouts. And Catherine, I really am thrilled about your new poetry. Tell me about it. Are you carrying over your Impressionist theme?"

"Thank you, Dr. Andrews." Catherine accepted the change in topic as a peace offering. "I guess you would say my general theme is Memory. But it does use Impressionist techniques."

For the next twenty minutes, they discussed poetry and parted on cordial terms.

As she left the office, she came up with a very different idea about how she would find the answer to her line of inquiry about the girl who cried. But right now, she was late for lunch with Dr. Harry.

She went out the Woodstock Road exit and, striding with a brisk pace, she made her way down to Cornmarket Street.

* * *

"So she turned off the spigot, did she?" Dr. Harry commented. "I wonder why? She was cooperating so nicely!"

"I think she suddenly realized how intrusive all my questioning was. Frankly, I was surprised she told me as much as she did!"

"At least she gave the appearance of being open. What she actually told you was that except for the anonymous threats the subject was a closed book, so there was nothing to tell."

"Until she got to the last bit. She clammed up in the end. I think she realized she hadn't handled it as well as she should have."

Since it was not term-time, Dr. Harry was not wearing his gown. Instead, he wore a blue oxford cloth shirt and a Christ Church tie under a navy blue blazer. Thus, his eyes looked bluer than ever and intense, causing her to avoid them.

"You know, you look quite lovely today," he said.

"We'll get along a lot better if you don't make this personal, Dr. Bascombe," she said.

"Yes. After all, it could lead . . . well . . . to canoodling, and we can't have that."

She was suddenly stifling, particularly in the popular pub packed closely with tourists.

He leaned forward on his elbows. "I've spent the morning in the archives of the *Oxford Mail*. The hullabaloo last year over Lady Margery Wallinghouse's book of poetry was quite a thing. I copied down the actual review she sent to the publisher as it was given in the paper."

He passed his notebook over to her. It appeared to be a black and white cardboard covered exercise book. Lord Harry's printing was sprawling and idiosyncratic. After struggling to become familiar with it for a moment, she read:

Lady Margery Wallinghouse's attempt at poetry is regrettable. Her images are hackneyed, her similes trite. It reads like a nursery rhyme. It is hard to believe it is the fruit of an Oxford education. Definitely give this one a miss.

Anger kindled in Catherine's breast. "How utterly horrid! How could she be so cruel? She knew exactly what she was doing to Margery's dreams. I have read the poetry. It is a little old-fashioned like I told you. But it is not *bad*!"

"Do you think this is a motive for murder?"

"Margery would never murder anyone. But how could she even bear to come to that dinner last night?"

"Either she is very thick-skinned, or she did have a motive," said Dr. Harry.

Catherine gave a little shrug. "I wouldn't have called her particularly thick-skinned. Most poets are, as you know, more sensitive than your average person. Particularly when it comes to their work."

"Lady Margery is the tall one that looks like a model, yes?"

Margery wouldn't like being identified that way. She thought people who judged her by her looks weren't taking her seriously. She purposely scorned makeup. "Yes."

"She was seated at my table. I just remembered she came in late. After the others were seated."

This was news. "How late? Could she have been in the ladies' room?"

"Probably not, unless she was ill or something. She didn't come in until the fish course."

Dread suffused Catherine's breast. Could her friend, someone she had known intimately during her university years, really have committed murder?

"I can't believe it, Dr. Bascombe. I know her too well to think she could have . . . *strangled* anyone."

"Let's put it this way," he said. "You're a poet. What if Dr. Chenowith had aimed her academic poison at you? What if she had made it her business to see that you never got published?"

"I wonder . . . What if there were a reason why Dr. Chenowith was so vicious other than her feeling the poetry was without merit? What if she had a personal grudge?"

Dr. Harry sighed. "Unfortunately, that does happen. It's one of the curses of academic life. One likes to feel that Oxford dons are above that sort of thing, but a select few are not. You said earlier that you had an idea of how to find out about the student she caused to cry. What are you going to do?"

Catherine looked around to make certain no one was listening to them, but everyone was completely wrapped up in their own concerns and lively conversations.

"There is a scout who has offered to help me," she said, just loud enough for Dr. Harry to hear. "She would know how to find out who it was. There is always heavy drama in the dorms. The scouts know just about everything that goes on, I'm convinced."

"Good plan. I, too, have various sources at the different colleges. I'll try finding out if there's any dirt on the two male professors."

"Good. I need to find out the reason Margery was late to the dinner. She was at the sherry party. Maybe my friend Dot knows something. She may remember what cab she went into The Mitre."

"She wasn't in my group," said Dr. Harry.

"It would be a good idea for us to see how each of the guests got to The Mitre. Who *was* in your group?"

"I'm not sure that will do us much good. Our cab left after yours. I don't know how long afterward, but our driver was pretty sharpish for making him wait so long. He charged us extra. There might have been plenty of time to do the deed. But we had Professors Stephenson and Williams and the platinum blonde aboard."

"Anne Tomlinson. So that leaves the dean and Margery unaccounted for."

"Do you think the dean could have done it?" He grinned. "I say, that would make a wonderful leader in the *Mail*: 'Women's Dean Does Don to Death.'"

"Don't even think it!" Catherine said with a shudder.

He smoothed his mustache, the piratical glint in his eye. "By your account, she did behave a bit suspiciously."

"That had nothing to do with the murder. She was protecting one of the students."

"Joking aside. How do you want to proceed?" he asked, leaning forward on his forearms.

Catherine forked some pork pie into her mouth as she thought as she chewed. "It only now occurs to me, that the reason the dean was protecting that student was that she might have thought she had a motive for the murder. I must find out who she is. I'll set my spy to work."

"And talk to Dot about Margery."

"Yes. And you're going to dig for dirt on the professors."

He took a notebook out of his breast pocket. "I'll write down the names of those who drove with me plus the dean and Lady Margery. I'll check with my university gossips. Shall we meet tomorrow morning and compare notes?"

"That would be good. I don't want to miss services at the Christ Church Cathedral. After that?"

"Sure. Let's take a walk this time. The Botanic Gardens? I could meet you outside the Cathedral."

"That sounds lovely."

"I do come up with the lovely idea occasionally."

Catherine smiled and left him in the pub, sipping his second pint.

* * *

Catherine found Dot in the Senior Commons Room drinking coffee.

"I'm sorry I've been so elusive," Catherine said. "I had a pub lunch with Dr. Harry."

"Really? Yum," teased Dot.

"We *really* are trying to work this case. I've already spoken with the dean this morning. Not much help there, but did you know that Margery was late to the dinner last night? I don't think she strangled Dr. Chenowith, but that's motive and opportunity.

The police are going to look at her pretty thoroughly. Do you know why on earth she came to the party? You couldn't have paid me to come if Chenowith had put me through the wringer like she did poor Margery."

Dot lit a cigarette. "She did tell me she's seeing an alienist. Maybe she's being told to face up to things."

Catherine made a face. "Poor Margery. How abysmal."

"Her husband is rather like a boxer's trainer if what I hear is true. He thinks she's is a good writer and Chenowith be damned."

Catherine began pacing. "Do you have any idea why she took so much longer than anyone else to get to The Mitre from here?"

"Sorry. I haven't the slightest. She was at my table. She just joined us with a 'sorry,' as I remember. No explanation. Have you seen the *Mail* this morning?"

"No. Is there a copy here?

"Anne gave me this before she went off. Dot handed her the newspaper, folded with the story about the murder face up on the front page:

OXFORD DON FOUND STRANGLED IN SOMERVILLE COLLEGE CHAPEL

Dr. Agatha Chenowith, a member of Mrs. Virginia Woolf's Bloomsbury set, was killed last night at approximately 8:00 pm. She is thought to have been on her way to a college dinner honoring Dr. Sarah Sargent at The Mitre in Oxford.

Police speculate that the murderer was someone known to her, possibly another guest at the function.

There followed a list of their names. Catherine was described as a former student of the victim. If the police had found anything concrete, they weren't sharing it with the press.

Dot ground out her cigarette in her saucer and leaped to her feet. "Well, I'm off to ring my boss. He won't be happy about me being detained here over a murder investigation."

"Before you take off, any idea where Anne went?"

"Blackwell's. We may not see her for hours."

"Thanks." Catherine bade her friend good-bye and went back upstairs to find Jennie. The scout was in the room Margery had used, changing the bed linens.

"I see as you'll be stopping here a few days, then," said the scout.

"Yes," said Catherine. "You said you wanted to help me. I have a question for you."

The scout stood up straight, a gleam in her eye. "What is it, miss? I'll help you any way I can."

"I know you scouts are the heartbeat of the college. You know everything that goes on."

"Well, I don't know about heartbeat, miss. But we get to hearing a fair lot of things."

Catherine sat in the room's armchair. "Do you recall an incident where one of the students was made to cry over something that Dr. Chenowith said to her? It might have been something to do with her poetry."

"It doesn't come to mind, miss, but I'll think on it. And I'll ask Susan and Mary. They're the other scouts that are here during the Long Vacation."

"Thank you. Have you done Miss Tomlinson's room yet?"

"Did Miss Tomlinson's before yours. You know Lady Margery's husband's come, and they've moved to the Randolph."

"Do you mind if I have a look around?"

"Do you think you might find a clue?" The scout brightened.

"I don't know what I'll find, honestly," said Catherine over her shoulder.

There was nothing to find, unfortunately. She studied the desk blotter, hoping to find an impression of a letter Margery might have written. No joy there. She looked through the dust bin. Nothing. Also, nothing in the cupboard or under the bed. So much for an amateur sleuth's luck!

She was leaving the room when she ran into a policeman no doubt bent upon the same errand. He was a stout individual wearing a trench coat. Catherine was surprised the police had not been there already that morning. Wouldn't they know the scouts had done the rooms?

"I'm with the Oxford Police. If you've been in Lady Margery Wallinghouse's room snooping," he declared, "I'll have to ask you to turn over anything you found, miss."

Something about the man was off. Was it his unmatched socks clashing with his lofty demeanor? She decided to bluff it out. Looking at him right in the eyes, she said, "I'd like to see some identification."

To her surprise, the man turned on his heel and ran back down the hallway. Instinctively, Catherine ran after him, clattering down the stairs. They ran across the quad, but he outpaced her and eventually disappeared through the west porter's entrance into the traffic of Walton Street.

Chapter Five

Thoroughly disgusted with herself, Catherine asked the porter to ring the police.

"I'm Miss Catherine Tregowyn, a witness in the Chenowith murder," she told the dispatcher. "I found a man claiming to be police searching the rooms at Somerville college. When I asked to see his identification, he ran. I lost him, I'm afraid. But I think someone should take down his description."

"Hold the line, miss. I'll put you through to Detective Chief Inspector Marsh."

When the detective came on, she repeated her story.

"We don't take kindly to police impersonations. They're a crime, as you probably know. Would you please come down to the station, miss? This may be the break we need. We can have you work with a sketch artist preferably while the details are fresh in your mind. Could you be here at three o'clock?"

"You're on St. Aldate's Street, is that correct?"

"Yes, miss. In the City Hall."

"I'll be there."

Prior to leaving for the police station, Catherine decided to check Anne's room before the woman returned from Blackwell's.

Jennie had already made the bed and scrubbed out the washstand. Catherine wasn't exactly certain what she was looking for. She found that when it came down to it, she was squeamish about opening Anne's journal or even her dresser drawers. Her appointment diary and telephone book lay open on the desk. Flipping through that was unproductive of anything except giving Catherine a nervous stomach.

Some detective I am!

* * *

It was a stiff walk to the south side of Oxford, but she shunned the idea of a cab. Catherine loved walking through the city, and she had time. She was very glad she had packed a pair of stout walking shoes.

The walk was a favorite of hers. She walked down St. Giles, passing St. John's College. The road then split to accommodate the gem of St. Mary Magdalene's church which had sat in the middle of the ancient thoroughfare since the twelfth century. She passed Balliol College and the Martyr's memorial, the somber spire commemorating the death by burning of Archbishop Thomas Cranmer during the English Reformation.

As usual, when passing by all this history, Catherine's mind boggled at the chance she had had to study in such a place. Her own family history included martyrs and freemen, lords and ladies. One day she was determined to trace it all and construct a family tree for the children she still hoped to have.

Of course, children presupposed a husband. She allowed her mind to dwell for a moment on Rafe. Since her girlhood, she had always supposed she would marry him. But now she wasn't certain that was at all likely. With an effort, she pushed the problem away. It would do her no good to dwell upon it now.

She had arrived at Christ Church, Dr. Harry's college with its lofty cathedral. It was her favorite of all the colleges, with its Tom Tower (named after its huge bell), large Tom Quad, and of course the magnificent cathedral. On a whim, she went through the porter's gate and asked the wizened man if he knew if Dr. Bascombe was in college at the moment.

"I'm a colleague from Somerville College, Miss Tregowyn."

"I'll just ring his rooms," the porter said.

Dr. Harry apparently answered. The porter informed him, "Miss Tregowyn at the gate for you." He motioned for Catherine to come around to the lodge entrance and handed her the telephone.

"I'm on my way to the police station. They're going to have me work with a sketch artist on a rendering of a man I caught at the college today snooping and impersonating a police officer. I thought you might want to come along and see if you could identify the sketch. It may be someone connected with one of the professors you are looking into."

"Jolly good. I'll be along in a minute."

Catherine took the opportunity to stroll into Tom Quad and gaze about her at the honey-colored walls. She loved Oxford, never more than when she took the time to walk about and enjoy the atmosphere—the soft light, the medieval architecture, the whisper of brilliant minds. She could lose herself here again, but what purpose would that serve? She needed to be out in the world with her East End lads who probably would never have much connection with learning—really learning—except what she could give them. She dreamed that maybe one or two of them would catch a love of knowledge from her and run with it, someday qualifying for a place at Oxford funded by a generous scholarship.

Dr. Harry joined her.

"Hullo! What's been going on?" he asked.

She recounted her adventure at Somerville that afternoon.

"Who the devil could the fellow be?" Dr. Harry pulled at the tie about his neck. "How very exasperating!"

It was a short walk from Dr. Harry's college to the Town Hall where the police station was. Detective Chief Inspector Marsh greeted them and offered them coffee while they waited for the sketch artist to arrive.

"Was the man well-spoken?" the detective asked. "Did he speak like a Toff?"

Catherine had not even thought of this detail. "Now that you mention it, it was odd. He spoke like a professor, full of authority. That must be what tipped me off to ask for his identification. Who but a professor would speak like a duke and wear unmatched socks?"

Dr. Harry laughed. "Well, we'll see if I recognize the man. Aside from his socks, how was he dressed?"

"I couldn't really tell. He wore a trench coat. His shoes were just brown oxfords. They didn't give the impression of having been recently polished."

They were given an interview room to work in when the sketch artist arrived. She was an attractive young woman who looked like a student. It transpired that she was an artist with a degree from the Slade. Her name was Robin.

"I'm working on my portfolio here in Oxford," she said. "The colleges and the gardens are wonderful material. I offered my services to the police. I've done this sort of thing in London."

Robin started by asking the general shape of the man's face.

"Sort of like a rectangle—wide brow and double chin with a dimple. He had jowls," said Catherine.

They moved on to the positioning of the eyes, shape of the nose. The hardest thing to get right was the mouth.

"His front teeth overlapped just the slightest bit. Oh, and ears. His ears were large, and they stuck out from his head."

After an hour and a half, the sketch was complete.

"Well, Dr. Bascombe?" Catherine asked.

"You know, I've seen this fellow. He's part of a group that drinks at The Bird and the Baby."

"I assume you are talking about The Eagle and Child?" asked Detective Chief Inspector Marsh. "Does he do so frequently?"

"Yes. I don't know any of his compatriots, but they all seem older—not students. Probably professors."

"So I was right," said Catherine with satisfaction.

"Maybe not. He's just one in a sea of faces. You know how crowded the pub gets," said Dr. Harry. But that dimple in the chin is kind of a tip-off."

"We'll have one of our detectives take the sketch over there and ask the barmen," said the policeman. "Now, Miss Tregowyn, we'll need your statement, and then you're free to go."

* * *

"Shall we take an evening walk along the Isis?" asked Dr. Harry as they left the Town Hall.

"That sounds good. It got very warm in there," Catherine fanned herself with her hand.

"There's usually a breeze off the river this time of day," he said. "What do you think of this business?"

"It's amorphous. Too many possibilities. The only ones with real alibis for the time of the murder are Dot, the warden, Dr. Sargent, and me. We were in the first cab. Was there any particular reason your cab didn't leave until awhile after ours?"

"Your friend wanted to go upstairs after drinks and 'freshen up.' She said she'd be a few minutes. So I took my time, too. When I got to the cab, I was the first one there. She came right along. We waited on the other two professors and then the cab was full, so we took off."

"By my friend, you mean Anne, the platinum blonde?"

"Yes."

They had reached the Isis and the promised breeze. For a moment, Catherine stood in its wake, took off her hat, closed her eyes, and let it ruffle her shingled hair. "So," she said, her eyes still closed, "None of you have an alibi for the time of the murder."

"You shouldn't stand at the edge of Isis with your eyes closed next to a murder suspect. It's very foolish."

Her eyes flew open. "Much as I dislike you, I can't see that you've got a motive."

"Surely an aspiring poet like yourself takes *Journal of Modern Verse.*"

His reference to her as "aspiring" put her teeth on edge. "Oh, yes! How can I forget when it made me feel so vindicated! Dr. Chenowith gave you a rancid review in there, didn't she?"

"I despised the woman, I freely admit. I only went last night to honor Dr. Sargent, whom I adore."

"Your admiration of her is mutual, I know."

"What a wretched place Oxford is!" he exclaimed suddenly.

She stopped on the footpath. "Most people think just the opposite."

"Do you?" he asked.

"Well, I admit this murder has given me pause. I do see your point. Do you really think it is the result of professional animus?" she asked.

"No one knew how to inspire that emotion more than Agatha Chenowith. Surely you knew that, even though you were her fair-haired girl?"

"Well, I must admit I thought her treatment of Margery was terribly unfair. And I know Marge has suffered agonies because of it," Catherine said.

"The dislike of her extended to many of the other colleges as well. It hasn't been good for Somerville. I expect Dr. Sargent would have had a much nicer turnout for her farewell last night if it weren't for Dr. Agatha Chenowith."

"You're right. I never realized that. If what you say is true, that isn't good for Somerville. And, somehow, I expected a larger crowd last night. I wonder if the dean was aware?" she said.

"I don't know how she could help but know."

Catherine stopped. She exhaled slowly. "Between you and me, they've offered me Dr. Sargent's position."

"Even though you haven't a doctorate?"

"I'm to study for it and obtain it within three years."

"So you've decided to take the job?"

"No, actually, I have already decided to stick with what I do.

I like my independence, and I've sensed some of what you say about the Oxford community. But I didn't ever think it would lead to murder."

"What is it you do, besides writing verse?" he asked.

"You forgot the adjective. Possibly *execrable?*"

"Don't put words in my mouth," he advised.

Catherine was oddly reluctant to reply. But at last, she answered, "I tutor little boys in the East End who are having difficulty learning to read or with their sums."

"Hmm." He looked at her closely.

"What does that mean?"

"Noble of you. I suppose you're a Communist?"

"Of course, I'm not a Communist!"

She stood her ground for a moment and then turned down the path that traversed Christ Church Meadows.

He hastened to catch up with her. "So why do you do it then?"

"I happen to love little boys and want them to get a good start in life."

"You really think you can make a difference?"

"At least it's worth a try. Now go away. I've had far too much of you for one day." She branched out from the path, making her way across the open meadowland.

Chapter Six

By the time she had crossed the meadow and arrived at Broad Walk, she was far too tired to return to Somerville on foot. Walking back to St. Aldates, she flagged down a cab to take her the rest of the way. It was only then that she realized she had missed her concert in the Music Room. Dot must be worried. Regret tugged at her. Catherine loved Chopin. She could only hope that the sketch the police artist had made would lead somewhere eventually.

Though it was past her work hours, Jennie was awaiting her in her room. The white-haired woman had fallen asleep in Catherine's armchair, but she awoke at the first sound.

"Oh, Miss Tregowyn! I am that glad to see you. I was worried, and so was Miss Nichols."

"Why were you worried, Jennie? I'm not a student anymore." Catherine laughed. "I get along just fine in London, you know."

"Have you had anything to eat?"

"No, as a matter of fact, and I am wretchedly hungry."

"I'll just pop down and check the larder. I know we have cheese and biscuits. Mayhap there's some fruit as well."

"That sounds heavenly. Thank you," said Catherine. "I'm going to take a quick bath. I feel quite grimy."

When Catherine returned to her room, she found Jennie had been as good as her word. She had even fixed her a cup of tea.

"Wonderful! This will do nicely."

As soon as Catherine sat and had her first biscuit and cheese, Jennie said, "I was able to find out the answer to your question, miss. The girl who cried?"

Catherine was surprised. "Excellent work! Who was it?"

"A girl named Lady Rachel Warren. An earl's daughter she is. There was a fuss, that's why Mary remembered it. Her parents took her out of school and wrote a complaint against Dr. Chenowith."

"Oh, dear. It does sound serious. Good work, Jennie. Did you happen to find out any details about the incident?"

"So 'mat about a poem she wrote. The girl, I mean."

"Good. I mean, it must have been rotten. Poor Lady Rachel. Do you know anything about who her parents complained to?"

"Some board. Sounded like high muckety-mucks."

"The Board of Trustees?" Catherine asked, holding a biscuit halfway to her mouth.

"That's it," said the little scout, beaming.

"That's serious." And yet the dean had made it sound like she was just mentioning it in passing. It must have raised an unholy stink. No wonder she had been reluctant to name the girl.

"Got anything else for me to do, then?" asked Jennie. Eagerness shone out of her little brown eyes.

"Not at the moment. You've done marvelously well. Thank you. I knew you would come up trumps."

"I'll keep my eyes and ears open," the scout said.

"Be careful," said Catherine, suddenly concerned. "I don't want you to lose your job over this."

"I've been a scout for a long time, miss. I reckon I know how to keep my job."

* * *

Catherine had not intended to stay at Oxford longer than the weekend, but she had planned on going to services at the Christ

Church Cathedral before she left, so she had packed her favorite suit—a powder blue linen with a fitted skirt that had stitched down pleats to the knees and hung to mid-calf. She had brought her matching cartwheel hat the brim of which she wore turned down on the right side of her head.

As she was leaving, she noted the packaged advance reader's copy of his poetry from Dr. Stephenson sitting on her desk. She had brought it with her from London thinking she might have time to read it. Well, perhaps later on.

Catherine took a cab to the Cathedral. She was very happy to see that the world-famous choir was singing for the service. Settling into her seat, she contemplated the vaulted ceiling and the beautiful stained glass with its musical motif. The Cathedral always calmed her with its dedicated space and light in a world where those commodities were often sorely lacking.

The choir was sublime. Hearing its songs echoing hauntingly off the walls and columns was worth her entire trip to Oxford. It carried her away from the sordid crime and the questions it had generated. By the end of the service, she had completely forgotten she was to meet Dr. Harry.

But there he was, waiting for her as she left the Cathedral, dressed in his blazer with a red carnation in his lapel. Her heart gave a little leap, surprising her. How could she possibly be attracted to that mustachioed rogue?

"You're looking very glam," he greeted her.

"I think we said everything we needed to say last evening," she said.

"You're still angry."

"Certainly not. Only tired of you. And hungry."

"Sunday dinner at The Mitre. My treat. I've even rung them up. They're holding a table for us."

Sunday dinner at The Mitre meant roast beef and Yorkshire pud. Her stomach growled. *Betrayed by the flesh*. How could she answer no?

Without replying, she merely fell in with him as he began to walk the short distance to the High Street and turned toward the restaurant.

"Because of you, I missed my Chopin concert last night," she said.

"My charm can be an inconvenience," he said.

Shaking her head, she didn't reply. They crossed to the other side of the High.

When they entered the restaurant, she breathed deeply of the savory smell of roast beef.

"This was an inspired idea," she admitted.

They were seated at a small table in front of a window. It was perfect.

While they awaited their food, they sipped Chablis, and she said, "I do have some news."

She told him about Jennie's nugget of information.

"The Board of Trustees, eh? I wonder if Chenowith got a dressing down."

"Possibly. That kind of thing is hard to keep quiet. You were right about Chenowith damaging the college's reputation."

"The family must have money and influence. An ordinary incident like that rarely makes it to the Board of Trustees."

"There could have been more to it. There must have been some kind of emotional trauma. We only have the scouts' version."

"True. I have some news, as well. Last night I went back to the police department and borrowed the sketch for the evening. I inquired of my drinking pals about the man in the sketch. It was definitely worth the bother. He's pretty distinctive looking. Turns out he drinks with dons from St. John's. At a stab, he's one of them. No one could remember his name from the pub, but I imagine the police will make short work of that. I took the sketch back this morning. They were glad of the information."

"Pardon me for ever doubting you," she said.

"I will pardon you just about anything," said Dr. Harry. "He's probably another one of us poetry people, like Stephenson and Williams."

"Wouldn't you know him, then?"

He considered. "I should. Maybe he's more in Williams' line than mine."

"Early Teutonic period, before it branched off into early English."

"Right. Pretty arcane stuff," said Dr. Harry.

Their dinner was served, and if Catherine had been standing, the sight of it would have made her weak in the knees. She dug into her roast beef. For a moment, their conversation ceased.

"It's interesting. I find the development of poetry fascinating," she said. "It's rather like how painters have learned to use the medium of paint differently down the centuries; only the poet's medium is words."

"And I doubt whether there is any place in the world you can study all stages of that development better than here."

"I'm sorry," she said, after sampling the excellent Yorkshire pud. "I seem to have carried us off-topic. Do you think the police will arrest the St. John's man if they manage to locate him?"

"I think they will. I can't imagine what he will have to say for himself. Snooping around a female dorm? Impersonating a police officer?"

They made short work of their dinner, and afterward, over coffee, Dr. Harry decided to see if he could use The Mitre's telephone to ring the police station. He disappeared briefly into the back regions of the restaurant.

"No joy," he said, upon his return. "They identified him as Dr. Christopher Waddell of St. John's all right, but he has taken off."

"Taken off?" echoed Catherine.

"Disappeared. Vanished. With all the belongings he could carry, apparently."

"Hmm." Catherine weighed this information with surprise. "That puts rather a serious complexion on things, doesn't it? A don leaving his college with no explanation."

"Murder *is* serious," Dr. Harry said.

"So they think he is the murderer?"

"If they didn't think so before, they surely think so now," said the professor.

"So he got into the college without the porter's knowledge, and just happened to run into his quarry by the chapel as she was hurrying off to an engagement . . ." Catherine posited.

"They could have planned a rendezvous. Chenowith might have thought he just needed a few moments of her time."

As she cut her beef, Catherine considered this. "Yes. That makes sense. But what could possibly have been the motive?"

"Maybe we'll never know," said Dr. Harry, filling his pipe.

Catherine thought over this possibility. She was not satisfied. "Do you think he will be named the murderer at the inquest?"

"No." The professor tamped down his tobacco. "What evidence they have doesn't even have a firm connection to the case. We don't know why he was in the dormitory or if it had any connection at all to the murder."

"It's very strange. I suppose if there is an open verdict of murder, the investigation will proceed."

"Yes. I'm not out of the woods yet," he said, puffing his pipe.

Catherine had a sudden thought. "They might even think you recognized him and warned him."

"I'm afraid they do think that. They asked me about it, anyway. They want to see me again."

She was surprised at her own alarm. "Oh? And you're just sitting here calmly enjoying your pipe?"

He grinned a particularly insouciant grin. "They can wait. Gives them a chance to go through my digs anyway."

"You're infuriating!" she exclaimed. In reality, she was a little afraid of him. She had allowed herself to become too comfortable with the professor, even beginning to overcome her dislike.

"Did I tell you how that hat becomes you?" he asked.

"No. And you shan't have the chance. I'm leaving." Taking up her clutch bag, she rooted for currency to cover the amount of her meal and left it on the table.

* * *

Catherine walked back to Somerville by way of Turl Street onto Broad Street and thus to the Martyr's Memorial and St. Giles. She was thinking furiously and was nearly run down by two different bicyclists.

Was Dr. Christopher Waddell the murderer? What in the world was he seeking in the dormitory? He had been in Margery's room. Margery was a suspect.

Catherine's thoughts took an about-face. What if she had been looking at the picture from the wrong perspective? What if he was not looking for something, but was going to plant something? Something that would strengthen the case against Margery? Evidence that would carry that case forward past motive and opportunity? Well, if that was his intent, thank heavens she had caught him at it. Or what if he was working with Dr. Harry Bascombe? Her Sunday dinner companion *could* have warned Waddell. What on earth could their motive be? Did they have something against Dr. Chenowith personally or professionally? It was impossible to imagine what that could be.

CHAPTER SEVEN

Dot was waiting in her room when she returned. She had almost forgotten about her friend.

"What on earth have you been up to?" Dot asked. I haven't seen you since yesterday morning!"

"I went to services this morning and then out to dinner with Dr. Harry. He's with the police now. Or anyway he should be unless he too has disappeared."

"He too? What are you talking about?"

Catherine told Dot of the happenings on the day before when she had discovered the intruder and helped the police.

"Oh, and Jennie came through with a bit of information." She related the story of Lady Rachel Warren, Chenowith's insult and the report to the Board of Trustees.

"My! You have been busy! Need a Watson?"

"I could use a Sherlock to tell you the truth. I don't know which way to turn at this point. I'm in something of a dilemma. Is Harry Bascombe guilty? Or is this Christopher Waddell the murderer?"

"Surely Waddell is more likely than Bascombe!"

"I would hope so. Then there's also this story with Lady Rachel. I feel I need to look into that."

"Tell you what! Let's go down to the library and look at

Debrett's. We'll find out who her father is and where he lives. I've got the motor, remember. We can drive off and do a bit of sleuthing."

"We're not supposed to leave Oxford until after the inquest, but I suppose we could leave word with the porter where to find us. At least the police will know we haven't disappeared."

"I'd better dress up some if I'm going to meet an aristocrat," said Dot.

* * *

Debrett's had yielded the information that Lady Rachel Warren was the only child of the Earl of Carroway whose principal seat was in Buckinghamshire—just a few hours away.

"Perfect," said Dot. "We won't even be gone overnight if we're lucky."

"Let's pack a toothbrush and a change of clothes, just in case," said Catherine.

It was a lovely day for a drive—no fog, rain, or clouds to be seen. *Ah, July.*

Once they got to the town of Dawley, they stopped at The Horse and Dragon for a pub snack and directions to Carroway Castle. It had been a bit too noisy for conversation in Dot's motor with the top down, so while eating pickle, cheese, and peasant's loaf, they planned their strategy.

"We should give false names, I think," said Dot. "In case they check on our cover story with the Board of Trustees."

"Right. I'll be Miss Jane Featherstone. I think I belong to *The Spectator* magazine."

"I've got my camera in the boot," said Dot. "I'll be your photographer, Miss Olivia Manchester. I've always wanted to be called Olivia."

The first bit of trouble they ran into was the guard at the gatehouse. Obviously, the earl valued his privacy. Catherine made a swift change of plans.

"I'm Miss Jane Featherstone of Somerville College. I am here to see Lord Carroway on behalf of the Board of Trustees," she said. She could feel the shock emanating from Dot beside her at the wheel. "This is my secretary, Miss Olivia Manchester."

"Are you expected?"

"No. But I am certain his Lordship will want to speak to us."

"His Lordship doesn't see anyone without an appointment, and scarcely anyone with an appointment."

"What about Lady Carroway?"

"I shall see if she is available."

While the guard rang the house, Dot hissed, "Have you any idea how much trouble we will be in if they happen to ring the Trustees?"

Catherine nodded. "I'm willing to chance it. But you can stay out of it."

The guard returned. "You are to park in the front-drive. Lady Carroway will see you in her sitting room. The butler will show you the way."

As they drove down the long, poplar-lined drive to the castle, Catherine said, "Golly, I haven't seen a real live butler in ages."

"Have you ever heard of Carroway Castle?" asked Dot.

"Never. But I don't know much about County Bucks."

The drive took a sharp curve, and suddenly the golden-stone castle came into view. It was surprisingly medieval. There was a grass planted moat and a drawbridge with a coat of arms displayed above it.

"I wonder if King George stays here on weekend visits," said Dot. "It's grand enough."

Once they were across the drawbridge, crenelated towers guarded the castle keep where the living castle stood. Catherine couldn't imagine living in such a place. There were few windows and centuries' old conifers shrouded the building.

Dot parked the car in the circular drive. Catherine was seldom intimidated, having grown up on a large Cornish estate, but this place was overpowering.

A butler in full butler-kit answered the knocker.

"We are Miss Featherstone and Miss Manchester to see her ladyship," Catherine said.

The butler bowed and pulled the door open widely. "Good afternoon. My lady is taking tea in the west sitting room. She wishes you to join her."

They followed him down a dark inner corridor lit only by oil-burning sconces, into a room at the west end of the castle. There a series of small windows let in the western sunlight, and a tiny woman with dark brown hair streaked with gray sat behind a large silver tea service.

"How do you like your tea?" she asked, without introduction.

"I am Miss Featherstone, your ladyship. I take my tea with milk and sugar. Thank you."

"I am Miss Manchester, my lady. I take lemon, please."

"Have a seat, have a seat. If you're not slimming, the lemon seed cake is very good."

Catherine accepted her tea from Lady Carroway and sat in a green damask chair. The whole scene reminded her of tea on the best china with her Granny when she was a child. Dot seated herself next to her ladyship in a chair with a needlepoint cover.

"You've come from the college? You may not see our daughter."

"No," said Catherine. "I quite understand that. She has been through enough. We were scheduled to come this afternoon to see how the family is getting along; however, now we have some news that may interest you. Perhaps you have seen it in the paper."

The little lady, whose face was surely prematurely lined, tilted her head to one side. "We don't read the news or listen to the wireless. Not since the War. Too upsetting."

"Dr. Chenowith was murdered on Friday evening at the college," said Dot with the air of someone who could not restrain herself.

Lady Carroway blinked and stared. Then she dropped her teacup with a clatter on the wooden floor. It shattered by her feet.

"Murdered? Friday evening?" she repeated. What little color she had possessed left her face, and her lips trembled.

"Yes," said Catherine. "I'm afraid so."

Lady Carroway sat bolt upright. "Gel!" she all but shouted to Dot. "Ring for the butler." She nodded toward the bell pull in the corner.

Setting her teacup on the table, Dot got up and pulled the bell pull. The butler entered almost immediately. Catherine suspected he had been lingering outside the door.

"Simmons. His Lordship is working on his stamps, I believe. Tell him his presence is required most urgently."

Catherine shot a glance at Dot and said, "We did not mean to alarm you."

The lady folded her lips against her teeth and said nothing. In a few moments, they heard shuffling noises through the open door to the corridor. In walked what appeared to be a very old man. His jaundiced skin hung in heavy folds over his face, he dragged his feet, and his breaths were heavy rasps.

Catherine and Dot leaped to their feet and held out their hands, introducing themselves.

"My husband served as a major in the War. He lost a leg and was gassed," his wife explained. "Now you can see that he couldn't possibly have committed murder," she said. "No matter how strong his motive."

"Murder?" repeated her spouse in a deep, chesty voice. He fell into a storm of hard coughs. "Who was murdered?" he gasped.

"The Chenowith woman," said his wife. "Now, gels, perhaps you will leave us in peace."

Lord Carroway stared at them, his face contorted in a mask of hate. "Persecuted my daughter," he said. "Wouldn't leave her be."

The bout of coughing overcame him, and he fell. The butler entered from the hallway and helped his lordship into a chair.

Catherine was completely tongue-tied. Dot took her arm and said, "We'll leave you in peace. We're desperately sorry. For everything."

Horrified by what she had seen and heard, Catherine allowed Dot to lead her away from the pathos. It was with difficulty that she left the castle, however. She felt as though she ought to do something, say something.

"Those poor people," she said finally, once the front door shut behind them. "Those poor, poor people. I've never seen anyone who was gassed in the war."

"Most of them didn't live long," said Dot. "I'll bet you anything you like their daughter is the world to them."

"Still, it was very queer."

"Very."

As they sped away, Catherine said, "Why do you suppose Lady Carroway immediately jumped to the conclusion that we were there to get his alibi?"

"Well, we were," said Dot.

"But we're not the police!"

"Do you suppose ... I mean ... What if murdering Agatha Chenowith is something he has threatened to do? Often? Maybe he sent her the death threats! And, what did he mean about persecution? What has happened to their daughter?"

"Perhaps," said Dot, "She's mentally unhinged."

"Perhaps *she* killed Dr. Chenowith," said Catherine.

They sped down through the plane trees toward the village. "Pub," they both said at once.

The diamond-paned windows of the Horse and Dragon where they had dined earlier showed a full complement of locals laughing and settling in for an evening of relaxation before the work-week began the next day. Dot and Catherine walked in, squeezed between the patrons, and ordered—Catherine a lemon squash, and Dot a pint of lager.

They sat on stools at the bar and listened to the conversation around them. Catherine was still recovering from the scene at the castle, while Dot, more outgoing than she was, struck up a conversation with a woman on the stool beside her.

Ever direct, Dot said, "We were just up at the castle. I haven't been called 'gel' since my granny died."

"Oh? And what would you be doing up there?" asked the large woman next to her. Catherine noticed she was dressed in a printed jersey, no doubt her Sunday best.

"We're looking for our friend, Lady Rachel Warren."

"No joy, I suppose," said the woman.

"Nope," said Dot with a sigh. "Wouldn't even talk about her."

"Not surprised. Barmy, she is."

Catherine joined the conversation, "Really, truly? We were at school with her."

"Hmm," said the woman. She drained her beer. "Everyone knows she's barmy." With that, she slid off her stool and said, "Hope you find her if that what's you want."

They weren't able to make much more headway, though they stayed another hour at the pub. Apparently, it was well-known that Lady Rachel was "barmy," but no one had the least idea where she was. Some speculated that she lived, unseen, at a room in the castle, but the servants never spoke of her. Others had it that she was a "loon" kept somewhere in a bin for crazy people.

As Catherine and Dot were both tired, they decided to stop overnight at the pub in the room available upstairs. After they brushed their teeth and lay in the big, cushy four-poster merriment was still proceeding full strength below.

Catherine said, "I think another talk with the dean is in order. Maybe she knows where Lady Rachel is."

"Good idea. Now, shut off your head, Cat. I need to sleep," said Dot.

Chapter Eight

The following day, Catherine and Dot pulled into Oxford around noon and decided to have lunch at a tiny restaurant near the college. The rain was coming down in sheets when they ran inside.

Both women ordered the vegetable soup and sticky buns.

"I think we should split up the inquiries," said Dot. "I'll run Anne to earth and see what she has to say."

"I think I'll have another go at the dean and then see Dr. Sargent. I also need to find out what's new on the Christopher Waddell investigation."

"Who?"

"The man I caught in Margery's room. The St. John's don who disappeared. All of which means I have to call Dr. Harry, unfortunately. I could do without speaking to him."

"Why? I've always found him charming. Too charming sometimes, actually," said Dot.

Catherine ignored this observation. "Actually, from him I learned that the dean was a bit late to The Mitre. She and Margery both arrived late. Everyone else came in one of the two cabs. Maybe Anne knows something about that. I seem to recall she and the dean were sitting at the same table."

"And maybe the dean knows where Lady Rachel is," Dot said.

"Let's write down our questions before we get muddled," Catherine suggested.

They both dug in their handbags for the little appointment diaries they carried. In the back of them was a place for notes.

* * *

The dean offered to see Catherine that afternoon at three o'clock. Dr. Sargent was in her office, so Catherine was able to meet with her at once. She entered to find her tutor in the midst of boxing up her many books.

"Hello, Tregowyn! I'm packing up my life, as you see."

"May I help?" asked Catherine.

"It would be a great help, actually, if you would unfold those boxes in the corner and tape the bottoms shut for me. I am trying to be efficient and have this done by the end of the week. I'm going on holiday next Monday, you see."

"Ah! I envy you," said Catherine. "Where are you going?"

"I'm making my first trip to the South of France. I'm going to do nothing but lie in the sun and read."

"Sounds heavenly. Especially when we're in the middle of a deluge outside."

"I understand they're looking for Dr. Waddell in connection with the murder," Dr. Sargent said.

Catherine was startled. "However did you hear that?"

"Word travels fast around Oxford. It's the scouts, I think. Whatever do they want with poor, inoffensive Christopher Waddell?"

"I caught him in Margery's room, and he posed as a policeman. That's against the law, apparently, but not anything so major that he should flee Oxford! Apparently, he took everything but his books."

"Whatever would he want in Margery's room? How very peculiar!"

"I have a theory that he was trying to plant some false evidence against her. She is the only one the police have found with a motive for the murder. You know—the business with her would-be publisher and Dr. Chenowith's review."

"Ah, yes. Well, Ackerman's no murderer. You and I both know that," said Dr. Sargent roundly. She was a tall woman with jowls which quivered when she was indignant.

"I don't believe so, either," said Catherine. "I know the whole business with her poetry was upsetting to her, and her husband only added to the problem with his lawsuits, but that wasn't her doing. It quite embarrassed Margery, I think."

"Yes. Sir Herbert is a bit of a loose cannon. But he's on her side, which is heartening."

"Yes. He does seem besotted with her," Catherine said.

Her tutor looked up from her work and into Catherine's eyes as though she were going to say something, but evidently thinking the better of it, she went back to packing books.

For a moment, they worked in silence. Catherine got the last of the boxes built and began taping. "I met Lady Rachel Warren's parents yesterday," she said in what she hoped was a casual tone.

"Ah . . . the earl and his wife. How on earth did you meet them? They never leave their castle."

"Dot and I went in search of them, actually. We heard about their animus against Dr. Chenowith. I thought it might be interesting, in light of the murder, to hear their side of the story."

"You thought that poor man strangled Agatha? Why I don't think the earl capable of breaking open his egg for breakfast! So ghastly, what happened to him in the War; I pray there will never be another one like that," Dr. Sargent closed her box with a violence that suggested she was closing the conversational topic as well.

But Catherine pressed on, "It was very disturbing. Lady Carroway insisted that we understand there was no way her husband was physically capable of committing the murder. And that before we even hinted that they might be involved. She actually said he couldn't have murdered her, 'no matter how strong his motive.'"

"How very odd!" exclaimed Dr. Sargent. "She just popped out with that out of nowhere?"

"Yes. It made me think. I heard that Dr. Chenowith received threatening letters. Do you suppose one of the Carroways sent them?"

"I have always suspected them, as a matter of fact," said Catherine's tutor. "The notes began during the dust-up over their daughter. I know Lord Carroway was feeling quite impotent over the situation, and I fancy those are the kind of people that send such things."

Catherine taped a box with careful precision. She asked, "Any idea what became of Lady Rachel?"

Her tutor sighed. "You are certainly very inquisitive."

Catherine tried a grin. "I'm a suspect. Haven't you heard? Dr. Bascombe and I discovered Dr. Chenowith's remains. I'm trying to clear my name."

"That policeman must have shredded tissue paper for brains."

"Lady Rachel?"

Dr. Sargent became brisk. "All I know is that they were bound to commit her somewhere. She had a bit of a breakdown. I believe her to be by the sea."

"And we live on an island, so that is no help, whatsoever," mumbled Catherine as her tutor turned her back and went to collect more books.

"What are you going to do in your retirement?" Catherine asked.

"I'm not really retiring, just refocusing. I'm going to start a day school for girls."

"How lovely. Where are you going to do this?"

"In Devon. I've always loved it there. My family used to take our holidays there when I was a girl. But I don't think I could live without teaching. So that is what I'm going to do."

"I hope you'll keep in touch," said Catherine. "Remember I'm from Cornwall. I holiday in the West Country, as well. I could pop in to see you on my journeys home."

"That would be famous. I'm certain I'll be ready for a little adult company."

With the further winding down of the conversation, Catherine helped her mentor pack up the remaining books and then took her leave in order to keep her appointment with the dean.

* * *

"You visited the earl? Miss Tregowyn! Have you any idea the trouble we have gone to here at Somerville to resolve that more than difficult situation?" Catherine could have sworn she saw the dean's hairpins shoot out of the coronet on her head as she bristled. "If this interference is an example of what your investigation is going to cause, I demand that you cease it at once!"

Catherine stood her ground under the force of the dean's wrath. "I am almost positive they were responsible for the threats Dr. Chenowith received. Dr. Sargent agrees with me."

"Sarah Sargent always was indiscreet! What else did the woman tell you?"

Surprised at the venom in the dean's tone, she carried on, "She has no idea of Lady Rachel's whereabouts. Do you?"

"If I did, I wouldn't tell you. The girl is nothing but an embarrassment to our sex and the college."

"Because she broke down under persecution by a professor who was supposed to be her mentor?"

"Persecution?" cried the dean.

"That's what the earl called it."

"He's a weak, disillusioned man," the dean fairly spat.

"He was all but gutted by the War, fighting for his country. I don't call that weak," said Catherine. She had never once suspected the dean's venomous disposition. She dug in her heels. "The police will want to know where Lady Rachel is. They are fixing their minds on our Margery. You know she is innocent, and I suspect you also know why she was the object of Dr. Chenowith's wrath." She added the last bit off the top of her head, realizing as she said it that it was probably true.

The dean's eyes narrowed, "You think you are so wise, Miss Tregowyn, but your present course will only lead to disaster for this college."

"A murder of one of our dons committed by one of our alumni is not a disaster?"

"I tell you once again. You will cease this investigation!"

"Dean, I am suspected as well. As a woman and a scholar, I will not sit by and allow me or one of my friends to be arrested for this crime. Unlike you, I believe that finding the truth is in the best interests of my alma mater."

With these words, she left the office of her former dean, determined to discover what had tipped the woman over the edge.

CHAPTER NINE

Catherine tried to control her shaking hands as she mounted the stairs to her room in the dormitory. She hoped the dean did not remember that she had given her permission to stay here. Once in her room, she boiled water on her gas ring and made a cup of tea to steady her nerves. Never had she heard or known the dean was such a termagant.

For the first time, she wondered about Dr. Sargent's retirement. She was still comparatively young. Did it have something to do with the dean? And what about the strange look Dr. Sargent had cast her way when they were talking about Dr. Chenowith? Was there some dirt there, too? Seeing as how the woman was murdered, there must have been plenty of dirt somewhere. Was it over the Lady Rachel situation? How was she ever to know if she could not find the young woman?

Catherine sipped her tea and ruminated as she looked through her window out over the quad. There was little to see. Thunder grumbled in the distance. What drama she had stumbled onto? Things were clearly amiss here in the deceptively gentle world of Oxford.

Soon Dot came in, along with Anne. The Jean Harlow looka-like did not seem the least like a scholar. Catherine was glad to see them.

"You managed to stay dry, I see," she said.

They held up their umbrellas. "But it is beastly soggy out there. I'm cold," said Dot. "What are you drinking?"

"Tea. I'll make you some," said Catherine. "You must be missing your twins," she said to the blonde. "Has anyone heard when the inquest is to be?"

"Thursday, they told me," said Anne. "And yes, I am missing my children frightfully. They are too young to speak on the telephone, more's the pity." She seated herself at Catherine's vanity stool. "Dot tells me you're looking into the murder."

Catherine set the kettle to boil on her gas ring. "Yes, much to the dean's chagrin. She's quite upset with me, at the moment."

"Chenowith wasn't liked much; I can tell you that much," Anne said. "And, of course, she's been beastly to Margery."

"I'm getting the feeling that she wasn't popular," said Catherine. "Do you know any particulars?"

"She was always sticking her nose in. And, quite frankly, she was dishonest. I know that's a horrid thing to say, but, to my sorrow, I have proof."

"Anything you'd care to tell me about?" Catherine poured boiling water into her teapot over the tea ball and left it to steep for a moment.

"Only if you promise not to construe it as a motive. I'm not guilty, I swear," said Anne.

"Do tell!" said Dot, who was reclining against the pillows on Catherine's bed.

"You know that my father died last year?" asked Anne.

"No, I didn't," said Dot. "I'm sorry. He was a prof at Merton College, right?"

"I didn't know either," said Catherine. "I am sorry, too. But I remember meeting him in the dining hall one night. You brought him for dinner, right? He taught Greats."

"Yes. And he had the most divine collection of first editions. After his death, my brother and I were a bit strapped for cash to pay the death duties. We culled his collection and saw that he had some duplicates. There were two *Tale of Two Cities* and *Vanity Fairs*. We consulted Sotheby's informally and learned that if they were in mint condition, which they were, they would be worth a tidy sum. Enough to pay death duties and have something put away for the twins."

"Go on," said Dot.

"Dr. Chenowith was one of their 19th Century experts on valuation. She learned at her father's knee apparently and was much respected. She gave it as her opinion that the Dickens was only worth a fraction of what we were expecting because it was part of a rogue second printing that had been fraudulently labeled 'first edition.' She claimed that that particular press did that with Dickens often to bring in more money.

"Sotheby's was forced to disclose this 'fact' at auction and sold it at a fraction of its worth to a man whom, upon investigation by yours truly, turned out to be an agent for Agatha Chenowith. It now sits on her bookshelf as part of her private collection of First Editions."

"That's dreadful!" exclaimed Dot and Catherine together.

Anne's hand was shaking with remembered anger, and thinking of the tea, Catherine poured out and handed the women their cups. "Yes. It was rather shattering."

"The picture emerging of the good Dr. Chenowith is surprising," said Catherine. "And she's not the only one." She told her two friends about her conversation with the dean. "It was all very Jekyll and Hyde."

Both women appeared stunned. "The dean threatened you?" said Dot.

"Definitely. And now I'm wondering about *her*. You sat at her table, didn't you, Anne?" asked Catherine.

"I did."

"She wasn't in either cab. Was she late getting to the dinner?"

"Yes. And a little breathless," Anne said. "She apologized but didn't offer any excuse."

"Hmm," Catherine replied. "Well, I think we need to put her

up there with Christopher Waddell and Lady Rachel as suspects. I refuse to include Margery."

Anne was clearly puzzled. "Who are Christopher Waddell and Lady Rachel?"

Dot explained while Catherine looked absently out the window again. When their friend was brought up to date, she said, "I'm going to ring Dr. Harry. He might have heard something further about Waddell. I can't imagine what motive he would have for doing away with Chenowith, but what in the world was he doing up here if he wasn't involved?"

"Oh," said Anne. "Dreamy Dr. Harry!"

"Down, girl," said Dot. "You're a married woman."

* * *

Dr. Harry suggested they meet at The Bird and Baby for drinks. She agreed and proceeded to make herself presentable. At least the rain had stopped. While she had been on the telephone down the hall, Anne and Dot had left her room, so she changed out of her frock and donned her white linen suit. If only she had known she would be staying, she could have packed more clothes. Fortunately, Jennie had pressed the garments for her.

The scout came to the door while she was dressing, and Catherine invited her in.

"I tried to get into Dr. Chenowith's room today to search around like, but the police have put sealing tape on the door," Jennie said.

"I was sure they would have," said Catherine. "At least until the inquest is over. They have probably found everything that is to be found there."

"Per'aps they didn't look under the mattress. You'd be surprised at how many people in this college hides things under the mattresses."

"Good thinking, Jennie! Do you do for the dean?"

"Not me, miss. That be Mary's job."

"Well, never mind. I'm off for drinks with Dr. Bascombe. Mind you don't get into trouble because of me."

The scout just grinned.

Chapter Ten

Dr. Harry awaited her in an inglenook of the pub. "I ordered you a lemon squash. You don't like beer, do you?"

"Not much," she admitted as she slid onto the bench opposite him. "Thank you. What have you been up to while I've been out of town?"

"Out of town?" He grinned, and she found herself wishing he weren't such a heartthrob. It got in the way of her thinking.

"To wildest Bucks." She told him about her visit with the earl and his wife. "I would love to be able to question their daughter. She has a good motive, and she's 'barmy,' according to the locals."

"Hmm. Interesting. Any ideas on how to find her?"

"I've asked Dr. Sargent and come up blank. When I asked the dean, however, it turned into Guy Fawkes' Night."

"Huh. More to that poor girl's problem with Chenowith, do you think?"

"I'm realizing the victim was not lily pure. My friend, Anne, the blonde, you remember, took some additional swipes at her person." She related the story of the first editions.

"You're right. The woman is emerging as what they call an unsavory character." He sipped his beer. "Her behavior towards Lady Margery and Lady Rachel seems not only ill-natured but full-on bullying. And the episode with your friend Anne is downright criminal. Can Somerville have been harboring a socio-path?"

"I think that's taking it a bit far. But she certainly was not all she seemed."

"Perhaps her position as an admired member of the intelligen-tsia went to her head, and she believed she was entitled to being above the laws of ordinary decent behavior."

"It could be, I suppose. I am bracing myself to face her con-temporaries in Bloomsbury. I don't suppose you'd care to go with me?"

"That would be jolly good fun! This murder must have shocked them down to their socks."

"You're not going to be all sour grapes about them, are you?"

He laughed. "I knew Lytton Strachey, and he liked my work well enough. I really don't feel inferior, my dear."

"Still, the review from Dr. Chenowith rankles."

"It does, I'll admit. Whatever else she was, Agatha Chenowith was a scathing critic." He settled back into his bench, beer glass empty.

"I guess we need to remember people aren't all good or all bad," said Catherine. Leaning forward, she asked, "What can you tell me about Christopher Waddell?"

"I've been looking into his life, as you can imagine. He taught classes exploring the connection between myths and legends and the creation of nations. Was of the belief that the Church plunged civilization into the Dark Ages."

"That's not an unusual position," she remarked. "I don't sup-pose you'll join me in having a pork pie?"

"That sounds a remarkably good idea. I'll force myself through that madhouse up to the bar and order them."

When he returned, pies in hand, she dug into hers. Vegetable soup seemed hours ago. "So, the professor is a Marxist, I pre-sume?"

"Actually, not. It seems that he's a fascist, or at least has fascist leanings."

"According to. .?"

Dr. Harry said, "His colleagues in the department who *are* Marxists, I admit."

"So, he's not part of a conspiracy or anything," prodded Catherine.

"Well, something was going on in his life. Apparently, he had become secretive and temperamental. Given to making rash statements about the injustice of the Versailles treaty, and the praiseworthy rise of a strong leader in Germany. He was not in favor of the Labor Government."

Catherine felt as though she had awakened Through the Looking Glass. Now they were dealing with fascists? "How very strange. What could such a person want in Margery's bedroom?"

"I think your idea that he was planting something was right. He wanted her to take the fall for the murder. Maybe he's rabidly anti-aristocracy or something. She's not Jewish, is she?"

"I have no idea. Why do you ask?"

"That's one thing I'm sure of. Waddell is anti-Semitic."

"It seems like he's anti-everyone."

"A little paranoid, certainly," agreed the professor. "But more to the point, what connection could such a person have to Agatha Chenowith?"

"You mean why would he murder her?"

"Right."

"I have no idea. She wasn't political that I ever heard. Her whole life was poetry and literature."

"Maybe there was a personal connection. He wasn't married."

"Now, that's an idea. She was pretty anti-man, but maybe he was the one to break through that. He wasn't bad looking. Just a bit overweight," Catherine mused.

"Or maybe he was a fan of hers. Maybe his attentions weren't welcome. You know strangling is one of the crimes of passion."

"Yes. Waddell could have detained Chenowith on her way to the dinner, declared himself, met with a rebuff, and attacked." She sighed. "Oh, this is all too ridiculous." She took another bite of her pie. It was delicious.

"Equally ridiculous—maybe he was acting on behalf of poor Lady Rachel . . ."

"Yes. That may seem ridiculous, but it seems more probable than a *crime passionel*."

He finished up his pork pie. "Well, all I have to say is thank heavens we finally agree on something."

"Yes. Christopher Waddell shall remain an enigma."

"I had slightly more luck with Dr. Wesley Williams,"

"Oh, yes?"

"Well, not in terms of the crime, which he had no reason to commit that I can see, but I did find out something rather interesting." He began fiddling with his pipe. "While remaining with Balliol and giving the odd lecture now and again, he is actually something hush-hush with the government."

Catherine laughed. "But don't you see? Now we must face the possibility that Chenowith was assassinated!"

"By headscarf," he said, keeping a straight face.

"Her poems were actually some sort of code," added Catherine.

"She was secretly working to overthrow the government," Dr. Harry said.

"There must be hallucinogens in this pie," Catherine concluded.

"Then there's Dr. Anthony Stephenson . . ."

"Oh, heavens!" Catherine exclaimed.

"What is it?"

"He sent me an advance readers copy to read. He's publishing some poetry and wants a review. I keep forgetting I must get to it."

Dr. Harry got his pipe going. "Well, in any event, the man is clean. Exactly who and what he says he is."

"He restores my faith in Oxford, then. It's been a trying couple of days."

"I think you need a walk in the fresh air," Dr. Harry said.

They made their way out of the pub to find that it had started raining again. Dr. Harry had brought an umbrella, fortunately.

"Let's walk back to Somerville if you don't mind. You can come in to visit in the Senior Commons Room until the rain stops, at least."

There was an enforced intimacy about sharing an umbrella with someone. Dr. Harry held the umbrella over them with his right hand, and his left went gently around her waist. His hand on the small of her back caused a tingle there. How ridiculously susceptible she was!

She began to ramble about her encounter with the dean and how shocked she had been.

Dr. Harry said, "My guess is that Dr. Andrews has to contend with rather a lot of prejudice from otherwise all-male Oxford. She is probably exceptionally sensitive to any scandal."

"But I tell you, she was practically rabid. It was though someone flipped a switch and she saw *me* as the enemy. We have always been on such cordial terms."

"You have been a great asset to Somerville, though I hate to admit it. I can see why you would be puzzled. But the dean is highly regarded also," said Dr. Harry.

"How far would she go to keep the college's name sacrosanct?" asked Catherine. "I am inclined to put her under the list of suspects. Perhaps Chenowith had committed some sin more than usually unpardonable. Maybe she was part of something truly scandalous that we know nothing about."

"I see we're back to the assassination theory."

"If you had seen and heard her, I think you would find my suspicions valid," she insisted.

"I will take it under advisement," he promised.

When they reached Somerville, he greeted Hobbs, the porter, but declined her invitation to join her in the Senior Commons Room.

"I have plans for the rest of the evening. Another time I would find it delightful," he said.

He left her in the quad outside the door to the hall, cheeks burning in embarrassment.

Every time I begin to see him as human, he goes and says something that restores my dislike! He could have simply said, "No, thank you." Instead, he has to humiliate me.

* * *

Catherine determined that she would spend her evening reading Dr. Stephenson's poetry manuscript. Making herself a cup of Ovaltine from the provided supplies, she settled at her desk.

Two more days until Rafe gets home. He will expect me to meet his ship. And when I don't, he won't find me in London, either. Perhaps I'd better drop a line to his flat.

Using the college stationery she found in the desk, Catherine dated her note and then paused, trying to decide what to say. Finally, she began:

Dear Rafe,

I'm sorry I wasn't there to meet your ship! I have been detained at Somerville College in very mysterious circumstances indeed! I am investigating a murder. Of course, I am a suspect. As yet, I haven't been arrested, just under suspicion. Dot and I are staying in the dorms. Will be here at least until Thursday when the coroner's inquest is scheduled.

If you're at loose ends, you might come up.

Dying to see you, of course.

Cat

Addressing the envelope, she found a stamp in the drawer, left by some kind student, and propped the letter on the mantel for Jennie to drop in the post. Then, putting Rafe and all the complications he brought to her life out of her mind, she turned to Professor Stephenson's manuscript.

To her surprise, the poetry turned out to be Victorian in flavor. The words flowed and were the tiniest bit reminiscent of Tennyson. The meter was very predictable.

Was it her imagination, or had she read this before? Not only did it feel predictable but vaguely familiar. Of course, her mind was a mish-mash of Victorian poetry, having taken her degree in the subject. But after she had read halfway through the manuscript, she began to suspect that Dr. Stephenson wasn't original.

Her mind kept going back to the mass of papers she had received from Edith Penwyth's daughter. The poems by her lover that she referred to only as 'S.' Most of Penwyth's poems Catherine had used in the biography she wrote or edited into a new book of her poetry.

Now she recalled the visit she had made to Edith Penwyth's daughter four years ago, and the thrill it had been to see the unpublished poetry in the poet's own handwriting. There had also been a journal, covered in water-stained pink silk. In it, she had recounted her steamy love affair with an amateur poet. His poetry had made an impression. There had been reams of it. Catherine had mentioned him in her book, of course. Surely, they had a copy of her book at the college library. She had included just one of his poems, as it was an answer to one of Penwyth's.

It was full dark now and raining, but outside her window, she could see the lights of the library beckoning. She was tired of sitting. After standing up and stretching, she realized she had no torch. Perhaps Dot did.

However, when she knocked on the door to Dot's room, her friend did not answer.

"Oh, well," she said aloud. "I know my way well enough."

Dressing in warmer clothes, which included a scandalous pair of flannel trousers, she pulled on a jumper and took her umbrella with her. At the last minute, she grabbed Rafe's letter. She could post it outside the library. As she descended the stairs and went out into the quad, she began to think she was slightly addled to be going after her own book at the library when it was coming down in sheets.

She had to cross the quad and hoped no one was watching as she stepped on the sodden grass. It was strictly forbidden to do so, but she wasn't about to go around the long way in this weather. Catherine shivered.

When she reached the door of the library, she scuttled inside, closed down her umbrella, and shook it. Who would be working here out of term time on a Monday evening?

She came upon a small group of older women sitting in a semi-circle listening to Dr. Harry, of all people. Standing just out of sight behind a bookcase, she listened to him do a reading of his poetry. So, this was his engagement. He was presenting to a book club.

Not wanting to be caught listening to him, she retraced her steps and went up the back staircase to the biography section. There she found her book shelved neatly in the Ps. Opening it on the spot, she paged to the part about Penwyth's lover. There was the poem.

I do not seek for Arthur, no
Nor broken chancel far below.

The greatest knights, the grandest kings
Once marched where now the waxwing sings.
Their hoofbeats echoed in the hills
On paths o'ergrown with daffodils.

The verdant green of England's breast
Obscures the humble and the blest.
Her golden sun and gentle rain
Wash down upon the ancient plain

And wipe away the transient fears
Of distant drums of yesteryears.

Yes! I thought that sounded familiar. I wonder how much Dr.
Stephenson plagiarized. I have heaps of these poems at home.

She needed to borrow this book. As a graduate, she still had
privileges at the library. Taking the back stairs again, she went
down to the ground floor. There was a sleepy young woman
behind the check-out desk. Just as she was signing for the book,
she heard the chatter of female voices. Dr. Harry's reading must
be concluded.

She scurried out the door, back into the rain. With all the witnesses emerging from the library, she dared not walk across the
wet grass this time. Instead, she followed them around the paved
walkway that skirted the quad towards her dormitory. The ladies
branched off at the porter's lodge, and she walked on a few steps.

Out of nowhere, before she could do much more than register-
ing the presence of another person, she was coshed on the head
and fell to the ground.

* * *

She awoke to someone pulling her eyelid open and shining a light
into her eye. She was most awfully cold.

Where am I? What's happened?

Catherine was lying on a rather hard bed, covered by nothing
more than a stiff, white sheet. The person peering into her eye was
a man.

"Ah, you have come to yourself!" he said heartily. "That was
a very nasty hit you took. I'm afraid you have a concussion. I'm
Dr. Ryan."

Her teeth began to chatter. "I'm freezing."

"You're in shock." A nurse materialized with a stack of folded
blankets she tucked around Catherine.

Another person came into view. Dr. Harry. In her vulnerability, she was conscious of the urge to curl away from him, but her limbs were too heavy.

He spoke. "What've you been getting up to that's caused someone to try to kill you? You were hit with a cricket bat! Did they tell you I found it at the scene?"

Her head hurt so badly Catherine couldn't think.

"I found you on the walkway near the porter's lodge," Dr. Harry told her.

Moaning a bit, she tried to sit.

"No," Dr. Ryan said. "You stay down. You're in the Radcliffe Infirmary. You must stay down. I'm afraid if you get up too soon, you'll lose consciousness again. We need to keep you awake. We don't want you slipping into a coma."

"May I?" Dr. Harry asked the doctor as he brought a straight-backed chair to her bedside.

"Yes. Anything that'll keep her awake."

"The police are coming. They want to question her now that she's conscious." He looked into Catherine's eyes. Worry clouded his. "I'm afraid this was attempted murder, darling."

The "darling" glanced off her. She heard it but, in her pain, discounted it.

"Just stay with her," Dr. Ryan said. "Call me if there's any change."

To her, he said, "We can't give you anything for the pain, just yet. It might cause you to lapse into a coma. Bear with it as best you can."

It's all very well for him. He hasn't got sixteen hammers beating in his head.

"Can I ring anyone for you?" Harry asked.

She managed to ask him the time.

"Quarter to one. You were out for a while. We didn't know if you were going to regain consciousness. You gave me quite a scare," Dr. Harry said.

She wouldn't have Dot awakened at this hour. When was it when she left the library? Who had done this to her? Why?

"Edith Penwyth," she murmured.

"Who?" asked Dr. Harry.

"Penwyth's lover."

"Darling, you're not making sense. That happened in another century."

She was too tired to explain. Closing her eyes, she turned her head away.

"You must try to stay awake. Where were you going at nine o'clock at night?"

"Library," she said.

"Why?"

"Copy of my Penwyth book."

Conversing sapped her of what little vitality she had.

"Ah," he said. "Well here is Detective Chief Inspector Marsh, come to question you. Do you want me to raise the bed just a bit?"

"No," she said.

The handsome detective looked down at her from his great height. "Getting ourselves in trouble now, are we?" he asked heartily.

She grinned feebly. "Not canoodling."

"Then who have you been harassing?" he asked.

"Everyone," she said. "Dr. Harry knows."

She realized her mistake in referring to Bascombe this way but cared little. Everything took second place to the pain she was trying to endure.

The professor told the policeman about her interviews at Carroway Castle and her disagreement with the dean. "Neither of those would appear to account for the attack. The earl and his wife are old and ill. And I can't see Dean Andrews wielding a cricket bat. There must be ramifications to her questions that we don't realize. Serious ramifications, apparently. To someone who is deathly afraid."

"You found her, I take it," said the policeman.

"Yes. I was just coming out of the library, where I had given a reading. I don't know the names of all the ladies who attended, but the library will have a list. It was the Monday Night Reading Group."

"You saw no one on the path or on the quad?"

"Just the ladies leaving." He thought for a moment. "I dimly recall some scraping, like boots or something, but it was raining hard. A regular cloudburst. There was thunder, too. I didn't see anyone, but then I hadn't a torch."

"I already questioned the porters at both ends of the campus," said Marsh. "They saw the Book Group ladies leave, but no other action around that time."

"Waddell hasn't turned up?"

"No. You think this might have been he?"

"I think we have to consider the possibility. I've investigated him a bit. Did you realize he was somewhat of an extreme thinker?"

"In what way?" asked the Detective Chief Inspector.

"He's a fascist. No reason to think he would hurt Miss Tregowyn, though."

"She can identify him as the man she saw in the dormitory, but I'm inclined to think that had more to do with the Chenowith murder than with right-wing thinking," said the policeman.

"Yes," Dr. Harry agreed. "But how? According to Miss Tregowyn, Dr. Chenowith wasn't political, and his politics are the only things of interest about Waddell. Unless you're passionate about myths, which she wasn't."

It was galling to Catherine to be discussed as though she weren't there, but she had no idea who would come after her with such a weapon.

"Weren't canoodling," she said again, feeling as though sleep was going to overcome her in spite of the pain.

Dr. Harry chuckled.

"Thank you for bringing us back around to the basics, Miss Tregowyn," said the policeman.

He left soon after that, and Catherine realized they wouldn't be making an arrest anytime soon. If only the pain in her head would stop!

Chapter Eleven

When morning arrived, the doctor had been replaced, but Dr. Harry was still there, valiantly attempting to keep her awake without a lot of success. He read to her from a society tabloid and a fishing magazine, the only literature available.

"I reckon you can tie a trout fly with the best of them," he told her.

They were served an early cooked breakfast of eggs, toast, bacon, and tomatoes, which she scarcely touched.

"You need to be relieved," she said. "You need some rest."

"I'm a night owl," he told her. "Used to surviving on very little sleep."

"Very little is different from none."

"First, if you feel up to it, I'd like to know why you were at the library checking out your own book of all things."

"Miss Penwyth's lover," she said.

"You said that already."

She summoned her wits. "He wrote poetry. Never published to my knowledge."

"And . . . ?"

"I quoted some of it in my book. I needed to look at it."

He frowned. "I don't think I'm particularly dense, but you're still not connecting with me."

She sighed. "I've been reading Dr. Stephenson's advance reader copy. The poetry seemed similar to Penwyth's lover's stuff. But I wanted to be sure."

"You're telling me he plagiarized?"

"Yes. He did. I'm almost positive. I have heaps of his poetry at home. He included it in all his letters to her."

"Hmm. I wonder if that relates to our mystery," Dr. Harry smoothed his mustache. Even with his morning stubble, he was still good-looking. Catherine turned her gaze away. He continued, "Does he know you know he plagiarized?"

"I don't know how he could. I know he read my book years ago, but I doubt that he would remember a little fragment by an anonymous poet. He would never ask me to read his ARC if he knew."

"Let's say Dr. Chenowith discovered the plagiarism somehow. That could have been a motive for murder. You are going to have to be very careful, darling. And I think we should let the police know."

"Would you call the dorm, please? If someone answers, ask them to wake Dot. She can bring the advanced readers copy. It's on my desk."

* * *

Dot arrived at the infirmary an hour later, and finally, Dr. Harry left on a wave of cautions to be careful and not to confront Stephenson on her own.

"Sir Galahad, is he?" Dot asked. "Whatever happened to you?"

Catherine briefly sketched her adventure and then, since there was no one to tell her not to, fell deeply asleep.

Sometime later, she was awakened, and a new doctor examined her pupils.

"There is still evidence of your concussion. Could you turn

your head to the side, Miss Tregowyn? I need to examine the wound."

Until then, she hadn't been aware that she had one. The pain in her head had obscured any other pain she might have. To her dismay, part of the back of her head had been shaved.

"Good thing cloche hats are in fashion!" Dot said.

"From the size of this lump, you are lucky to be alive, Miss Tregowyn," said the doctor.

Catherine felt another unwelcome flash of vulnerability.

"From now on, I'm your shadow," said Dot. "What in the world were you thinking to go out in the dark without a torch and all alone?"

"I guess I didn't realize I was in danger. I still don't know who it can have been. Dr. Stephenson has no idea I think he plagiarized his book."

"What are you talking about?"

She told her friend about her discoveries of the night before.

"What are you going to do about it?" Dot asked. "He's on the brink of publication."

"I haven't decided. I don't want to embarrass the man. Maybe some of it is original. I have a pile of S's poetry at home with my Penwyth papers."

"We'll go down to London as soon as you're out of this place."

* * *

Dot stayed with her until nine o'clock that evening when Dr. Ryan was once more on duty. He declared it safe for Catherine to take pain medicine and sleep. After an only semi-restful night, she was discharged the next morning with instructions to be safe and avoid reinjuring herself.

She and Dot wasted no time motoring down to London. The sounds of her friend's motor aggravated her headache, but Catherine tried to endure as best she could. Dot dropped her at the flat and went to her own residence to pack some clean clothes for the inquest the following day.

It was hard to believe that tomorrow was already Thursday! Rafe's ship would be docking. She tried hard to name what she felt, but after a year without his company, she felt only numb at the idea of seeing him again. And the pain in her head obscured any serious thought.

Catherine greeted her maid, Cherry, and treated herself to a soak in her wonderful Victorian bath.

"Miss, what have you done to your beautiful hair?" Cherry asked with horror.

"I was clonked on the head and have a concussion. There are a few stitches under the bandage, they tell me."

"Whatever have you been up to?"

Since Cherry was in her confidence, Catherine spent a half-hour responding to the maid's query, telling her about the murder and her investigations.

"Now, I must look for something in my papers. It's going to be a job. When will I ever get organized?"

"I don't think being organized is one of your strengths, miss," said Cherry. "If only you'd let me help you . . ."

"If I don't do it myself, then I'll never be able to find anything."

"You can't find anything now," said the maid.

"You're right. Oh, don't let's discuss it! It makes my head ache to think of such a project."

After dressing in gray flannel trousers and a sailor blouse, Catherine proceeded to tackle the stack of papers she had accumulated for the Penwyth book. She had thrown them together and deposited them in her wall safe. Not very scholarly of her.

At least, S's papers were all in the same envelope. Finally laying her hands on it, she drew it out of the safe. She sat at her desk and opened it. Scanning the sheets of poetry and comparing them to the ARC, she was dismayed to see that they had been copied word for word by Stephenson. Where had he encountered them? But, more importantly, what was she going to do about it?

Should she confront Stephenson directly or should she go to his publisher? Much as she hated to admit it, she decided she should consult with Dr. Harry.

Dr. Chenowith could have known. Catherine remembered that she had given her four or five of the poems as a forensic experiment. The professor had offered to read them, and (as an expert in Victorian verse) try to pick up some phraseology or another clue which might link him to a known poet. It would have been a coup if Catherine could have named the reclusive Penwyth's poet lover in her biography. But, though Dr. Chenowith had studied them minutely, she found she couldn't name a poet.

If Stephenson had given Dr. Chenowith his ARC, would she have recognized the poems? Of course, she would! Surely she would have confronted Stephenson. Had she done so at the sherry party? Could they have been the motive for her murder? At this rate, everyone at the ill-fated dinner was going to have a motive. But this was the most serious motive yet. Exposure of his plagiarism would ruin Dr. Stephenson's reputation and career.

She sat up straight and paid for the abrupt movement with pain. If Chenowith had told Dr. Stephenson of the connection between S's poems and Catherine's book, wouldn't Dr. Stephenson be anxious to silence *her* as well? Before she read his ARC? Could it be Dr. Stephenson, who coshed her? Of course, this was all supposition. She didn't know if Chenowith had even confronted Stephenson at the party.

Thinking back, however, she did remember that they had been having a confrontation. And Stephenson was in the second taxi. The one that had been late. Could he have used the time gap between the end of the sherry party and the departure of the second taxi to strangle Dr. Chenowith? Yes. He could have.

When Dot arrived moments later, Cherry served them a late lunch of tinned tomato soup, biscuits, and cheese at the tea table in the sitting room. Catherine couldn't bring herself to eat. The pain medicine and the pain itself robbed her of her appetite.

Catherine said, "Stephenson plagiarized his book. I have the proof."

"Crikey! So now what?" asked Dot.

"I think we have to go to the police. I remembered that Dr. Chenowith knew Penwyth's lover's poetry. I gave her some of it to study to see if she could recognize it as belonging to a Victorian poet whose work she knew. If Stephenson gave her an ARC, too, which he probably did as she's an influential reviewer, she would have recognized it. She wouldn't have hesitated to confront him about it. She could have done it at the sherry party."

Dot considered this. "Cat! Do you realize if she did that, Stephenson was most likely your attacker? He meant to kill you before you read the ARC! I mean, there is more than just his book on the line. His whole career is at risk! And his life, if he killed Chenowith. We've got to get you to the police."

"I have no proof."

"The police need to question him. Maybe he'll crack."

"It's rather shattering," Catherine admitted. "Even if he didn't commit the attack on me, he's another suspect in Chenowith's murder. So now we have at least two suspects other than Margery—Dr. Stephenson and Lady Rachel. But no proof against either one."

Dot said, "We're going straight to the police as soon as we get back to Oxford."

Catherine replied, "Even if he didn't attack me or kill Dr. Chenowith, he can't be allowed to publish plagiarized work."

"Just let the police take care of it."

"I don't know that they understand the scholarly mind. They might not see this as a sufficient motive for murder."

"Dr. Harry can make them see. Stephenson's committed an infamous act, by our standards. He's fully cognizant. He didn't do it by accident."

"It's really hard to believe. He's such a timid fellow," said Catherine.

"Don't let that fool you. He's about to lose everything he cares about. And his life is at stake if he murdered Chenowith."

Catherine said, "Dot, this is so wretched. He was in the second cab. He had the opportunity. It doesn't take long to strangle someone. And if the murderer used her scarf, it wasn't planned."

Cherry came in to remove the dishes and serve coffee.

"Don't go soft on him," her friend advised. "It was still murder. And he may have tried to murder you, as well."

"That could have been Waddell," said Catherine. "I'm the only one that can identify him."

"Or, I suppose someone else we haven't uncovered yet."

Catherine considered this, her mind going back to her confrontation with Dr. Andrews. "The dean is very afraid of something. The more I think on our conversation, the more I believe that fear was behind her anger. And I don't imagine she is particularly attached to Dr. Stephenson. Not enough to be afraid and angry on his behalf. And I can't see her swinging a cricket bat."

"Perhaps he's her secret love child or something," said Dot with a bark of laughter. "The ages are right!"

Catherine smiled, then pressed her forehead with the heel of her hand. Her suspicions had taxed her brain to the fullest extent. The pain was exquisite. "Now, dearest friend, I'm afraid I need an hour or two of rest before we drive back. You can occupy yourself, can't you? There S's love letters to Miss Penwyth."

"That sounds jolly. Are they on your desk?"

"Yes. Somewhere." Catherine rang for Cherry who saw her to her room, removed her dress, and handed her a light wrapper. Then she tucked her mistress up in her bed.

Catherine lay in the gloom. Her room had always been somewhat masculine with the deep, charcoal gray walls of the rest of the flat—they showed off her light-colored upholstery brilliantly. But in a bedroom, it was not the least bit her idea of a color for a boudoir. Oh, well. She drifted into sleep.

Her dreams were not restful. A doctor who resembled Professor Stephenson was peering into her eye with a pencil torch. "Ah, well done! A concussion for certain. She will be dead by nightfall."

At his side stood the dean, Christopher Waddell, and poor

decrepit Lord Carroway. On the other side of the bed stood an infuriated Dr. Harry, brandishing a cricket bat over her bed. He had grown a rather spectacular beard and sported a gold earring as well as a gold incisor. "What do you want with her?" he asked. "Her poetry is not even passable!"

She woke with a start as Dot crept into the room. "I'm afraid we must go," she said. "I'm sorry to wake you."

"No, she said. "You are right. I think Cherry's got all my things packed. Would you ring for her?"

The maid was able to get Catherine fitted out in her dropped waist pink frock. Then they tried the matching cloche hat. Catherine winced, but it would have to do.

Cherry and Dot were able to carry her suitcases, and Catherine managed the hat boxes. They strapped them on the boot of her friend's motor, and soon she and her friend were driving through the outlying areas of London on their way back to Oxford.

Between the noise of the traffic and Dot's own car, conversation was impossible. Catherine closed her eyes and tried to prepare for her encounter with the police. The drive seemed to take forever, and her neck was sore from twisting her head to the side against the seatback to keep from laying her wound on it directly.

When they arrived at Oxford, they called Dr. Harry to meet them at the Bird and Baby where they intended to have a late pub supper before descending on the police department. Catherine carried S's poetry.

When he entered the pub, Dr. Harry came straight to her side and kissed her cheek. "You look like the devil," he said. "Did you sleep at all?"

"Thank you so much," she said. "I haven't slept much, but we have a motive for Dr. Stephenson. Let's order, and we'll tell you about it."

He seated them at a table in the back and procured three orders of fish and chips.

"Spill it, ladies," he said after he returned to them.

Catherine told him about giving Dr. Chenowith copies of S's

poetry to study. "She would have examined it minutely," she said. "If Stephenson was handing out ARC's for review, I have no doubt he would have given one to Chenowith. And I'm certain she would have recognized the poetry."

"You think she confronted him?"

"It would have to be after he spoke to me at the sherry party. At that point, he was still eager for me to review his manuscript. But afterward, I recall him having some sort of heated discussion with Dr. Chenowith. That may have been when she told him. It wouldn't have mattered to her that they were at a public function. It would have been just like her."

"So, you think he murdered her?"

"At least he's a strong suspect," Dot said. "And if Dr. C told him about the connection with Catherine, he is certainly the one that tried to kill her with the cricket bat."

"You're right. I hope you've decided to tell the police about this discovery."

"We wanted to tell you first," said Catherine. "We want you to come with us to describe how serious an act of plagiarism is for a scholar. That he will lose his reputation and his career. We have no proof, you see, and they might not see the motive as sufficient."

"I'm determined to come with you. He certainly has a motive. The only thing that troubles me is what in the world he was doing strolling around Somerville with a cricket bat?"

"Yes," mused Dot. "That is a problem. Unless . . . could he have called her from the pub intending to have her meet him, while he planned to lie in wait for her in the shrubbery? When he heard she was out, he could have just concealed himself near the dorm and waited for her to come back."

"Of course!" Dr. Harry exclaimed. "Brilliant!"

* * *

The police station at the Town Hall was quiet when they arrived, and Detective Chief Inspector Marsh was off duty. A baby-faced constable was at the desk.

Catherine addressed him, "I'm Miss Catherine Tregowyn. An attempt was made on my life two nights ago at Somerville College. I'm here to make a statement. I have the name and evidence for a probable suspect. He is dangerous, and I believe he needs to be brought in for questioning. Detective Chief Inspector Marsh is handling the case. It is related to the Chenowith murder, of which this man might also have been guilty."

The constable was flushed red, and his eyes were round by the end of her statement.

"One moment, miss," he said. He picked up the telephone and rang the Detective Inspector on duty, relating the essence of her statement.

Moments later, a tall, mostly bald man with a rim of red curls above his ears appeared at the front desk. "Miss Tregowyn?" he asked.

"I am Miss Tregowyn," Catherine said.

"Would you step back this way, please? I am Detective Inspector Lawrence. My sergeant and I will take your statement."

"I would like Dr. Henry Bascombe to accompany me. He also has evidence to give."

"And this other young lady?" the detective asked.

"Miss Dorothy Nichols. She is here for moral support. The attack the other night left me with a concussion, and she has been my caretaker."

"Very well. You may all come back."

They traipsed back to the bowels of the building and found themselves in a small, featureless interrogation room. The Detective Inspector introduced them to Sergeant Hawkins.

After they sat down, Catherine asked, "Are you familiar with the crime?"

"I just grabbed the file. If you give me a moment, I will look it over."

The three of them watched him as he read through the file and looked at the photographs of her wound.

"All right. You say this is also related to the Chenowith murder?"

"Yes. We believe so," said Catherine. "I must say we have no proof, but we have enough motive that I think Detective Chief Inspector Marsh will want the man to be brought in for questioning."

"All right. You may begin your statement. My sergeant will take it down."

Catherine gave her account, trying to make it as straightforward as possible. She gave the DI Dr. Stephenson's ARC as well as the copies of S's poems she had kept in her safe.

While she was doing this, Dr. Harry said, "For a professor at Oxford, a charge of plagiarism is akin to a charge of murder. When this becomes known, not only will he lose his publishing contract and most likely be sued for costs by his publisher, he will lose his position at Merton college, and will lose his reputation to the point that he will be unable to secure another post. The degree of his panic should Miss Tregowyn make this connection to 'S' would certainly be a motive for an unstable man to commit murder. As long as he is at large, Miss Tregowyn's life is in danger."

Detective Inspector Lawrence cleared his throat. "Dr. Stephenson has a water-tight alibi for Dr. Chenowith's murder. He was raising an unholy ruckus at the Somerville College Library when he was told that because he wasn't a member of faculty, a graduate, or a student, he couldn't check out one of your books, Miss Tregowyn."

She was surprised, but said almost immediately, "That was most likely my book on Edith Penwyth. It had a quote in it from her lover, the anonymous 'S' of the poetry I gave you. If he knew about the book at that juncture, it all but proves Dr. Chenowith had just told him she had discovered his plagiarism."

The DI thought this over. "You're right. And while it clears him of the Chenowith murder, it does give him a powerful motive for yours. We will pick him up for questioning. Although, unless he was observed there is no proof."

Dot intervened, "He must know by now she is still alive. She spent the last two nights in the Radcliffe Infirmary. He may come after her tonight. You need to pick him up now!"

"I will make a call to Detective Chief Inspector Marsh," said the Detective Inspector. "He will decide. However, I can promise you that if we cannot find him tonight, he will be brought in tomorrow morning."

"That's not good enough," said Dr. Harry. "I know Marsh. Let me speak to him."

"Rather I suggest you take this young lady somewhere other than the dormitory to spend the night. She looks extremely tired."

"I'll go to the Randolph," said Catherine. "I *am* very tired."

"I will station a uniformed constable in the lobby if we can't lay our hands on Stephenson tonight," said the DI. "Now, on another matter, tomorrow is the inquest on the Chenowith murder, so Dr. Stephenson's questioning will have to wait until the adjournment. And Detective Chief Inspector Marsh will want to speak to you in person, Miss Tregowyn, before he questions Dr. Stephenson."

"I understand," she said. "If you'll excuse me, I'd like to go now."

"That will be perfectly fine. I believe you will be called as a witness tomorrow?"

"Yes. I was summoned by mail to be present," said Catherine. "I discovered the body along with Dr. Bascombe."

"I will see you tomorrow then."

* * *

Catherine saw that Dr. Harry was relieved to note that the Randolph had a desk clerk on duty through the night, as well as a doorman and a lift operator. He cautioned them all with a description of Stephenson and warned them not to tell anyone her room number on the telephone or in person.

By the time Catherine settled in her bed next to Dot, the pain in her head was so great, she didn't know if she would ever get out again. The pain medicine gave her wild but unremembered dreams, but other than that she passed an uneventful night.

Dot called the police station in the morning and determined that Dr. Stephenson was still at large. Apparently, he had fled.

Two men out there with motives to kill me.

She commenced to bathe and dress for the inquest.

* * *

Spectators and press crowded the Town Hall, but Catherine and the other witnesses sat sequestered behind a velvet rope in a section by an open window for which she was grateful. She was next to Dot on one side and Dr. Sargent on the other. Dr. Harry turned up at the last minute and showed her a wink before he sat down.

The coroner arrived, and they all rose until he was seated. He was a small man with an unusually skull-like head, his eyes deep in their sockets. He explained that the purpose of the inquest was to determine the cause of Dr. Agatha Chenowith's death. Several witnesses were to be called who had associated with her that last night.

First, the pathologist was called to the stand. He swore that death had occurred as the result of strangulation which had taken place at the so-called new chapel at Somerville College. According to the physical evidence, the body had not been moved from elsewhere. The means of strangulation appeared to be the scarf she was wearing at the time. When the pathologist was asked how long it would have taken to commit the deed, he answered that depending on the strength of the assailant, he estimated it would have taken anywhere from a minute to three minutes at the outside. Dr. Chenowith did not appear to have been a very strong woman.

Catherine was next to be called and sworn in. After she had

taken her seat, the coroner asked her to explain what she was doing in the new chapel at nine o'clock in the evening.

She explained about the sherry party for Dr. Sargent held in the Senior Commons Room at Somerville.

"There was a dinner afterward, held at The Mitre. When Dr. Chenowith proved to be missing during the toasts, the warden, Dr. Phillips, expressed alarm. We, along with Dr. Bascombe, another guest, decided to return to college to see if she was ill or injured. The scouts had already begun a search for her by the time we arrived." Here Catherine paused.

"It was my idea to have a look in the chapel as it was on the direct route from the SCR to where the cabs were waiting to take us to dinner. Also, it was one of the few buildings that would have been open. Dr. Bascombe accompanied me, and we began searching the pews."

Catherine found it necessary to stop a moment to compose herself as she remembered her discovery of the flaccid hand in the beam of her torch.

"I found her there."

A murmur swelled among the onlookers, and the coroner hammered his gavel.

"Now, Miss Tregowyn, please tell us who among those seated here attended the sherry party and dinner at The Mitre."

Catherine looked at those behind the rope and gave their names. "Dr. Anthony Stephenson was also there, but I don't see him in the courtroom."

"Thank you, Miss Tregowyn. Now, how and in what order did these various parties traverse from Somerville to the restaurant?"

"Miss Dorothy Nichols, Dr. Phillips, and Dr. Sargent and I walked from the SCR to the cab together immediately after the sherry party broke up. We took the first cab in line which had been called to wait for us. The other guests all followed eventually, though I don't know firsthand how they traveled there."

"Could any of the later arrivals have had sufficient time to commit this murder?"

Catherine's hands turned clammy, and a bead of perspiration traveled from her neck down between her shoulder blades. "I would rather not speculate on something so dire. There was one other cab, but there was not room for everyone in it. Its passengers arrived later than we did. I could not say with any accuracy how much later."

"Thank you, Miss Tregowyn. You may stand down."

Dr. Harry was called next. He was able to add the occupants of the second cab: himself, Mrs. Anne Tomlinson Stuart, and the professors Williams and Stephenson. He also gave an estimate as to the time the cab left. When asked if any of the occupants of the cab would have had time to commit the murder, he said he would rather not speculate on anything so damning.

"Isn't it true, Dr. Bascombe," asked the coroner, "that Dr. Chenowith gave a scathing review of your latest publication?"

Dr. Harry replied with his piratical grin. "These things happen. She was entitled to her opinion. I don't mean to sound like sour grapes, but Dr. Chenowith was not the best of friends with male professors in her field. She had yet to give any of us a glowing review."

He was told to stand down.

Both the dean, Dr. Andrews, and the other remaining guest, Lady Margery Wallinghouse, were asked to account for, in detail, their late arrival at the dinner following the sherry party. They both claimed to have had telephone calls to make—Lady Margery to her husband, and Dr. Andrews to her mother's nurse who was caring for her that evening in the dean's absence. The nurse, when summoned, confirmed the telephone call.

Sir Herbert Wallinghouse, a very handsome and appealing man, made a good witness for his wife's benefit. "She was calling to set my mind at rest. For various reasons, I hadn't wanted her to attend the dinner without me, and I was unable to go."

Catherine was interested to hear these new pieces of information, but could not quite bring herself to rely upon them—a spouse and an old family retainer? Not the ideal alibis.

The coroner, also, appeared to be skeptical, at least of Margery. He recalled her to the witness stand after hearing from her husband, and asked, "Is it true that you and Dr. Chenowith had a troubled history over a book of poems you wrote?"

Margery, dressed in sober black with an unimaginative hat (not at all her normal style), replied, "Yes. That is true."

"Perhaps you would enlighten the court," the coroner invited.

"I had a contract for a book, which Dr. Chenowith agreed to review at my publisher's request. I was quite shocked when, after reading the review she wrote, my publishers decided to revoke my contract. She had written scathingly of my work, which was a great surprise. She had read many of the poems individually and gave me to understand that she admired them."

"What action did you take? You must have been very angry."

"More hurt and puzzled. It was my husband who was angry. He sued the publisher. In the end, they arrived at a cash settlement."

"It puzzles me that you would attend this function for Dr. Sargent, knowing Dr. Chenowith would be there."

"I owe Professor Sargent quite a lot. And I didn't know for certain that Dr. Chenowith would attend. I wouldn't have thought she'd have the nerve for it, knowing that I would be there."

The coroner looked at Margery steadily as he asked, "And how did she treat you?"

"She gave me what used to be called 'the cut direct.' Fortunately, I had good friends there, as well as Dr. Sargent. My husband asked me to call after sherry to let him know if Dr. Chenowith was there, and if so, how it went."

"Thank you, Lady Margery. That is very clear."

The rotter! He thinks she did it, I'll wager. Catherine exchanged glances with Dr. Harry. He, signaling her with a raised eyebrow, evidently thought the same.

The coroner adjourned the court for luncheon, saying they would reconvene in two hours' time.

Dr. Harry shouldered himself over to where she stood. "At

least our canoodling didn't come into it," he said, looking down into her face. For the first time, she realized that he was quite tall. Since she was almost an average man's height, not many men looked down into her eyes like that.

"He's a beast. He thinks Margery did it. We shall have to prove him wrong," said Catherine.

"At least coroners no longer have the power to convict. He hasn't even called the police to give evidence. There's been no mention of Dr. Waddell, his strange appearance, and even stranger disappearance," said Dr. Harry.

"He hasn't even asked the members of your cab party to account for their missing ten minutes," she fumed. Turning to Dot, she asked, "What do you think?"

"I think they should check on Sir Herbert's whereabouts at the time. They are assuming he was home in Somerset. The exchange would have a record of a trunk call. He seems the more likely murderer to me."

"Brilliant!" Catherine gave her friend a quick hug. "Now, where shall we lunch?"

"Come," said Dr. Harry, "Be my guests at Christ Church."

"You won't find me turning down that lovely food," said Dot.

Over luncheon of roast beef, potatoes, French beans, and grilled tomatoes, they discussed the case against Dr. Stephenson.

"The police haven't been able to arrest him because he's disappeared," said Catherine.

"Yes. But it is rather a shame he has such a good alibi for the murder. I hope they can come up with some evidence that he was your attacker," said Dr. Harry.

"He seems like such a timid little man. It's difficult to imagine him swinging a cricket bat," said Catherine.

"He had a lot at stake," said Dot. "And remember that he raised quite a 'ruckus' at the library."

"Yes. He obviously has a violent side when threatened," said Dr. Harry.

"Dr. Chenowith herself wasn't above a spot of wickedness," said Catherine thoughtfully. "Remember Anne's first editions."

"She wasn't above doing things that weren't according to Hoyle, that's for sure," said Dot.

"It wasn't just men who found her a nasty bit of goods," said Dr. Harry.

After an excellent trifle for pudding, Dot and Catherine were led back to the inquest—one on each of his arms. Catherine's head was pounding out the rhythm of her heart by the time she took her seat.

During the afternoon, the court finally heard from the police, who told of the strange behavior of one Dr. Christopher Waddell. Catherine was glad of their evidence as it seemed to take the spotlight off Margery, save for the fact that there was not a scrap of motive to be had for Dr. Waddell.

In the end, the coroner said, "It is not my place to name Dr. Chenowith's assailant, but I feel we have heard plenty of evidence to declare that the woman met her death unlawfully by a person or persons unknown. The facts gathered in these proceedings will be handed over to the Crown's prosecutors, and charges will be brought in the future when a case is built, and a trial is held."

He banged his gavel and adjourned the court.

Chapter Twelve

As spectators and participants filed out of the Town Hall, Catherine spied Dr. Williams making for the cab queue on St. Aldate's Street. She knew that Detective Chief Inspector Marsh would want to speak to her, but it occurred to Catherine that now might be a good time to latch onto Professor Williams before he got back to his hush-hush job in London.

Notifying Dot and Dr. Harry of her intent, she told them she would meet them at the Eagle and Child after she had spoken to the professor.

"I say, Dr. Williams, what did you think of the proceedings?" she asked once she had said hello to the professor as he stood in the queue. "Have you ever heard of that fellow Waddell? There's at least a possibility that he might have been the one who coshed me."

"Coshed you?" The dapper little man raised his eyebrows. "Did I miss something in there? I must say it was deuced warm."

"I guess you haven't heard about my little adventure," she said. "I was hit over the head with a cricket bat in the Somerville quad."

"My dear! I'm so sorry. Whatever for, do you think?"

"I don't really know if it was Waddell. Others have motives, too." She refrained from getting into the case against Dr.

Stephenson as it didn't serve her purpose at the moment. "I don't know why he would want to, or even what he has to do with this crazy situation."

"Should you be standing about in the sun?" Dr. Williams asked. "How about if we go someplace for a drink. You're looking a bit peaked."

He helped her into the waiting cab and told the driver to take them to the Eagle and Child. Catherine appreciated the gallant gesture and was glad of their destination as it would be easy to catch up with her friends there.

The ride was a short one, and once they were inside, the professor found a seat for her in the pub's wood-paneled inglenook and went off to order her a lemon squash. By the time he returned with their drinks, she was feeling somewhat restored.

"I know Waddell slightly. He's a bit of an oddity, even for Oxford," he said. "But I can't for the life of me figure out what his connection would be to Dr. Chenowith or this investigation."

"I have heard he's a bit of a fascist," Catherine ventured, sipping her drink.

"He's right off his nut about Hitler, that's true. But, as far as I know, Agatha Chenowith wasn't political."

Catherine thought about this statement. "She was a woman of untapped depths; I'm finding out," she said.

"How do you mean?"

"In some ways, she wasn't very nice. She seems to have liked upsetting the apple cart."

"Well, I know her feelings about men. To my cost," he said with a short huff. "I have caught myself sometimes what it was that put her off our sex."

"Have you ever wondered how such a beautiful poet could be such a hurtful human being?" Catherine asked. She told him the story of Anne and her first editions, as well as the sad account of Lady Rachel.

"Present company excepted; poets can be odd. I think they put their brains in a different gear when they write."

"I wouldn't excuse myself from that stricture," she said. "It's true that I did like Agatha Chenowith, the poet, a lot better than Agatha Chenowith, the person."

"I'm just glad our orbits didn't intersect often," Williams said.

"Especially now that you're not at Oxford much," said Catherine. "Do you miss it?"

"Yes. We are doing some interesting things right now with the investigations in Norway. It's very exciting to find these stories so close to primitive thought that have been handed down over such eons."

"Early Teutonic legends, you said?"

"Yes. Oral tradition. None of it has been written down, so everyone is scrambling to transcribe. It's part of this remote peoples' consciousness. They don't even know how it has colored their perceptions of the world. Oddly, it makes one question one's own basis for reality."

"So . . . Wotan and that gang?" Catherine asked. She had always found the grim old legends surprisingly frightening. Bad fortune seemed to swirl through them with an uncomfortable arbitrariness. She had always thought the Greek and Roman myths more friendly and sensible by comparison.

"Yes. The essence of Richard Wagner, of course."

"And the legend of the Aryan master race," she said dampeningly. "Hitler loves Wotan, I understand."

The professor looked uncomfortable, so Catherine took pity on him and changed the subject. "And what exactly is it you're doing at Whitehall?"

"I advise in a general capacity. Nothing thrilling. Would you care for another drink?"

"No, thanks. I know you must need to get back to London. This has been a refreshing change from the inquest. Thank you for taking me under your wing."

"Maybe we'll see each other soon. I'm going to organize a little soiree when my lads get back from Norway."

"That sounds interesting," she said.

Only after Catherine had said goodbye and went to join her friends in another inglenook did she realize she had no more idea than before about what Professor Williams had been up to in his missing ten minutes.

* * *

"So?" Dot inquired, sipping on her lager.

"I muffed it," she said. "Got drawn in by the general perfidy of Chenowith and Teutonic Fairy Tales and completely failed in my mission."

"Well, what's your general impression of the professor?" Dot asked.

"Typical Oxford professor with his quaint enthusiasms. Even he was stung by the Chenowith scorpion, though he didn't give details. He said Waddell was odd, by the way, even by Oxford standards."

"How's your head?" asked Dr. Harry.

"Thumping. I'm in no shape to go to the police station, but I suppose I must."

* * *

The sergeant at the station desk rang for the Detective Chief Inspector, who appeared to greet Catherine and Dr. Harry. Dot said she would meet them at Somerville.

"Miss Tregowyn, Dr. Bascombe. I'm afraid I have some rather upsetting news. We haven't been able to lay our hands on Dr. Stephenson. We were unable to locate him at his college this morning. A watch has been kept there since then, and he hasn't turned up. As you noted, Miss Tregowyn, he didn't show up at the inquest."

Dr. Harry's hand went to the small of her back in a protective gesture. Catherine's heart jolted at this most recent news that the professor was still at large.

"Please come back to my office," the policeman invited.

The handsome Detective Chief Inspector's office was neat as a pin, which had the effect of irritating Catherine. Her life at the moment was anything but neat. Her head hurt, she was in danger, and the police had let her down.

"There is the consolation that if he knows you have been to the police, he knows he has nothing to gain by killing you," Marsh said.

"We can't be certain of that," said Dr. Harry.

"His colleagues at Merton said he hasn't been in college for a couple of days. The receptionist at the Radcliffe Infirmary says she took several calls from the Merton College exchange the night Miss Tregowyn was brought in wanting to know her condition. She explained that she could not give that information to anyone but family. That is the closest thing we have to proof that Dr. Stephenson was behind your attack. His apparent flight is also another indicator. Your *Life of Edith Penwyth* was also checked out of the Merton College Library by Dr. Stephenson the day of the attack, Miss Tregowyn. All these things, taken together, are damning."

"Does he have a motorcar registered to him?" asked Dr. Harry.

"Not that we have been able to discover. His family home is in Londonderry, Northern Ireland, but we imagine he will steer clear of there. We have notified the police there in any event."

"This is very unsettling," said Catherine.

"I advise you to stay in company," said Marsh. "And to keep your wits about you. However, I doubt he is going to show himself."

"Has he been in touch with his publisher?" asked Catherine.

"We rang them this morning. They have heard nothing from the professor. Naturally, they wanted to know our business with him. We told them he is a person of interest in an assault case.

They were not too happy about that. They agreed to cooperate and said they would let us know if they heard anything from him."

"Did you want to ask me any further questions after reading my statement from last night?" asked Catherine.

"No. It was very clear and complete," said the Detective Chief Inspector. "Will you continue to stay at Oxford? If not, I will need your London address."

She gave it to him along with her telephone number. "I don't know how long I will be staying here. At least through the weekend, I imagine. I will be at the Randolph. It's safer than Somerville."

Catherine stood. The policeman showed her and Dr. Harry out. "We will continue to have a uniformed constable in the lobby then."

"I'll drop you off at the Randolph and then go back to Somerville to collect Dot," said Dr. Harry.

"Could you also give Hobbs a message for me?"

"Of course."

Once they arrived at the Randolph, Catherine wrote out a message on hotel stationery and addressed it to Mr. Rafael St. John. She knew he'd be up at Oxford sometime looking for her. She handed the note to Dr. Harry.

"Give this to Hobbs and tell him that Rafe is a big man with curly black hair. No one else is to know where I am."

Dr. Harry pressed his lips together. "Rafael St. John? Who is that?"

She replied with spirit, "My sometime fiancé. He's just back from Kenya."

"Sometime fiancé?"

"It's a long story, and I'm far too exhausted to get into it at the moment. Plus, I feel positively grimy and must have a bath. Thank you for standing by me. Thank you for all your help."

"I will be in touch with you tomorrow," he said with all the firmness of a bulldog.

"Fine," she said. "Now I go to take my bath and have an early night."

* * *

Much later, when Dot was already asleep, and Catherine was sliding under her sheets, pink and fresh from her bath, Catherine heard the telephone.

"Bother!" she said. She rolled over and tried to block the sound with her pillow. It continued, however.

Finally, worried it might be something to do with her inquiries, she answered.

"Hello?"

"Cat?"

Her stomach performed a flip. "Rafe?"

"Cat! I'm here! Down in the lobby. I couldn't wait to see you, so I motored up from London."

In spite of all her efforts to dampen it, she felt the excitement Rafe's presence in her life always brought. Her fatigue fled, and her heart began to pound. "I'm in my pajamas. Give me a moment to get dressed, you bounder."

She hung up and brought her hands up to her burning cheeks.

What should I wear? Oh! What about my hair? I can't wear a hat at this time of night.

Dot rolled over. "Who was that?"

"Go back to sleep," she said. "Just Rafe."

Dot groaned and put her head under her pillow.

Catherine settled on her gray flannel trousers and a pale blue turtleneck jumper. She tied a matching scarf around her hair, arranging it in a floppy bow on the right side of her head. Adding a bit of powder and lipstick, she frowned at herself in the mirror.

Will he find me changed? Are those circles under my eyes?

She turned resolutely from the mirror and went out the door.

* * *

It had been many years since she had decided Rafael St. James was going to be the great love of her life. As far as she could recall, she had been ten years old the first time her brother, William, had brought him home from boarding school. She had gone back on that decision many times since, but the sight of him never failed to lift her heart. He was tall and powerfully built with a head of black curls—a gift from a Spanish ancestor—he tried unsuccessfully to tame

"Rafe!" she exclaimed upon seeing him.

His exuberance matched her own as he pulled her to him and twirled her around right there in the lobby.

"Stop it!" she cried. "I am no longer a hoyden, but a respectable graduate of this university!"

"How could I ever leave you for as long as a year?" he asked.

Catherine took the question to be rhetorical. "Have you eaten anything for dinner?"

"No. I drove straight up from London."

"Let's find you a beefsteak," she said. "You must be starved."

They left the Randolph and began walking toward the High Street. It felt so good to be next to Rafe again. She fell into step with him as though they had been together just yesterday.

"Have you a place to stay?" she asked.

"How long do you plan on being here?"

Catherine grinned. "I told you. I'm investigating a murder."

She might have said she had taken up opera dancing. "So you weren't joking in your letter."

"No. Definitely not. One of my former professors was murdered in the new chapel at Somerville." She gave him a very abbreviated sketch of the situation.

"Strewth! You discovered a body?"

"Yes. It was beastly. The police have several suspects, of which I am one."

"So naturally you feel you must look into it yourself."

"Naturally. I make a rather good detective, actually," she said.

They had arrived at the Carfax intersection, where the High

met St. Aldates. Catherine led Rafe to The Canterbury Room, an upstairs grill and restaurant where they served a decent steak. The maître 'd seated them at a table by the window.

"How's William?" she asked.

"Happy to be home. He didn't take to Kenya, as you probably know."

She had received but a few letters from her brother, but all were less than enthusiastic. "But you did. I'm surprised you came back."

"Needs must. The pater isn't well. He wants me by him so he can task me with all my duties. As usual, he feels that he is going to pass on. You know how he gets."

"Well, he does have a weak heart, Rafe."

He dismissed his father's health with a wave of his hand. "He will outlive us all. Mark my words."

"So, when do you go down to Kent?" she asked, looking her fill at his full lips and hooded brown eyes. She had missed him so much it troubled her.

"He has actually come up to London to the Mayfair flat. We're meeting with his man of business tomorrow."

"That sounds serious."

"Yes. He's transferring title of some of his holdings to me to begin looking after. Boring businesses in the North."

The waiter came, and Rafe put in his order. Catherine requested a slice of apple tart. Her grand luncheon at Christ Church remained with her.

"So," he said, placing his hands palms down in front of him and looking her in the eye. "When are you going to marry me?"

All Catherine's pleasure at seeing Rafe drained away. "We've had this out thoroughly, Rafe."

"But I'm a changed man, Cat. Kenya was good for me. At least give me a chance to prove it to you."

How many chances had she given him? Her head warned her heart.

She looked down at her hands linked before her on the table but said nothing.

"Six months," he said. "Give me six months."

"No engagement," she countered.

"All right," he agreed. "No engagement. But when are you coming back to London?"

"I don't know at the moment. There are things I need to follow up on here in Oxford."

"All right. Plan on me joining you here after I've done with the pater."

The white-aproned waiter served their food. Catherine tucked into her tart. "You didn't write much, but I read your pieces in the *Times*. Tell me more about Kenya."

Rafe, an excellent raconteur, spun tails of safaris and colonial life. "You can't even imagine the vastness of Africa. There is one grand vista after another. And the animals. I lived out all my boyhood fantasies—elephants, giraffes, lions! The whole country suited me down to the ground."

"I can imagine," she said with a smile.

"I think I might like to buy a coffee plantation. Of course, I would have someone else run it. I wouldn't want to leave England for good. How about you? Would you be willing to give it a try?"

Catherine's feelings were mixed. While it sounded a grand adventure, she knew to her cost that Rafe could make anything sound appealing. The problem was, his enthusiasms did not endure.

"I might enjoy a visit," she temporized.

"It's a beautiful place. So completely different from England."

"I love England," she said, knowing she sounded merely stubborn. She added, "But there are many places I long to visit. Italy, for instance. Greece."

"We could travel anywhere you like," he said.

"Italy, first then," she said. "For the art, the clothes, and the food. I long to visit Florence and Tuscany."

"When the time comes, I will buy your engagement ring there,"

Rafe said. "On the Ponte Vecchio. You will love all the little jewelry shops—some no bigger than a cupboard—all on this quaint
old bridge over the river."

"Then Greece. I want to see the ruins. I even know some Greek.
And I want to cruise the islands," said Catherine. She never hesitated to speak of her dreams to Rafe. He was the one who had
always encouraged her to become a poet. Some dreams came true.

"That is where we will honeymoon," Rafe decided. "There is
enough to see there to keep us for months."

If only. . . How wonderful life would be.

"When we go to Kenya, I will teach you to shoot. There is
nothing like a big game hunt," Rafe told her.

"I'm afraid I must draw the line at shooting. I would love to
see those beautiful animals. But I could never bring myself to kill
them."

He laughed. "Ever the idealist. Some of them might eat you.
We'll see."

Rafe made it all seem so real. So possible. Indulging her imagination, she spoke of Paris, Spain, and the Pyramids. They ended
the dinner in laughter and high spirits. By the time they got back to
the Randolph, Rafe had wrapped her up completely in his brand
of magic, and she was close to forgetting all that she had resolved
to remember. She hadn't even mentioned to him that someone was
trying to kill her.

At the door to her room, he said, "I will drive back to London
tonight, then. Here is something to remember me by."

He kissed her with a warmth that curled her toes. Nothing had
changed. But then, that was part of the problem. Nothing had
changed. She watched him walk away with regret.

How long will it last this time? Am I completely nuts?

Chapter Thirteen

Catherine didn't sleep much that night but tossed and turned over her inevitable reaction to Rafe. When she eventually slept, she dreamed of sailing in a leaky boat.

Dot woke her at what seemed like dawn.

She groaned. At least her head was a little better. She remembered she needed to get it checked at the infirmary today.

"How was Rafe?" Dot asked. "Has he cast his spell, once again?"

"He's the same," she said. "I'm to give him a six-month trial."

"He is the same."

"Yes. Still kisses like a dream."

"I need to go into work today, but I'll be back up here for the weekend. What are you doing?"

Catherine hoisted herself on her elbows. "I need to go to Somerville to speak to Jennie about Lady Rachel's friends."

"That's good. It's right by the infirmary. You need your head looked at."

"Inside and out, I'm afraid," said Catherine with a sigh. She said good-bye to Dot.

After a cooked breakfast in the hotel dining room, she stepped out into the fresh air and walked briskly to Somerville, hoping that Dr. Stephenson was not observing her.

Where had he gone? Was he lurking, trying to find her alone? Or had he given up on that idea, knowing she had already been to the police with her tale of plagiarism?

She had no answers.

Once at Somerville, she sought out Jennie who was changing linens and refreshing towels in the few inhabited rooms in the dormitories.

After inquiring after the scout's health, Catherine asked, "Jennie, could you try to find out the names of Lady Rachel's friends? I think maybe she might have been in touch with at least one of them since she left college. We have no idea where she is."

"I'll ask my friend, Mary. I think she may know. How is your head today?"

"I'm supposed to go to the infirmary to get the bandage changed. Bit of a bother, but I'm feeling all right."

The scout scrutinized her face. "You didn't sleep well."

"No," said Catherine. "It must be this beastly murder."

* * *

Catherine kept the promise she'd made to Dot and went to the nearby Radcliffe Infirmary to have her head checked, and her bandage changed. As she lay on the table in the treatment room, she thought through what she knew.

Surely the Detective Chief Inspector no longer suspected her of the murder of Dr. Chenowith. Why was she so driven to meddle in his investigation? Why did she think she could do a better job at it?

She shouldn't feel bad about Dr. Stephenson. She would have found him out eventually after the book was published. And he had tried to murder her.

Should she cease investigating? Still troubled by Lady Rachel, she thought she should at least eliminate her as a suspect. The police weren't even looking in that direction, as far as she knew.

Besides, it gave her something else to occupy her mind other than the man who had just returned from Kenya.

When she arrived back at Somerville, there was a message waiting for her from Dr. Harry. He had rung to invite her to "Guest for Tea Day" at Christ Church. He claimed to have some information to share.

Cheek! He knew she couldn't resist a clue.

She went to the room she had occupied and packed up all her possessions for the Randolph porter to pick up. Then, giving in to the demands of a headache on top of a sleepless night, Catherine decided on a bit of a lie-down. Jennie assured her no one would mind if she lay on the bed in the room she had occupied. She promised to make up the bed again. Catherine ended by sleeping away the entire afternoon.

* * *

Dr. Harry awaited her at the Christ Church porter's lodge to take her in to tea. She hadn't known how dressy she should be, so she was glad to see by his tie and navy blue blazer that she had been wise in the choice of her white linen suit and red and white cartwheel hat.

"Greetings," he said. "Did you make it to the infirmary today?"

He was every bit as handsome as Rafe in his own way. "I did. And I napped away the afternoon so I'm in fine fettle."

"Oh my," she said as they entered the dining room. "This is elaborate."

The complete tea consisted of tiered servers full of cakes, scones, and biscuits, plates of sandwiches and fruit, as well as complete silver tea services with pots of jam and clotted cream.

"I shan't want dinner, that's for certain."

Once they were seated, she said, "So what's the clue you have for me?"

"Well, I doubt it will make you happy, but I have cultivated a sergeant who is working on this case. Had a pint with him. If I approach him casually enough, he has proved to be not immune to my digging. He happened to mention that there was no trunk call made from Somerville to Somerset on the night of the murder. So, your friend, Margery's alibi has vanished. And there is the fact that she lied under oath, as well."

"Oh." Catherine felt as though the wind were knocked out of her. "That was a silly thing to do. She must have known they would check."

"She still maintains she called her husband," Dr. Harry said. "He just didn't happen to be in Somerset. He was here. At the Randolph."

"Oh, my. I suppose they checked that, as well."

"Yes. Sir Herbert was apparently out when she claimed to have called. The hotel rang his room, but he didn't answer. They were most helpful."

"Evidently."

Catherine thought about what she knew of Margery's husband. He loved his wife fiercely. The whole business of her poetry was important enough to him to have brought a lawsuit against the publisher who withdrew her contract. But was he hot-headed? Would he commit murder over such a thing? Catherine had no idea.

It is the sort of thing Rafe would do.

She brushed the thought away impatiently.

"So now he is a suspect, as well as Margery," she said.

"Yes. Perhaps we are going to have a plethora of suspects, and the problem is going to be choosing between them. There is Waddell, too."

"And I'm still going to try to follow up on Lady Rachel. My scout is trying to find out who her friends are. One of them might know where she is. But I agree. Waddell is a puzzle. How in the world does he fit in?"

Dr. Harry spread a scone carefully with clotted cream and topped it with raspberry jam. "If he hadn't disappeared, I wouldn't be thinking twice about him," he said.

"I know what you mean. By the way, this walnut cake is divine," she said.

"We seem to do our best detecting over meals," said Dr. Harry after finishing off his scone. "Speaking of which, a mate of mine saw you out to dinner last night with a chap."

"That was my chap." She tossed the words out like a challenge. "Rafael St. James."

"Is he the one who writes about Kenya in *The Times Sunday Supplement?*"

"The same," she said, obscurely glad that Rafe had acquitted himself so well in print.

"Glad to see him?"

"I am. He'll be coming up to Oxford next week if I'm still here, so you'll have a chance to meet him."

"Delighted, I'm sure," he said, his voice dry. "Can't say I think much of that type."

"What type is that?" she asked, affronted as though he had criticized a member of her family.

"Big game hunter, idle rich."

"He's not exactly idle," she said. "He's talked about buying a farm in Africa, and he's in London learning all about the companies he's inheriting from his father."

"And hiring someone else to run, I imagine."

She couldn't disagree. She took up his other point. "I don't like the hunting either," she admitted. "He wants me to learn, but I could never shoot anything like an elephant. It would feel like murder."

"So, there's hope for you," he said.

"What do you mean by that?"

He only raised an eyebrow and offered to refill her teacup.

Would he classify her as a member of the "idle rich?" Probably. Although she did have her East End boys. And her poetry, of course.

Steady on! Why does it matter what he thinks?

"We're going to honeymoon in Greece," she shot back.

"So, you're engaged?"

"Provisionally," she hedged. "I've been more or less engaged to Rafe as long as I can remember."

"What's stopping you?" he asked, his blue eyes keen as he examined hers.

"I couldn't begin to explain, and you wouldn't understand anyway." She took a cucumber sandwich and ate it as though it were an act of defiance.

"I'd be interested to know what Dot thinks of all this."

For some reason, Dr. Harry compelled her to be honest. "She doesn't like Rafe."

"I knew she had a good head on her shoulders."

"You haven't even met him!"

"Has anyone ever told you you're a bit dense at times?"

She felt herself color as red as the raspberry jam. Dr. Harry was interested in her romantically? No. He just liked a challenge. He didn't even like her. Besides, he despised her poetry.

He evidently decided a change of topic was called for. "So how are you going to track down Lady Rachel's friends?"

"I haven't got that far yet. I don't even have their names."

"You need a source in the Registrar's Office."

"With any luck, one of them will be in Debrett's like Lady Rachel."

Dr. Harry prepared another scone with cream and jam and placed it on her plate. "Eat. You're far too thin."

Ignoring him, she said, "I wonder if I ought to talk to Margery."

"I thought we might go dancing tonight," he said.

She looked at him as though she had misheard. "Are you joking?"

"Not a bit."

Without thinking, she ate the cream scone. She loved to go dancing, and it had been ages. And she wasn't *actually* engaged. Then she remembered.

"I have a shaved spot and a big white bandage on my head."

"Wear a thing in your hair. You know. One of those bands with feathers sticking out."

"How enterprising you are! What sort of feathers do you recommend?"

He grinned at her. "Ostrich. Dinner first?"

"I already told you that I shan't need dinner tonight. This tea will just about set me up for life."

"All right. I'll call for you in my motor at eight o'clock. There's a dance on at the Town Hall. The band is supposed to be good. You tango, I hope?"

"With pleasure," she said and gave a little laugh. She could only imagine what it would be like to tango with a pirate.

* * *

Fortunately, Catherine knew of a costumier near the covered market who was happy to rent her a feathered headpiece that successfully covered her bandage. There were plenty of dancing frocks there, as well. Oxonians loved to dress up without spending much money. She found an ivory gown with black feathered shoulders and hem and a smocked bodice that fit her to perfection.

As she walked back to the Randolph with the hired clothing, her spirits were high. There was a message from Jennie awaiting her.

Mary knew one of Lady Rachel's friends. Her name is Honorable Gwendolyn Fellingsworth. She lives in Hampshire, but Mary didn't know any more than that. I hope this helps.

An Honorable! Well, that was a piece of luck. She would be in Debrett's. But that would be left until tomorrow. Now she needed a bath.

Her belongings from Somerville awaited her in her room. She extracted her oil of gardenia and poured it into her bath in the old Victorian tub and allowed herself to soak.

Catherine couldn't believe that Dr. Harry was anything more than a flirt, although he had been wonderful to her when she had been coshed. But they were incompatible. Her poetry was the best part of her, and he utterly rejected it. Why did she have to keep telling herself that? Was she actually in danger of falling for the man?

No. Of course not. Unfortunately, she was mad about Rafe.

Chapter Fourteen

Dr. Harry in full evening kit was a sight to behold. Simply put, he was gorgeous. The stark black and white of his clothing played up his resemblance to Douglas Fairbanks, and the flash of his smile was devastating.

What am I doing?

"You look marvelous. Nothing like a convalescent," he told her. "And the headpiece is a success."

"Thank you. I haven't been dancing in a long time. I'm looking forward to it."

The Town Hall had been transformed. The walls were lined with ornamental trees and flowering shrubs in containers. A white gauze sheet stretched above them at ten feet, lowering the ceiling. All the light was provided by gas lamps.

The band was sensational. Dr. Harry asked her to dance immediately. It was a Fox Trot, and Catherine had to admit he was a wonderful dancer. He fixed her with his sapphire gaze and said the last thing she expected.

"I was certain Penwyth was an agnostic. That was the worst of it."

Gathering her wits, she said, "No. She was definitely a transcendentalist. She knew it was unfashionable, but she was."

"I forgive you for being right. Is there any chance I can look at her papers sometime?"

A kernel of disappointment bloomed in her breast. "Is that what this evening is about? You could have just asked. You didn't need to bring me dancing."

He grinned. "Since I made your acquaintance, I have been prey to two warring factions in my consciousness. Number One: I have always wanted to dance the Tango with you. Number Two: I have been angry you beat me to Penwyth's biography. I can now admit that it was a good thing for my own scholarship on the woman was completely amiss, and you saved me a great embarrassment. But I still want to dance the Tango with you."

His words countered her disappointment, and she began to feel more at ease, but still a bit on guard. "I am trying to get used to your frankness," she said.

The dance ended, and they made their way to a side table which had been set up to hold punch and miniature pastries. "I'll let you sample the punch and tell me what variety it is," she said.

He took up a cup and sampled it. "Rum," he said. "Not too strong. Fruity."

She had detested rum ever since an incident at Dot's coming out party when she had been distressingly ill. "I'll pass on it, I believe. But these look amusing." Catherine sampled a tiny chocolate cream puff.

With a cloth napkin, he wiped a tiny bit of cream from her upper lip. The gesture was intimate, and she unconsciously touched the place with her tongue.

"You will finish by driving me round the bend," he said. "Let's dance again."

"It's a Rhumba," she said. "I don't know how."

"I will teach you then," he said. "As evidence that I am over being shown up by a female undergraduate."

"But I don't think that you are," she said.

"But I am working on it," he said. "And you are helping."

He taught her the Rhumba box step, and she caught on quickly. A spot of heat bloomed in her breast as they danced.

Stop it! He isn't Rafe!

The attraction she felt was as welcome as a nail file against her bare skin. Catherine was relieved when the dance ended, and she spotted Margery and her husband across the room.

"You must come to meet the Wallinghouses. I see Margery," she said.

"I remember her from the dinner, but I don't think we've ever been introduced," he said.

They fought through the thick crowd until they achieved her objective.

"Margery! I'm so happy to see you. Sir Herbert, good evening."

Her friend exclaimed over her dress and kissed her cheek.

Catherine said, "I'd like to introduce my friend, Dr. Bascombe. Margery, you may remember him from dinner at The Mitre. Dr. Bascombe, meet Sir Herbert Wallinghouse and Lady Margery."

The baronet was tall and balding. He was handsome in a very English sort of way with a thin, long nose, a broad brow, and large, deeply set eyes. The men shook hands.

Dr. Harry wasted no time on trivialities. "Horrible thing, murder," he said.

"Ghastly," said Margery. "And the police have us in their sites."

"Not really!" said Catherine.

"You know all the business about my poetry. They are convinced one of us did it for revenge."

"Poetry as a motive for murder. Only in Oxford," said Dr. Harry.

"I'm working on a few other angles. I know you aren't guilty," said Catherine.

"This new suspect has a poetry motive, as well?" asked the baronet.

"I shouldn't say anything about it, but I can tell you that we're not certain poetry has anything to do with it," said Catherine.

"Thank you for looking into this," said Margery. "Now that we know we aren't being singled out, maybe I can enjoy the dancing a little more. And maybe the police will let us go home tomorrow."

Catherine felt a little uneasy. Had she had been so anxious to reassure her friend that she had spoken up when she shouldn't have? Detective Chief Inspector Marsh was not going to be pleased with her if he found out.

"I haven't talked to you since Dr. Chenowith's review of your book," she said to Margery. "I have never understood it. She liked the poems you submitted to her individually. It doesn't make sense."

"I know. It was the greatest shock of my life, I think."

"What I am learning about her makes me realize she wasn't a particularly nice person. Did you ever do anything to offend her in any way?"

"She took against me from the time I married. You know how she felt about men, right?"

Catherine thought about this for a moment and then objected, "But Anne married. And Dr. Chenowith was always perfectly cordial to her. Even when she went platinum blonde."

She was aware that the baronet was shifting uneasily on his feet. "Let's dance, Margery," he said. "Good to meet you, professor. Good to see you, Catherine."

As they moved off, Dr. Harry said, "That man has something in his craw."

"I agree. Something is making him tremendously nervous. He's always been the soul of politeness, and that was downright rude."

"It's something to do with Chenowith, I'll wager," said Dr. Harry.

"But how would he even know her? She was an academic; he's a wealthy aristocrat."

"How did he meet Lady Margery?"

"At a coming-out party in London. It's been about four years ago now, during our last year at Somerville."

"He looks quite a bit older than Lady Margery."

"He is. There's a fifteen-year age difference. It never mattered to her, though."

"How old was Chenowith?"

"Approaching forty, I would say. But the way she wore her hair aged her. She could have been younger."

"I'll wager she knew Sir Herbert and he knew her. Very well."

Catherine considered this. "Yes. You could be right. He never came to Oxford that year. Even though they were engaged. I didn't meet him until the wedding."

"Do you know where he went to university?"

"I don't."

"A look in Debrett's will inform us. Dr. Chenowith was at Somerville, am I correct?" he asked.

"Yes, but she didn't like men."

"Maybe he's why."

The music changed. Suddenly the room came alive. It was a Tango.

She watched as Dr. Harry shook off his preoccupation.

"All right, Señorita. You will not escape me now."

Her partner took on a new personality as they moved onto the dance floor. His every move was cloaked in drama. Laughing, she joined him in the game, locking her gaze with his, miming deep passion. They stepped carefully and deliberately. Soon a circle had cleared around them as people drew back to give them room to perform. When the music ended, there was applause.

Dr. Harry gave a flamboyant bow and Catherine curtseyed. She hadn't had so much fun in a long time. Her partner told her she had to have a glass of punch after that, and she regretfully agreed. She was thirsty, but she hoped the result would not be disastrous.

"That was smashing," she said, borrowing Dot's favorite word.

"Utterly," agreed Dr. Harry. "You are the perfect partner. Does your Rafael St. John dance?"

"Very unwillingly," she answered.

"How did you meet?" he asked, his voice casual as he sipped his punch.

"He came home from school with my brother when I was ten. It was love at first sight." She put her cup down on a convenient tray. "But let's not talk about Rafe. Let's dance again."

They danced until the band packed up at one a.m. Catherine chased every serious thought from her head, and when the band left declared herself to be starving.

"I don't suppose we could find bacon and eggs anywhere," she said.

"Oysters, yes. Bacon and eggs, no," said her partner.

They headed for Carmichael's on the High Street, and each consumed a dozen raw oysters. Dr. Harry quoted Ogden Nash limericks one after another. It was the perfect cap to the evening.

When they stood outside her room at the Randolph, Catherine told him, "I haven't had such a lovely time in years. Thank you so much."

"What are you doing tomorrow?" he asked.

"Trying to track down Lady Rachel. Dot will be here in the morning."

"I am going to ferret out acquaintances of the elusive Dr. Waddell. I am determined to find out what the man is up to."

"Good idea," she said. Standing on her toes, she kissed his cheek. "Goodnight, Señor."

"Adios, Señorita."

She carried the memory of his smile with her in all her preparations for bed. Then she slept long and deeply.

CHAPTER FIFTEEN

Dot woke her at ten o'clock.

"Here I rise at dawn and drive up from London, ready for the hunt, only to find you still abed!"

"I went out dancing," she said dreamily.

"Dancing?"

"With Dr. Harry. We did the Tango. It was more fun than anything."

"Dr. Harry, huh? At least it wasn't the wastrel. Up, up, up!"

Catherine dressed quickly in her pink frock and hat while Dot ordered coffee and a bun for her from room service.

They found Dr. Harry waiting in the lobby below.

"Hullo, Señor!" said Catherine. "What are you doing here?"

"I thought I might help in the search for Lady Rachel. Saturday is not the easiest day to track down inhabitants of the men's colleges."

"We have to stop at Somerville to check the Debrett's in the library," said Catherine.

"My carriage awaits," said Dr. Harry. "I am ready to perform chauffeuring duties for the day."

She looked at him suspiciously. "Are you sure you're not acting as bodyguard?"

"Well, that, too. I won't be totally at ease until Stephenson is brought in."

"They didn't bring Stephenson in yet?" asked Dot.

"They haven't found him. Hence the bobby in the lobby here," said Catherine.

"Oh, dear. Surely, he knows that horse has already bolted. He must know why the police are after him."

"He called the infirmary," Catherine said. "He knows I survived the blow. We think that's when he took off."

"Well, I think my driving is probably better than yours," Dot said to Dr. Harry. "But I won't mind being chauffeured for once. You will be a grand help if we should have a puncture."

* * *

Dr. Harry waited by the porter's lodge in his Morris motor while Catherine and Dot performed their errand at Somerville.

At the library, Dot found the *Debrett's Peerage,* and they looked up the Fellingsworth family of Hampshire.

"Gwendolyn's father is Lord Robert, the second son of the Marquis of Debenham. The Debenham family seat, Brookshire Hall, is near Winchester, it looks like," she said. "New Alresford. It doesn't show Lord Robert's residence. We will have to place a trunk call to Brookshire Hall to find out. Where shall we ring from?"

"Hobbs will let us ring from the porter's lodge if we leave him money to cover it," said Catherine. "At least, that was the policy when we were up. I had to call Cornwall often when my mother was so ill."

The porter was indeed amenable. It only remained for them to ascertain the cost of the call from the switchboard operator at its conclusion.

Dot made the call. "Brookshire Hall in New Alresford, Hampshire, if you please."

The operator told her to ring off and wait for her call to be connected. While they were waiting, Dr. Harry, who had apparently grown tired of his motor, arrived at the lodge.

Catherine greeted him, "We are waiting for a call from Hampshire. Trying to locate Lady Rachel's friend."

"So she was in Debrett's?" he asked.

"Yes. An honorable. Niece to the Marquis of Debenham," said Catherine. "We're calling the family seat to try to find her."

"Is her father Robert or Alexander?" asked Dr. Harry.

"Robert," Dot said.

"I might have more luck. The marquis was up at Christ Church before the War. He actually made it through. He is an active alum. I know him."

"You're heaven sent then. We're trying to locate Gwendolyn—family name Fellingsworth."

The operator rang through, telling them she had Brookshire Hall on the line. At a nod from Catherine, Dr. Harry took the receiver.

"Hullo! This is Dr. Harry Bascombe calling from Christ Church at Oxford. Is this Lord Debenham's butler?"

"It is. Quarrels, Dr. Bascombe."

"Quarrels, yes. I remember. I don't wish to bother the marquis if I can help it. I am trying to ring his brother, Lord Robert. Have you his direction?"

"He lives here on the estate. The exchange will know. Redford House."

"Thank you so much, Quarrels. The family is at home, I take it?"

"Yes. You will find them all in residence, Dr. Bascombe."

"Thank you."

Dot took the receiver from Dr. Harry and asked the exchange for the charge on the call. Catherine left the requisite number of shillings with Hobbs. Then she thought to ask him, "May I leave a message to be delivered to the scout, Jennie, Hobbs?"

For a moment, the porter looked a bit sour. Then he said, "Yes, miss. I suppose I could take it over there before I go off duty."

"I would appreciate it. It has to do with Dr. Chenowith's murder investigation."

The man brightened. "I would be happy to take a message, miss."

Catherine wrote out a message for Jennie, telling her that if she had any further information about Dr. Chenowith, she could always call and leave a message with her maid in London. She left her telephone number.

"Thank you, Hobbs."

"It looks like we're off for Hampshire," said Catherine as they climbed into Dr. Harry's motor. "Let's hope Miss Fellingsworth knows how we can find Lady Rachel."

"You realize it's all of fifty miles to New Alresford," said Dr. Harry.

"Not as far as London," Dot assured him. "And how did you know that is where we are headed?"

"I told you. The marquis and I are acquainted."

As they took off down the Woodstock Road, Catherine spared a thought for Rafe. For someone unofficially engaged, she was certainly spending a lot of time with this man.

* * *

A light rain fell as they made their way south to Hampshire. Dot had insisted on sitting in the second seat, so Catherine was left to sit next to Dr. Harry in front. After the hilarity and intimacy of the night before, she felt quite silly and awkward.

As they drove through the curvy lanes to the major roads, Catherine asked, "Are you working on any poetry at present?" she finally thought to ask.

"You jest. Surely you have noticed I am fully engaged in proving I was not canoodling in the Somerville new chapel on Friday last."

"Right. It has taken me out of my normal writing routine, as well. I appreciate your help. But tell me, how do you go about composing? Do you write out your stream of consciousness and then compose it into a poem? Or do you start right out composing it in the proper form?"

"I suspect you of trying to milk me of my secrets."

"You're the one who offered to drive. Now that I have you captive, at least I can use the time productively," Catherine said.

"Well, as a matter of fact, I compose naked at the Botanic Gardens during the new moon."

Both Catherine and Dot giggled. "I shall write a biography of you and put that in," said Dot. "It would make me a fortune and would increase your sales a thousand-fold."

"There's that," said Dr. Harry. "Or we could romanticize this mystery a bit and write it as a Sherlock Holmes with Watson and his cousin up from the country."

Dot laughed. "I vote for you as the cousin up from the country. Catherine is obviously Sherlock."

"Yes. I'm more the Lord Peter Wimsey character," said Dr. Harry.

"You flatter yourself," said Catherine. "You are not a bit like Lord Peter."

They bickered in this manner for all of fifty miles. By the time they reached Hampshire, they had invented a wholly new character, based on Lord Harry, the viscount, who worked for the admiralty masquerading as a pirate on the high seas. Catherine thought he seemed quite pleased with his alter ego.

"Coming up: the Hampshire Downs. Made of chalk, in case you were wondering," announced Dr. Harry.

* * *

New Alresford turned out to be a charming town with a spacious main street. Lined with Georgian residences and shops, Broad Street had trees planted down its center. On one of the side streets, they located a picturesque pub called the Dog and Rooster.

When they entered, they found it paneled in dark wood, sparsely lit. Leather-covered benches flanked oak tables.

"What'll it be, ladies?" asked Dr. Harry.

"I'll have the Ploughman's Lunch," said Dot after reading the chalkboard above the bar.

"Same," said Catherine. "And a shandy."

Dr. Harry ordered a pork pie with a pint of lager, and they settled in a booth.

"Poor Lady Rachel. I feel like we're hounding her," said Catherine.

"We need to follow it through," said Dr. Harry. "It's a legitimate line of inquiry."

"I hope we can eliminate her as a suspect," said Dot. "Poor girl."

They fell to talking about the beauties of Hampshire, and Dr. Harry confessed to the fact that he had been raised not far away from New Arlesford. "I have a great fondness for this part of the country and its sheep," he said. "I come from a long line of wool merchants."

Catherine felt the importance of the seemingly careless utterance. He knew her background quite well—daughter of baron that she was. And the fact that she could sustain herself on the slim royalties from a book of poetry spoke for itself. Not only was her father a peer of the realm, but a wealthy peer.

Since the war, the barriers between the classes had been shifting, and after attending university with scholars such as Dr. Harry, whose family made their money in "trade," Catherine no longer viewed those walls as insurmountable.

"So that is how you come to know Lord Debenham! Have you ever met Lord Robert?"

"A time or two. He's rather vain but other than that he's a good bloke. I don't know his daughter, the Honorable Gwendolyn, however."

"Well, that can't be helped," said Dot with a little giggle. "Though it would have been quite fun to see you charm her."

"There is nothing to prevent that course of action if you think it best," he said with a grin.

"You really are a pirate," said Catherine, laughing.

Dr. Harry knew the way to the Debenham estate and they came upon Redford House at the end of a drive that took them through a lane of towering oaks that had been standing for centuries.

It was a large and sturdy red brick house of Georgian design with multiple chimneys and black shutters. Dot was afraid the three of them would overwhelm the poor Gwendolyn, so she stayed behind in Dr. Harry's motor.

When the butler answered the door, Dr. Harry passed him their calling cards. "We're here to see the Honorable Gwendolyn Fellingsworth. We have just motored down from Oxford this morning," he said.

The butler inclined his head. "I will see if she is receiving."

At length, they were guided to a sitting room with a view of the flower garden, which Catherine took to be a good sign. Though she hadn't sought it, she was grateful for Dr. Harry's presence. Too grateful, perhaps.

She drew the conclusion from her surroundings that, though a younger son, Lord Robert was prosperous. The room was freshly outfitted in glazed chintz upholstery in a navy blue and coral floral pattern. The walls were coral, and a navy blue Aubusson carpet lay at her feet. Fresh roses graced the tea table in an antique Chinese vase.

Miss Gwendolyn Fellingsworth proved to be a large, athletic-looking girl with brown shingled hair and golden eyes.

"Should I know you?" she asked rather grandly upon entering the room.

Catherine smiled. "No, I shouldn't think so. I was a few years ahead of you at Somerville. This is Dr. Harry Bascombe, a professor at Christ Church. We're here hoping you can talk to us about Lady Rachel Warren."

"Why?" asked Gwendolyn. "Why do you want to question me about Rachel? Hasn't she had enough trouble?"

"That's just it," said Dr. Harry. "The college greatly regrets what she has been through and thought she ought to know that Dr. Chenowith has passed away. There is no reason for Lady Rachel not to return to Somerville. I, myself, will be teaching Modern Poetry now."

This was the first Catherine had heard of this, and she suspected him of inventing it on the spot.

"Passed away? Dr. Hatchet? That's very sudden, surely. How did she die? Is it too much to hope that someone murdered her?"

Catherine exchanged a look with Dr. Harry. He spoke, "The cause of death has not been determined."

"The administration wanted to make a special effort in Lady Rachel's case, to let her know that they are keeping a place for her for the Michaelmas Term."

"Even I know there's a lawsuit afoot against the college on her behalf. Bending over backward, are you?"

Catherine found the girl very impertinent, but she could not wholly blame her. The story they were spinning sounded every bit like what Gwendolyn had in mind.

"Rather," she said. "The problem is, we haven't the least idea where she is. We'd like to inform her in person. Can you help us?"

"I'm afraid not. I wouldn't do it even if I could. Your lot have caused the poor girl to have what they are calling a nervous breakdown. She's in seclusion. Even I can't see her, and I'm her closest chum. She's locked down, so she can't get out, either."

Lady Rachel couldn't have done it. "Oh, golly. Is she violent then?" asked Catherine with assumed horror.

The Honorable Gwendolyn's eyes narrowed, and she looked hard at both her visitors.

"I'm sorry," Catherine said. "I shouldn't have asked that. I feel so sorry for the poor girl and what she has gone through."

"No, she's not violent, but I know you!" exulted Gwendolyn. "You're that poet! The one Dr. Hatchet was always going on about. One of her former students. She gave *you* glowing reviews!"

Catherine sighed. *How did I ever think I could pull this off?*

"Yes. I'm that poet. But it doesn't follow that I was starry-eyed about Agatha Chenowith. That I don't believe that in your friend's case, the lawsuit was justified. Dr. Chenowith did a grave injustice, not just to Lady Rachel, but to Somerville College and Oxford."

"There we are agreed," said the young woman. "Leave your address, and if I hear anything about Rachel, I will think about letting you know. It all depends upon how she is getting on."

Catherine took out another of her cards and printed her London address on the back. "I am staying at the Randolph in Oxford at the moment, and I can be reached there. But after next week, I expect I will be back at my London flat."

The student rang for the butler to show them out.

"It's lucky she doesn't read the newspapers," said Dr. Harry once the front door of Redford House had closed behind them. "Dear Agatha's murder was reported quite vividly in *The Daily Mirror* and *News of the World*."

"Even so, she smelled a rat," said Catherine. "I'm sorry I was so ham-fisted. But at least we found out what we needed to know. She couldn't have done it. She's in a lockdown facility."

Chapter Sixteen

Catherine gave her report to Dot. "You are so much more gifted at dissemblance than I am. It should have been you who went in with Dr. Harry."

"I don't know whether you realize it or not, but you just called me a liar," Dot said with a laugh. "Oh, well. Nothing ventured, nothing gained."

"I have a proposal," said Dr. Harry. "My home isn't far. Why don't I drive you around there where we can be sure of a welcome and a good meal? We can either drive back to Oxford tonight or better yet, in the morning."

"Excellent idea," said Dot.

Catherine felt overwhelmed. Was she ready to meet Dr. Harry's people all at once like this, with no preparation? Why would he want her to?

As though reading her mind, he said, "Never mind about meeting the parents. They always spend their summers at the seaside with my sister's family."

"In that case, I would love to see your home, if you have a spare toothbrush. I imagine the home of Dr. Harry Bascombe is a tourist site hereabouts," said Catherine.

He laughed. "Not quite. But it is comfortable, and I haven't visited for a while. Always good to keep the servants on their toes."

Dr. Harry's house proved to be a Georgian manor similar to Redford House. It sat on a rise looking down at a small lake with a willow.

Lovely. Why does he pretend to have no money?

An aged and bent butler's face lit when he saw Dr. Harry. "Master Harry! It has been a long time since you've visited."

"Too long," admitted Dr. Harry. "And you see I've brought my friends—Miss Tregowyn and Miss Nichols. We've been down this way on college business. Any chance we can get a meal and beds for the night?"

"Of course. I am only sorry your parents aren't at home," said the butler.

"I didn't know until this morning that I was headed this way, or I would have written. We'll just go into the drawing room. If you could bring tea, it would be appreciated. I imagine the view of the flower garden is lovely as usual."

"It is. And no one here to enjoy it," mourned the butler. "Mr. Hansen has been doing battle with aphids all summer as they've been at the roses. But he's winning."

Catherine was enchanted with the drawing room, which was not anything like what she expected a wool merchant would have. It was decorated in the Art Deco style with modern chrome and leather furniture, geometric carpets in red and black, and abstract art upon the walls.

"This is inspiring!" she said. "What an interesting room!"

"My mother's the artist," he said, indicating the paintings. "She took classes at the Slade before she chose to attend medical school."

This was so unexpected Catherine found all her ideas about Dr. Harry in disarray. "But . . . with such a modern woman for a mother, how can you be interested in Victorian poetry?"

"Nature seeks a balance, I guess. I don't favor the moderns much. I think they lack grace."

"But society evolves," said Catherine.

"History has also shown that eventually, every society declines. To tell you the truth, I believe Britain is in decline and has been since the War."

Though this was not an original idea, Catherine had never heard it espoused by anyone as young as Dr. Harry. Seating herself on a black leather and chrome tubular chair, she rallied her thoughts.

"While that may be true in some respects, I must say, that for women, things have moved forward. We have the vote. The marriage laws have changed so that we are no longer chattel and we can initiate a divorce. Women like your mother are accepted for their intelligence. Things are finally starting to move forward for our gender."

"You and my mother would get along splendidly. And I do agree about women. It's just that Britain's days in the sun are numbered. Despite some rough edges, America is evolving into the new world power. And, if we don't stop them, Germany will be, too."

Dot entered the conversation. "I agree. About Germany, at least. Hitler isn't doing a comic turn. And no one is stopping him."

"The last war sapped our energy and took away our will to police the world," said Dr. Harry. "And we will live to regret it."

"Oh, golly," said Catherine. "I hope not."

The tea cart was wheeled in, and she gave her attention to the selection of cakes and sandwiches, pushing the dire concerns down inside her where she kept such things. There simply couldn't be another war. Britain would never allow it. Would they?

There was a lemon cake, scones, and cucumber sandwiches.

"Not bad for spur of the moment," said Dot.

"The servants feed themselves well, even in my parent's absence," Dr. Harry remarked.

"Tell me about your father," said Catherine. "He must be a remarkable man to have married such a modern woman."

"He has one of the largest sheep runs in Hampshire. Other

merchants are expanding into retail, but he thinks the future of the industry is horizontal rather than vertical, so he keeps investing in land and sheep. Since their management is primarily in the hands of long-time employees, he has plenty of extra time. He's become a scholar. He took a degree from the London School of Economics and has now made himself into an expert on Locke and Bentham. Father spends his time writing articles for various journals. He is an anti-Socialist, which is not a very popular position right now, particularly at his alma mater."

"Ah!" said Dot. "I begin to see the roots of your thinking."

"Yes," murmured Catherine, "As do I. But surely you're not so conservative as to be a Monarchist!"

He laughed. "Calm yourself. It was the prime ministers of the Victorian age who made the country great. Not the queen. I applaud the parliament of those days. They made this country a fertile place for the explosion of ideas and inventions."

"You can idealize them only so far," said Catherine. "Poverty was terrible. Have you not read Dickens?"

"Ah, yes. The little boys of the East End. I forgot you were a Communist."

She restrained herself from throwing a scone at his head. "You polarize my charitable ideas to invalidate them. You know I am not a Communist."

"I move that we get back to the matters at hand," said Dot. "What should our next step be in our investigation?"

"You're right, of course, Miss Nichols," said Dr. Harry, cutting himself a large slice of cake. "I think Wallinghouse and Waddell are both deserving of more investigation. I believe you ladies stand the best chance of digging into the Wallinghouse situation. I need to look into Waddell's case. To me, he still seems the most obvious and viable suspect."

Catherine's temper flared. Who had appointed him the leader of their little band? She buttered a scone with great attention as she ground her teeth. "I also think the dean has something in her craw."

"Doesn't the dean have an alibi? A phone call to her mother?" asked Dot.

"That needn't have taken more than a minute," replied Catherine. "She has some connection to this murder; I'd be willing to wager. At the very least, she hasn't told all she knows."

"Very well. I see your point," said Dr. Harry with some annoyance. "I have no right to tell you what to do. But I still think you're admirably situated to look into the Wallinghouse affairs. I wouldn't be surprised if Chenowith were blackmailing Sir Herbert about a former love affair, or even just threatening him. I'm certain her treatment of his wife over the poetry collection really rankled."

"I wonder if the police found any letters or anything," mused Dot. "If so, they probably have no idea of their significance."

"I can find that out from my pet sergeant," said Dr. Harry. He stood up, stretching his neck from side to side. "I need a walk. Does anyone want to see the gardens?"

Dot declared that she did, but Catherine declined. "My head is aching rather," she said, knowing she sounded merely stubborn. She needed a nap. Last night's late hours had tired her more than she wanted to admit. Plus, she needed to escape from Dr. Harry for a while. His personality was threatening to overwhelm her. Tangos, unexpected wealth, his atypical parentage coupled with his archaic socio-economic ideas, would all take some processing. And, of course, there was still Rafe, whose appearance in her life once more demanded definition. The complications of that relationship made anything of the sort with Dr. Harry appear straightforward by comparison.

"Could your butler direct me to the room you would like me to have?" she asked.

"I'm certain he'll have it all sorted. I'll ring for him."

* * *

142

Alone in the contemporary teak wood furnished bedroom, Catherine found herself thinking about Margery. Dr. Harry was right about one thing. She was in the best position to find out the details of the Wallinghouse marriage. Secretly she worried about her friend. What if she was married to a killer?

Catherine had never taken to Sir Herbert, but Margery had been swept off her feet by him. He had mounted a determined courtship which included a daily letter, weekly deliveries of flowers and other gifts, and plenty of telephone calls. But he had never visited her at Somerville. It had seemed odd to Catherine at the time. Now that she suspected the probable reason for it—Agatha Chenowith—it seemed ominous. How could the man who had (as she suspected) carried on an affair with an intense and vindictive woman like Agatha Chenowith fall in love with an uncomplicated naïve girl like Margery Ackerman? Was it as straightforward as money and beauty?

There were plenty of debs every season with those attributes. Why Margery? Was the marriage in trouble? Was Chenowith a threat to it?

The only way she could see to find the answer was to rekindle her friendship with Margery. Her friend had always been her confidante when they were at school. Even more so than Dot. It was only her marriage and removal to Somerset that had put an end to their closeness. They had written at first, but over the years, that had tapered off. Looking back, Catherine could see that it had been Margery's doing. Her letters had become widely spaced and infrequent. Had she not wanted to confide in Catherine any longer? Was she afraid to admit that she had made a mistake in marrying Sir Herbert?

Rafe and his insistence on an engagement opened the door for Catherine to begin to write to Margery once again. No one knew the details of her ups and downs with Rafe better than Margery.

Sitting at the caramel-colored wooden desk in front of the window, Catherine searched in the drawers for stationery. She found several sheets with the house's address printed to the left.

Ordering her ideas and trying to dismiss her guilt over her deception, she wrote:

Dearest Margery,

I so enjoyed seeing you the other night at the dance and before that at Dr. Sargent's dinner party. Too bad it had to be upstaged by a murder!

As you can see by the address, I am taking a little visit to Hampshire. Dr. Harry Bascombe, whom you met at the dance, has invited Dot and me to spend the night in his family home as we were down here together on a bit of Somerville business. In fact, we have been trying to locate a student who was profoundly upset by Dr. Chenowith. Dr. Harry will be taking over from Chenowith and wants to convince the student to come back to Somerville for the next term. But we have had no luck finding her.

Actually, I am dying to confide in you as I used to. Rafe has resurfaced after a year in Kenya and wants to marry me. When I am with him, of course, I feel as though it is a wonderful idea, but when we are apart, all the doubts begin. I need to talk to someone who knows him as you do. Marriage is such a big step. How did you ever decide to take it?

Perhaps we could meet in London sometime soon? I would love to see you and get caught up.

Thank you.

Fondly,

Cat

After folding and sealing the letter, Catherine rooted in her purse for a stamp. Finding one, she stuck it on the letter and carried it downstairs to deliver to the butler for posting. He assured her it would go out by the next morning's post.

Her conscience troubled her a bit. Was she emotionally manipulative? Not if, as she suspected, Margery was in a troubled marriage.

The problem with this whole situation was that there were too many suspects, and none but Lady Rachel had yet been eliminated. It was difficult to go forward on so many fronts. Even Dr. Harry was a suspect. He had never really accounted for his missing ten minutes after the sherry party and before the cab ride to The Mitre. His interest in their investigation could be nothing more than a diversionary tactic. But then her head was aching, coloring everything darker than it probably was. How could she suspect someone for whom she was coming to have a reluctant attraction and fondness?

Weary of emotional gymnastics, Catherine belatedly took off her hat and lay on the red counterpane that covered her bed. She put her hand up to her bandage. Where was Dr. Stephenson?

* * *

When she woke, Dot was shaking her by the shoulder.

"Dinner, you slugabed."

Catherine opened her eyes slowly and had difficulty remembering where she was. She didn't feel at all refreshed by her sleep.

"Oh, golly, Dot. I can't believe I slept in my frock. It will be creased beyond anything."

"There's fresh trout on the menu," her friend said.

"That doesn't help. I need an iron."

"Sorry. No time."

Getting off the bed, Catherine used the sink in the corner to splash water on her face. She applied a fresh layer of face powder and some lipstick.

"You look splendid," lied Dot.

"Ha!" said Catherine. "My eyes are even swollen."

"Come on down for heaven's sake," her friend said. "It's dinner, not a beauty parade."

Dot could have done with a few repairs herself. Her face was shiny, and she had a ladder in one of her stockings, but Catherine did not point this out. Instead she followed meekly down into the drawing room.

Dr. Harry was mixing cocktails. Dot ordered a gin and tonic, but Catherine was still wary of alcohol due to her head injury. She asked for a lime and soda.

"Did you come to any earth-shattering conclusions as you pondered our puzzle?" asked Dr. Harry.

"No. I'm afraid I took a badly needed nap," she said.

"Good," he remarked. "Got to keep the mental machinery oiled."

Dot laughed. "Cat is famous for her naps. She sleeps like the dead."

Catherine shot her friend a look. "Yes. I always fight the desire to strangle whoever wakes me, so watch your step, Dot."

Dinner was heavenly, and Catherine was restored to good humor over the vichyssoise. The trout followed.

"Why do you go to such pains to cultivate the idea that you are in straitened circumstances?" she asked Dr. Harry.

"I prefer to be judged by my accomplishments rather than the wealth of my family," he said.

"That is admirable, I suppose," said Catherine. "Though hard for a woman to do. There are very few things a woman is allowed to do that can serve to support her monetarily."

Dot took up the conversation and talked about her job in advertising. She and Dr. Harry had a lively time discussing some of her campaigns advertising cigarettes and soap. Catherine let her mind wander.

For the first time, she wondered if Dot was interested in Dr.

Harry romantically. They seemed to be getting along like bread and jam, whereas Catherine was sulky by comparison.

She remembered the care he had taken of her at the Radcliffe Infirmary and the passion of their dancing. No. He was interested in *her*. But was she leading him on when all along she intended to marry Rafe? That wasn't fair to him or Dot.

And then she remembered her feelings of the night before. She hadn't imagined the romantic tension between them. What was going on in her heart? When had her feelings for Dr. Harry Bascombe changed? How could she feel such a connection with him when he had formerly been her foe? At the moment, she felt more connected to him than she did to Rafe.

So, what was she going to do about Rafe anyway? He would be coming up to Oxford on Monday. How did she feel about that? She had loved him through thick and thin for most of her life.

But she was anxious. Wary. Afraid that he would sweep her up and carry her beyond common sense. Kenya, for instance. Did she want to go to Kenya?

After dinner, they filed into the drawing room where Dot announced she was going to go up to bed. "I have to work Monday, and, unlike someone I know, I didn't nap. Thank you for driving today, Dr. Harry. I'm knackered."

Catherine was a bit uncomfortable being left alone with her host.

"Are you ever going to let me call you Catherine? Don't you think we have progressed beyond Miss Tregowyn and Dr. Harry?"

"I suppose," she said. "But you still don't like my poetry."

"I will call you Catherine in spite of that fact. Or perhaps you prefer Cat?"

"Not really. That's a school name. I'm grown up now."

His eyes sparkled. "You certainly are. Now. Tell me about this Rafe person."

She sighed. "I have known him since I was ten years old. I developed a pash for him then and have had one ever since."

"And how does he feel about you?"

"The same. But there are issues between us which are private, and I'm not comfortable discussing them. Even with him."

"Sounds messy and uncertain." They were sitting on a marshmallow-like leather loveseat, and he began to play with a tendril of her hair, triggering an electric fizz through her scalp down to her heart.

"Please don't do that," she said.

"You can't deny that there are feelings between us, Catherine."

"I know," she replied, lacing her fingers and squeezing them until the knuckles were white. "But we can't act on them. At least, not now."

"All right. But if your true intention is to refrain from enticing me, then I must warn you that you had better go upstairs. Right now."

She rose with jerky movements. "Goodnight, Dr. Harry."

"Goodnight, Catherine. It has been a splendid day."

She didn't sleep well that night.

Chapter Seventeen

Catherine insisted that Dot take the front seat next to Dr. Harry on the drive back to Oxford the following day. She listened vaguely to their conversation, which was drowned out in parts by the motor. Because of her lack of sleep, her head ached abominably.

When they pulled up at the Randolph, Dr. Harry assisted her to alight.

"Thank you very much," she said. "We did have a good day yesterday. It was lovely to see your home."

She shook his hand and walked through the Randolph entrance.

"There is a message for you, Miss Tregowyn," said the desk clerk.

"Oh, thank you," she said, taking the envelope he held out to her. Dot followed her, and they went up to their rooms.

"I must have a bath and change immediately!" she proclaimed, forestalling Dot's effort to chat. "I'm a complete grime!"

"Aren't you even curious about your message?" her friend asked.

"It's probably Rafe, and at the moment I must get out of these clothes."

"All right. I'll do the same," said Dot.

When at length she emerged from the bathroom in her dressing gown smelling of gardenias, she took up the envelope and opened it. It was not from Rafe, but from the dean—a request to ring her no matter when she arrived back at the hotel.

"Oh, golly," she said to herself. Going down the hall, she rang the number given in the message.

"Hello?"

"Dean, this is Catherine Tregowyn returning your call."

"Yes, Miss Tregowyn. I must tell you that Miss Gwendolyn Fellingsworth rang me yesterday to ask whether I was aware that you and Dr. Bascombe were searching for Lady Rachel Warren on behalf of the college."

Silence.

"I am afraid we led her to think that, yes," Catherine said, finally.

"I insist that you stop this ridiculous investigation into matters which are no concern of yours. What you did was unconscionable. I also must insist that you stay away from Somerville College and Oxford altogether."

"Were you aware that Lady Rachel had a nervous breakdown and is now in seclusion because of the incident with Dr. Chenowith?" Catherine asked.

"I was. But it is, I repeat, none of your concern."

Catherine saw red. "I will stay away from Somerville, but you have no authority over me, Dean. I will continue my investigation."

She rang off and went to Dot's room in a fury.

Her friend, also in her dressing gown, was at her desk writing letters.

"The message was from the dean. She heard from Gwendolyn Fellingsworth and commanded that Dr. Harry and I should cease the investigation. She wants me to stay away from Somerville and Oxford."

"Crikey! What did you say?"

"Basically, I told her she has no right to tell me what to do. But I think we're done here for the time being. Do you mind giving me a lift to my flat?"

"No, of course not. I have to go back down to London today because of work tomorrow morning. Did she know Dr. Harry was with you?"

"Yes."

Dot said, "I think you ought to ring him and tell him what happened. He may get called on the carpet as well."

"Good idea."

She took up the telephone and asked for the exchange to put her through to Dr. Harry Bascombe of Christ Church College. After several clicks, she was informed that Dr. Bascombe was on the line.

"Catherine?"

"Yes. Listen, I'm afraid I've just had a rather unpleasant conversation with the dean." She related the substance of her phone call. "I wouldn't be surprised if she tried to make trouble for you, as well. I thought I ought to warn you."

"The devil!"

"Yes. So I've decided to leave Oxford for the time being. I'm going down to London." She gave him her address and telephone number. "I've written Margery, so I expect to hear from her in a few days. Please let me know what you find out about Dr. Waddell and whether or not they pick up Dr. Stephenson."

"I shall. What a bother that you have to leave Oxford."

"If I think it's necessary, I'll come back up."

"Right," said Dr. Harry. "I'll stay in touch, meanwhile."

"Please. I want to continue this investigation."

"We have unfinished business in other areas, as well."

Not knowing how to reply to that, she rang off.

Catherine packed up all her things and carried them down to Dot's waiting motor car. It wasn't until she was riding down to London that she remembered Rafe. He was to have come up to Oxford this week. She must remember to call him from the flat and tell him of her change of plans.

* * *

The city seemed a bit steamy and grimy after the rarefied air of Oxford, but she was glad to be back in her flat just the same. The dean's actions were probably justified, but they annoyed her. What should she do while she was awaiting Margery's letter?

Frustrated, she culled through her mail. It was Cherry's day off, so she didn't even have her maid's company. But her publisher had sent a new contract, so there was that to see to.

As she perused the document, she suddenly remembered she needed to make contact with Chenowith's Bloomsbury coterie. Glancing at her mantel clock, she saw that it was already 6:00. Probably not the right time for a visit on Sunday night. And, to tell the truth, she was not feeling her best after two long drives and her confrontation with the dean. It would wait until tomorrow. She returned to her contract.

After marking several spots in red pencil, she inserted the document into a long envelope and addressed it to her solicitor. Then she made herself a cup of tea and opened a tin of soup for dinner. Later, after leaving the door on the latch for Cherry, she crawled gratefully into her own bed. Only then did she remember that she hadn't called Rafe.

Getting up, she padded out to the sitting room on bare feet and put a call through to his house a few blocks away. His butler informed her that Mr. St. John was out for the evening. She left a message for him stating that she was back in London.

For a change, she slept soundly that night. There were no dreams of a piratical professor or a tanned almost-fiancé just returned from Kenya.

She woke to Cherry, bringing her a cup of tea.

"The sitting room is a right mess, miss," she said. "What were you doing in there last night?"

Catherine blinked. "Mess? The sitting room?" As the words penetrated, she threw back her blankets and bolted out of bed. Without even pausing to don her dressing gown, she went into her sitting room where Cherry had already opened the blinds.

Papers were strewn everywhere, and her safe hung open. Her hands flew to her throat. *Someone was in here while I was asleep.*

Kneeling on the floor, she gathered up the scattered pages. Her first thought was that it was "S's" manuscript they were after. If so, then Professor Stephenson was the culprit.

However, the pages of the dead poet's manuscript were all there in a bundle with an elastic around them, just as she'd left them. In fact, all of her papers were there. As far as she could tell, nothing had been taken. Instead there was a note in bold, block capitals, left on her writing desk: *Cease your investigations or the next time I break in, it won't be to tamper with your safe.*

She felt a twist of fear in her abdomen. *What were they looking for? They could so easily have killed me as I slept! Would they have, if they had found it?*

Cold and vulnerable, Catherine stood shivering in her night-gown.

"What are you going to do, miss? Ought'n we to ring for the coppers?"

"What time did you get in last night, Cherry?" she asked.

"Ohh. The door was on the latch! That's how he got in! It was just before midnight. I didn't see or hear anything."

"Did you lock up, as usual?"

"I did."

"Very well," Catherine said. "Come help me get buttoned into something, and we will call the police."

* * *

The sandy-haired sergeant constable and his skinny superior, viewed the safe and the door, dusting for fingerprints. There were none. The note held none either.

"Obviously wore gloves," the skinny detective constable said. "I notice you've got a bandage on your head. Suppose you tell me what's happening here."

"I'm involved in a murder investigation up at Oxford," she

said. "I only got home to my flat yesterday. The woman who was murdered was called Dr. Agatha Chenowith, a professor at Somerville College," Catherine explained.

"Who cracked you on the head?"

"We are almost positive it was Dr. Anthony Stephenson of Merton College. It is a long story, but he was gone when the police went to bring him in for questioning. There is also another suspect, Dr. Christopher Waddell. He is a don at St. John's College, but he has also disappeared. This could be his work. You will want to talk to Detective Chief Inspector Marsh at Oxford. He has been handling the case."

"Did you spin the dial after closing the safe last time you opened it?" asked the policeman.

Catherine thought back to the day she had been here with Dot. "I can't remember. It's one of those things you do automatically, though."

"Well unless this were an expert safecracker, I'd say that you forgot this time," he said. "Have you checked over the rest of the flat to see if he tampered with anything else or if anything else is missing?"

"I have," Catherine answered. "My jewelry and silver are all there. And so are my papers. If he was looking for something, he didn't find it."

The detective fixed her with a steady look from his brown eyes. "What do you think he was looking for then?"

"I haven't the least idea."

"Hmm." The policeman ran a hand over the back of his head. "Well, I will talk to Detective Chief Inspector Marsh about this, but I can see that I don't have much of a case here as it stands, however, if you were to be murdered . . . Now that would be a different story. I would advise you to leave this to the police, Miss Tregowyn. Have you got someplace else you can stay until they catch the murderer?"

Catherine had no desire to leave her flat. "I will think about it."

"Do, Miss Tregowyn. And don't go thinking you're smarter than the police. This murderer has already killed once. He has nothing to lose by doing it again."

A chill swept over Catherine. *He's right.*

The policeman left her with his card. "Call if anything else happens. But please consider lodging somewhere else for a while."

* * *

As soon as the police left, Catherine rang Dot at her office.

"My flat was broken into last night. I never heard them. I was asleep the whole time!"

"Crikey!" said Dot. "What did they take?"

"Nothing. But they got into the safe and went through all the papers."

"Did you call the police?"

"I did. They're going to call Marsh at Oxford, but there were no fingerprints or anything helpful."

"I'm calling Dr. Harry right now," vowed Dot. "You need protection."

Her pulse quickened. "Actually . . . I thought maybe you'd let me stay with you," said Catherine.

"There's no room. My cousin's up from the country for fittings at the dressmaker for her wedding. She's got the couch. I'm calling Dr. H. right now."

Dot rang off.

Catherine paced her sitting room. She did, and she didn't want Dr. Harry. Right now, her feelings scattered about her like the papers on the floor. Bending down, she began to pick them up.

The telephone rang. She answered. Of course, it was Dr. Harry.

"I'm coming down right away," he said. "I can't believe you slept through that!"

"I can't believe whoever it was attempted it while I was home. But the door was on the latch, so he must have known!"

"Obviously, he was prepared to deal with you if you woke up. Be grateful he didn't wake you on purpose."

* * *

Cherry insisted on setting the sitting room to rights and hustled Catherine off to the corner bakery to lay in some pastries and sandwiches. Before she left, Catherine looked in her mirror. She was wearing the first thing she had found that morning, and it wasn't particularly flattering. She changed into a cocoa brown and white dotted frock with a dropped waist and pleats. Then she was tempted to change back. She was nothing more than a vain woman! What difference did it make what she wore for Dr. Harry?

After purchasing some French croissants and chocolate eclairs, Catherine also bought some ready-made chicken sandwiches and a carton of chutney. There weren't any pubs near her house, and Dr. Harry was bound to get hungry.

As she was on her way back to the flat, carrying her bounty, she ran into Rafe. Her heart dropped to her middle.

"Rafe! What are you doing here?"

His face lit with his killer smile. "Got your message this morning. It's good to see you, Cat."

"I've been run out of Oxford by the dean. Not that she has the authority. But it was the prudent thing to leave. There is something I probably should have told you," she said, nodding to the doorman as she entered her building.

His brow furrowed. "By that look on your face, it sounds like a story I need to hear. I've come to take you to lunch."

"I'm sorry. I'm expecting company," she said, indicating her shopping bag.

"I'll settle for dinner then." Leaning down, he kissed her on the cheek.

Just that moment, Dr. Harry sauntered into the lobby. He

stopped short. Catherine's feelings rioted. What was she supposed to do with these two men?

She said. "Here he is now. Dr. Harry Bascombe, meet Rafael St. John. Rafe, this is my colleague, Dr. Harry. We have been working on unraveling this mystery together."

The men shook hands, and she watched them size each other up. Rafe was the taller and more imposing of the two.

"Why don't we go upstairs?" she said. "I have sandwiches and chutney. Also, some eclairs—chocolate."

"My favorite," said Rafe. She threw him a quelling glance. Staking his claim over chocolate eclairs? This was ridiculous.

They went up in the lift, and everyone was very quiet as the operator worked the controls.

"I like your building," said Dr. Harry finally.

"My family has had the flat forever," she said. "But I'm the only one who uses it. My brother has rooms which he prefers when he is in town, and my parents are quite content in Cornwall."

When they entered her domain, Cherry was putting out the tea things.

"Oh, Mr. St. John! I didn't expect you. I'll just bring another cup." She took the shopping bag from Catherine. "And I'll put these out. Won't be a moment."

Catherine explained to Dr. Harry, "Cherry has been with me since before I was a deb. She thinks of herself as one of the family. She even criticizes my poetry. You have something in common."

She resolved to keep her hat on, though it would seem strange. She didn't want Rafe seeing her bandage until she had told him about Dr. Stephenson.

The men settled down on opposite vanilla-colored leather sofas. Catherine took the chair between them. This situation was surprisingly uncomfortable. She was worried far too much about what each of the men was thinking.

She said to the Oxford man, "Rafe has just returned from a year in Kenya. He was there with my brother, William."

"And what did you think of the colony?" asked Dr. Harry.

"Marvelous place," said Rafe. "I could settle there easily, but I'm afraid Catherine would miss England too much."

"Oh?" Harry said, raising his brows. "I wasn't aware you were going to be married."

"There is nothing settled," Catherine said. As Cherry set down the extra cup and the tray of sandwiches and plates, Catherine began to pour tea. "How do you take your tea, Doctor?"

"Lemon, no sugar," he said.

"Would you care for a sandwich? And some apricot chutney?"

"Please."

She thought she saw the edge of his mouth twitch as though he were hiding a smile. He was enjoying this! Glaring at him, she passed his tea. From that moment, she ceased to care about what he thought and relaxed.

"I suppose you know about the events of this morning?" Dr. Harry said.

Rafe scowled. "What events?"

"The break-in," Harry said lightly, sipping his tea.

"What's this?" Rafe demanded, accepting his cup from Catherine. "Is this what you were going to tell me?"

"Partly. I had a visitor last night. Don't worry. Nothing was taken, and I didn't even know it happened until I woke this morning," she said.

"What was your first clue?" Rafe asked, sarcasm edging his voice.

"My safe door was hanging open, and there were papers strewn about. I have no idea what they were looking for."

"I don't suppose you've called the police?"

"Of course, I have. They're going to cooperate with the Oxford police. This obviously has to do with our investigation."

Rafe looked as though he had tasted something bad. "Well, I'll leave you to it, then." He set down his cup on the refurbished old sea chest that functioned as her tea table.

"You don't want a sandwich?" she said.

"You weren't expecting me," he said, rising.

"Dot was the one who called Dr. Harry," she found herself protesting.

Dr. Harry grinned, shamelessly.

Rafe just shook his head and made for the door. "I'll check with you in a day or two."

"Don't sulk for heaven's sake," Catherine said. "It doesn't become you."

"Huh!" he remarked cryptically on the way out.

When the door had shut, Dr. Harry said, "Sorry to upset the apple cart." He didn't sound sorry at all.

"As I said, nothing's been decided yet." She poured her own tea and spooned some chutney onto a plate. Its burst of flavor restored her good humor. "You did rather egg him on, you know."

"He was sickeningly proprietary. I don't like that in any man. Now have you deduced anything from this break-in? You can take your hat off now. Mr. St. John isn't here to see the bandage you haven't told him about."

"You purposely gave him the wrong impression," she said.

He grinned.

Exasperated, she changed gears. "Look here. Someone must be pretty desperate to have carried this out while I was home. And that desperation is recent. After all, I've been out of the flat for over a week. That would have been a safer opportunity."

Catherine took a sandwich and ate it with absent-minded enjoyment. "Now that you're here, it might be a good time to talk to Chenowith's friends in the Bloomsbury group. Maybe she hinted that something was amiss."

"Do you know any of them?"

"There is one lady in the group that I know somewhat. We share the same publisher. We've met at receptions. I could call on her, I suppose. If you came with me, it wouldn't seem that I was after gossip, but that I meant business. You said you knew Lytton Strachey. You probably have a reputation in that group. She might be willing to talk if we were together."

"Shall we go this afternoon? I'm assuming you know where she lives?"

"I can find out from my editor," she said, eager to try this new lead. What side of herself did Agatha Chenowith show to her Bloomsbury friends?

CHAPTER EIGHTEEN

Rosemary Siddons had welcomed Catherine's desire to visit her that afternoon. Catherine and Dr. Harry arrived just after two, and Miss Siddons greeted them with a welcoming smile. A short, round woman, she had a pleasing face, unlike the long, thin, almost horsey-faced Virginia Woolf. Sensibly dressed, Miss Siddons did not betray in any way the fact that she had a brutally incisive mind.

Her flat was medium-sized and sparsely decorated with mismatched furniture and primary colors. It faced west and enjoyed an abundance of whatever sunlight there was to be had.

Catherine introduced Dr. Harry as "a colleague from Oxford."

"I hope this doesn't prove to be a waste of your time," she said once they were seated. "We are here to talk about Agatha Chenowith. It was our misfortune to have discovered her body."

"Oh! How awful for you," said the little woman.

"Well, the police did rather suspect us at first, which made us decide we should look into the matter ourselves and try to find out things the police might not be aware of."

"How enterprising of you! I certainly applaud your efforts."

Catherine went on, "I know she was a member of your literary circle, and you are the only one I know myself. That's why we've come to you."

"I knew her quite well as it happens," Miss Siddons said. "I am so glad you are looking into this. The police aren't aware of this part of her life, apparently. None of us have heard anything from them."

Catherine was relieved. They had been right to come. "Naturally, we won't share anything with them that doesn't have a bearing on the case. I think she had more friends here in London than she did at Oxford."

"Yes. Agatha was quite a devotee of our little group. We were fond of her and tremendously shaken by her death. I was sad that they didn't have a memorial service for her. But I suppose it's because she hadn't any people. No family to speak of."

"We didn't realize that," said Dr. Harry.

"I have her ashes," Miss Siddons said. "No one else claimed them. I shall scatter them in Wales. She used to love to take hiking holidays in Snowdonia, though she hadn't gone there for the last couple of years."

"I never knew that about her," said Catherine. "I'm so glad she had such a good friend in you."

They had taken seats in front of the empty hearth, and now their hostess offered them tea.

Thinking perhaps it might put the lady at ease, Catherine accepted. A servant appeared, and Miss Siddons ordered.

Dr. Harry fired the opening volley. "We believe Dr. Chenowith may have been murdered because of something she knew."

"Are you a poet, Dr. Bascombe? I feel sure Agatha has mentioned you."

"She didn't think much of my work," he said with a grin. Catherine wondered suddenly if he was as unaffected by Chenowith's criticism as he appeared.

"Very strict tastes, Agatha had. She preferred women's poetry, in any case," said Miss Siddons.

"So I had gathered," he said. "I'm certain she told you about Dr. Stephenson and his plagiarism. He has an alibi for the murder, so we are looking for other motives."

They spent a moment listening to the lady's invective against plagiarism. "Agatha was very disturbed," she concluded.

"Can you think of any other things she might have known that would have been as dangerous to her as Dr. Stephenson's plagiarism?" asked Catherine.

Tea was brought in, and while watching her pour, Catherine was certain that the woman was pondering what she should tell them.

"Milk?" Miss Siddons asked her. "Sugar?"

"Both, please," said Catherine.

"I'll just have lemon, if you don't mind," said Dr. Harry.

When they were all served, she said, "There was something quite weighty on her mind the last time I saw her. She was exceedingly perturbed. I'm sure you know she was very protective of Somerville, and I got the sense that this involved someone at the college."

"Oh, golly," said Catherine, taken aback. She was so startled, she set her teacup down on the table, afraid she might drop it. What had Dr. Chenowith been involved in?

"That's why she wouldn't tell you," said Dr. Harry. "You aren't a Somervillian."

"Yes. That's what I believe." Miss Siddons's brow furrowed in distress and tears formed in her eyes. "Her loyalty could have cost her life." She took a handkerchief from the sleeve of her cardigan and blew her nose.

"On the other hand," said Dr. Harry, his voice bracing. "We have another suspect. Were you aware of her affair with Sir Herbert Wallinghouse?"

Miss Siddons perked up at once, obviously glad to change the subject. "Oh, yes. She felt horribly rejected by his choice of wife." Catherine secretly applauded Dr. Harry for confirming his suspicion about the affair.

Miss Siddons continued, "She and Sir Herbert had a very cerebral type of relationship. Not to say it wasn't physical as well. And then he goes and falls head over heels for an empty-headed deb. A marked beauty. Fifteen years his junior. It almost destroyed Agatha. He never offered her marriage, you see."

Catherine kept her temper at this description of the brilliant Margery. "Were you aware that Lady Margery was a guest at the sherry party the night of her death?"

"While that might have bothered Agatha, it wouldn't have mattered to Lady Margery. She knew nothing about the affair. Sir Herbert made sure of that."

"What do you mean?" asked Catherine.

"He paid Agatha to keep quiet. It was demeaning, and I didn't think she should have accepted the money, but she was always hard up. Lately, though, since Lady Margery's pathetic attempt at poetry, she was very tempted to tell her. I'm sorry to say, Agatha did have a horribly jealous streak. She wanted to really wound the woman with that review she wrote and sent to the publisher."

The idea of Dr. Chenowith harboring such hatred for Margery made Catherine feel ill. She doubted very much that the payment arrangements would have been Sir Herbert's idea. It was much more likely that the don had blackmailed him out of her bitterness. "It sounds as though Sir Herbert may have had a motive, even if Lady Margery didn't."

"I thought of him right away for the role of murderer, I am sorry to say," said Miss Siddons. "I did like him at one time."

Catherine tried to quell her worries over Margery's family and said, "You are quite helpful, Miss Siddons. We are most terribly grateful."

"This whole business is shocking," said Dr. Harry. "Did you ever hear that she had received death threats?"

"Yes. She laid them squarely at Lord Carroway's door. That's the father of one of Agatha's students. Agatha had criticized her, and Lady Rachel went into a decline over the incident, apparently. She's in some kind of home. The whole thing was absurd."

"Patently," agreed Dr. Harry.

Catherine could only think of the poor man she and Dot had visited, old before his time, wheezing out his words.

Dr. Harry said, "It occurs to me that you might be able to shed some light on one more thing. There's this don, Dr. Christopher Waddell. He was caught impersonating a police officer in this case, and now he's gone and disappeared. He was at St. John's College. Did Dr. Chenowith ever make mention of him?"

The little woman puckered her brow. "Dr. Waddell. St. John's." She took a sip of tea. "No. I don't think I ever heard the name. Is he a poet?"

"No. The only thing remarkable about him is that he's a bit of a fascist."

"Well, Agatha certainly had no time for Hitler. That I can tell you. But I never heard her mention him, that I can recall. She used to unburden herself to me, you know. College communities are so inbred. It is almost impossible to keep one's personal life private. I was completely removed from Oxford, so she felt she could talk to me."

Though her feelings about Miss Siddons were mixed at best, Catherine said, "I'm glad she had a friend like you."

"She quite liked your poetry, you know," said the woman.

"She was very kind to me," said Catherine, trying to sound sincere. It was hard to feel any liking for the woman who had so hated Margery. Had Sir Herbert killed the woman? Was it the shadowy Dr. Waddell? Or even the dean? Catherine had more questions now than before they had arrived.

She switched the topic to whether or not "dear Agatha" had been composing another work before her death.

"Oh, yes. She was always composing. I am her literary executor. I'm working with her publisher now to publish her last poems."

"I know her collections always had an overall theme," said Catherine. "What was she writing about when she died?"

"All her latest poems were about betrayal in one form or another. Quite heated. Bitter."

"Huh," pronounced Dr. Harry. "To be quite crass, they will probably sell well in light of her murder."

Miss Siddons nodded her head sadly. "True."

"Tell us about your own work," invited Dr. Harry.

"Oh, I'm an essayist. No poetry. I write under an assumed name. You would be quite shocked to know who I am, but I'm not going to tell you. Only Agatha knew." She smiled serenely.

They stayed on another half an hour discussing the various accomplishments of members of the Bloomsbury set. Miss Siddons seemed to take great pride in all their accomplishments. Catherine deduced that she was a lonely woman.

As the clock on the mantel struck four, they finally took their leave.

* * *

In the cab back to Mayfair, Dr. Harry said, "Our victim was one bitter woman. It's a wonder she had any friends, but Miss Siddons seems to have been quite enmeshed in her life."

"Perhaps the lady doesn't have any other friends. Her identity as an essayist isn't as private as she thinks it is. And her work is the kind that makes many enemies."

"Now you have me curious!" the professor said.

"You won't hear anything from me. I'm in my publisher's confidence."

When they got back to Catherine's flat, she found that Rafe had called and left a bouquet of red roses for her with Cherry. The card said simply, "Remember me."

Rafe wasn't the hearts and flowers type, so the offering was a surprise. From the startled look on his face, she could tell the gesture was a bit disturbing to her companion. She imagined it was not often Dr. Harry came up against competition in the arena of romantic relationships.

"Cherry, could you put these in that crystal vase and place them in my bedroom on the chest?"

"Yes, miss."

"We shall have to talk about him eventually," he said.

"I don't see why," Catherine said. In a brusque tone, she said,

"Rafe's really none of your business. Now let's go into the sitting room. What else haven't you told me about your visit to the police? Did you ask if they found any love letters in Dr. Chenowith's rooms? And what about Dr. Waddell?"

Dr. Harry sat on her leather sofa. "There were some old letters, but the envelopes were gone, so they couldn't tell who they were from. They were all signed, 'H.' At this point, I decided not to enlighten them. I knew you wouldn't want your friend, Margery, involved before we determined whether it was warranted or not.

"As far as Dr. Waddell, nothing on his whereabouts. Nothing in his rooms that might help. Today I was going to start at St. John's talking to people to see if I could find anything out that might help us. But," he paused and looked into her eyes. "Obviously your safety comes first."

Catherine was touched by his concern, and lest he see it, she looked away.

"I wonder what there was that was so disturbing her—something to do with Somerville? I wonder whether it had to do with the dean?" Catherine mused. "I agree with Miss Siddons. Her loyalty could have cost Dr. Chenowith her life."

Her telephone rang, Cherry answered. The maid told her, "It's Lady Margery on the telephone, miss."

Catherine took the receiver from her maid's hand, "Margery! You got my letter?"

"Yes, Cat. I'm all agog to hear the latest with your Rafe and offer what advice I can. Although I must say, I'm hardly an authority on marriage."

She wondered at her friend's qualification. "Oh, I so appreciate it. I'm completely at sea over this."

"I can take the train up to London tomorrow if you can give me a bed for the night."

"Fabulous! Of course, I will."

"Good. I should arrive in time for luncheon. I'll take a cab to your flat, deposit my belongings, and we can be off to the Savoy."

"Sounds wonderful. I do look forward to having a proper gab-fest."

"Yes! Cheerio until tomorrow, darling."

"Bye," said Catherine.

After she rang off, she reported the news to Dr. Harry.

"So, she knows you want to question her about Dr. Chenowith?"

"Of course not. Sir Herbert may have killed to cover up his affair. We are going to discuss something altogether different. Before her marriage, she was my main confidante. I was even closer to her than to Dot."

A knowing glint came into his eye, but he kept his peace. Did he think he might come up in their conversation?

Just in case, she decided to puncture his conceit. "She knows Rafe rather well."

His brow contracted in annoyance.

"But I confess, I'm trying to get an alibi for Sir Herbert for the murder."

"I think we have to concentrate on him and Waddell. I think the dean is out of it," said Dr. Harry. We have to remember the way Chenowith died. The dean is smaller and older than she was," mused Dr. Harry. "I doubt she could have mustered the strength to strangle her."

"True," said Catherine. "Maybe the dean is only upset with me about the investigation because it reflects poorly on Somerville."

"That makes sense."

She longed to get into the murdered woman's rooms. Finally, she said, "The only thing I can think of is asking Jennie to make a thorough search of Dr. Chenowith's room. Maybe there's some-thing the police missed."

Her companion got up and began pacing the room. "There's got to be something somewhere that can help us."

He stopped his pacing and pulled out his pipe, which he began to fill.

Catherine mulled this over. "Miss Siddons is her literary execu-tor. Maybe there's some kind of abstruse clue in her latest poetry?"

"I think that lady would have told us. She was anxious to help."

"Well, it's worth a try," said Catherine. "I'm going to write Miss Siddons a note." She moved to her writing desk, took out her fountain pen and a piece of stationery, and began to compose.

Dr. Harry sat down and lit his pipe.

* * *

Dot telephoned when she got home from work, asking to be caught up on the progress of the investigation.

Catherine said, "Dr. Harry's here. Why don't you join us for a pub supper at that place by your work—what is it called?"

"The Spot, short for Spotted Pig," said Dot. "Sixish?"

"That'll just give us time to get there."

Catherine and the professor took the Underground along with the London hoards who were surging from offices all over the city. They arrived at six-fifteen. The pub was crowded with journalists from Fleet Street where Dot's office was located. Everyone was quite merry, holding their drinks aloft so they wouldn't be jostled by an errant elbow.

They finally reached the bar where they ordered two steak and kidney pies and two pints of lager. Finding a table was virtually impossible until they caught sight of Dot who was holding one down for them in the back corner.

They arrived at length and seated themselves.

"Phew!" said Catherine. "Thanks for getting us a table."

"You're welcome," Dot said. She appeared to be partway through her supper of fish and chips. "Now spill. Do you know who burgled you?"

"It must be someone who thinks I have something I don't have. We have worked out that Dr. Chenowith may have known something to the discredit of Somerville."

Catherine described their line of reasoning after their visit with Miss Siddons.

"You don't think that's a bit melodramatic?"

"What was Miss Siddons like?" asked Dot.

"It was hard to tell on such short acquaintance, but I suspect her of being spiteful, if not mean," said Catherine. "I was very careful to stay on her good side."

While she started on her pie, Dr. Harry filled Dot in on their conversation.

"Wow!" said Catherine's friend. "So, we've got a pretty solid motive for Sir Herbert."

"Margery's coming to Town tomorrow," said Catherine. "I'm going to see if I can find an alibi for her husband without tipping her off about the relationship with Dr. Chenowith."

"That's good. Do you think you need to go back to Oxford?"

"I'd love to have a look at Dr. Chenowith's rooms, but I will probably have to rely on Jennie since the dean has tossed me out."

"If they haven't started packing up her things," said Dot.

"She apparently has no family. Her things will probably be put somewhere awaiting the Chancery Court's decision about what to do with them. She left some kind of will because Miss Siddons is her literary executor," said Catherine.

Dr. Harry told Dot about Dr. Stephenson's alibi.

"Well, that eliminates him as a suspect," she said. "Aside from Sir Herbert, that leaves only Dr. Waddell of our known suspects."

Dr. Harry said, "When I go up to Oxford tomorrow, I am going to plague his college associates. There's got to be something somewhere that can shed light on why he was searching the dorm and then disappeared so completely."

Everyone concentrated on their meals as they thought. Catherine looked at her friend's familiar red head as she bent over her food and felt Dr. Harry's piratical gaze on her. She thought suddenly how lucky she was in her friends.

"Rafe sent roses," said Dr. Harry suddenly.

"Rafe?" Dot appeared astounded.

"I met him this morning. I shook him up a bit, I think. Thank you for calling me and telling me Catherine was in danger, by the way."

"Had to get some protection for Cat. I'll stay with her tonight," said Dot.

"Don't talk about me as though I weren't sitting right here," Catherine said, annoyed. To Dot, she said, "I don't mean to doubt your capabilities, but a stout walking stick and I would be a lot more protection than you if the burglar decides to revisit. Besides, I don't want to put you in danger, too."

"I'm to keep watch tonight," said Dr. Harry.

"I'd feel a lot less guilty if someone should hurt him instead of you," Catherine told Dot.

He grinned. "I see I'm expendable. Always happy to oblige."

"I'm putting Margery up tomorrow night," Catherine told her friend. Then she had a thought. "I'm persona non grata at Somerville right now, but I'm going to try to get Jennie to search Dr. Chenowith's room for anything the police might have missed. She could phone me and let me know if she finds anything."

"Good idea," said Dot. "I wish I didn't have to work. I could dash up there and take a look myself."

"This is really rather unsettling, you know," said Catherine, rubbing her arms as she felt a sudden chill. "It's not a game. Someone out there is a murderer, and that someone broke into my flat. What were they looking for? Why would they think I had anything?"

"I'll keep you safe," said Dr. Harry. "And we're going to find whoever it was."

Chapter Nineteen

Catherine rang Jennie that night when they returned to the flat. The scout agreed to take a look at Chenowith's room the next morning and smuggle out anything she found. She would take them in her cleaning cart, underneath the clean towels.

"I feel bad about asking her to do that," she said after ringing off. "I should be the one to do it."

"It's much less dangerous for Jennie. No one suspects her."

"But the golden rule scouts live by is not to steal from the rooms."

They were in the sitting room on separate sofas. Catherine felt a bit uncomfortable, knowing he was to stay the night and keep watch. She shifted uneasily where she sat.

"It just feels wrong," she said. "But I don't know what else to do. If we wait, even until the next day, they could take everything to Oxfam."

Dr. Harry took out his pipe. "To change the subject, is Rafe likely to show up tonight?"

"I doubt it. He said he'd see me in a couple of days."

"Good."

The single word dumped a load of guilt on Catherine's head. She knew Rafe would never understand Dr. Harry's vigilance. She hadn't even told him about the murderous attack by Dr.

Stephenson. It seemed to her suddenly that she was far too vested in this relationship with the professor. Their investigation was binding her to him emotionally. She stood up and went to the wireless. A classical piece was being broadcast by the BBC.

"Rachmaninoff's Second Piano Concerto," said Dr. Harry. "That's suitably ominous."

"The Russians are always ominous. Their poor souls are unsettled," said Catherine. *Like mine.* Going to her desk, she sorted through the afternoon post. There was a note addressed to her from Oxford—Balliol College.

"Would you mind if I opened this? It looks like it might be from Dr. Williams. He's the only one I know from Balliol."

"Proceed, by all means," said her companion.

Using her letter opener, she sliced open the note.

Dear Miss Tregowyn:

I should like to invite you to attend a little event at Balliol on Thursday evening. My lads conducting research in Norway made some interesting discoveries about early Teutonic legends and the development of the Anglo-Saxon language. This is the sort of thing I would normally have invited Dr. Sargent to attend, and she says you may be teaching in her place at Somerville.

The lads are going to share their discoveries over sherry and biscuits in the Old Common Room. It is very informal, but I would be delighted if you would attend. We will begin at seven o'clock.

Sincerely,

Wesley Williams, Ph.D.

Intrigued, Catherine handed the invitation to Dr. Harry, who read it as he smoked his pipe. "You are going to replace Dr. Sargent? You've said nothing about this."

"That's because, at present, I have no intention of doing so, but Dr. Sargent is hoping I will. The point is, Dr. Chenowith was very interested in this study in Norway. She blamed Teutonic legends for the whole idea of the 'master race.'"

"That must have led to tensions between her and the good professor."

"I know. He is besotted with the ancient legends. Now that I think of it, he told me that next month he is going to a conference in Germany where he is going to examine some sort of pre-Christian Teutonic document that was uncovered somewhere. Iceland or Greenland or somewhere like that, I think."

"He works for the Government, you said." He looked very professorial, holding his pipe with a musing look in his eye. "Something hush-hush. That document gives him a good cover for visiting Germany at this juncture," he said.

"I hadn't thought of that," Catherine replied. "I'm going to go to this, I think. It'll be a good excuse to go up to Oxford."

Her telephone rang.

"Hello?"

"Miss Tregowyn. Detective Chief Inspector Marsh here. I heard from the London police about the break-in at your flat. I just wanted to let you know that it wasn't Dr. Stephenson. We finally have him in custody up in Northern Ireland. He went to his grandmother's in Londonderry. They are sending him down here where we plan to book him for attempted murder."

Relief surged through her. "Thank heavens! It is good of you to let me know. As soon as I saw all the poems from the poet he plagiarized were still here, I knew it wasn't him, however."

Marsh asked, "Who do you think it was, then? Any ideas?"

Catherine struggled with her answer. "I'm not entirely certain what they expected to find," she said. "Nothing was taken, though the safe was opened."

"Yes. That's what I understand. Who has the combination?"

"My maid and I. The police here think I forgot to spin the combination dial when I last used it, but I would have thought that to be a reflex action on my part. Maybe my mind was on other things this time, however. The burglar could have just been lucky."

"You are extremely lucky he didn't cause you any harm. Are you staying there alone?"

A chill went down her spine. "No. I am taking precautions."

"To risk such a move, the perpetrator must think you have something that he wants rather badly."

"Or she wants," Catherine interjected, thinking of the dean.

"You have reason to believe it may be a woman?"

"I just think we need to keep an open mind," she said. "You may want to have someone come to London to interview a Miss Siddons of Bloomsbury. She was probably Dr. Chenowith's closest friend. She is her literary executor. Dr. Harry Bascombe and I called on her today."

"Oh? More amateur detecting?"

"She said the police hadn't shown any interest in her literary set. They were Dr. Chenowith's closest associates."

"Closer than the women at Somerville?"

"Apparently."

"I will send someone down. Suppose you tell me if you learned anything useful."

"General information about Dr. Chenowith's state of mind. I think it's important. Have you caught up with Dr. Waddell yet?"

"Haven't a clue about him. I found out his people are from the Isle of Man. We may have to send a detective there if this case doesn't break soon."

Catherine silently took in this information. Then she said, "Thank you for calling, Detective Chief Inspector. I don't expect my burglar to return, but as I said, I am taking precautions."

"Very good, miss. Cheerio."

She related the details of her conversation to her companion.

"The Isle of Man? Strewth! Not the easiest place to pursue an investigation."

Catherine considered. "I think there is more to be found at Oxford, in any event. If we still turn up nothing, Rafe can fly us to the Isle."

"He's a pilot?"

"Yes," she said with a sigh. "He's a bit larger than life—big game hunting, flying, mountain climbing."

"And how do you fit into this lifestyle?"

I'm not sure I know. That's one of the problems.

"That's enough about Rafe. My head is being tedious. If you don't mind, I think I'll call it an early night. I'll show you to your room. It used to be my brother's. I think he's left some things here. Let's see if we can find some pajamas."

She led him down the hall to the second bedroom which was painted a very masculine deep blue. Catherine was assailed by memories of her brother tearing through the flat as a boy, tormenting her by popping out of cupboards or from behind draperies and visiting her at night with his torch and checkerboard. She missed William and thought how she must ring him up.

"Try the wardrobe. There are some drawers in there with his things. Help yourself. The bath is down the hall to your right. Goodnight."

She left him standing in the middle of the room and retreated to her own domain. Why had she felt the sudden need to be out of the man's presence?

Her life was growing more complicated. As if her feelings weren't enough to manage with Rafe home.

Thank heavens Margery is coming tomorrow.

* * *

No burglar attempted to access the flat on Monday night. Tuesday morning, Cherry woke her, presenting her with her tea and the morning newspaper. Catherine's head was feeling much improved.

"How is Dr. Harry this morning?" she asked her maid.

"He's in the bath. I'm just boiling him an egg. I must get back to it."

"Fine, then. I'll have the same. With just toast."

"I have kippers."

"Save them for our guest."

She opened *News of the World*, which was her secret low brow addiction, to find the story of a mysterious corpse discovered behind a tobacconist's shop in the East End. The photo showed Dr. Christopher Waddell, obviously dead. He had been murdered several days prior. His identification showed him to be George Sullivan, but the address proved to be non-existent. The public was exhorted to help identify the man.

She restrained herself from picking up the telephone. She would leave that to Dr. Harry. Today belonged to Margery.

Dressing hurriedly in her pink hydrangea lounging pajamas, she took off her bandage and ran a comb through her dark brown hair. Her scalp itched fiercely. Leaving it uncovered, she pushed away from her mirror. Her heart-shaped face was white as a sheet, but she couldn't bother about how she looked now.

"Good morning," Dr. Harry said as she entered the sitting room. He was at the table eating kippers and egg. "You resemble a film star, darling."

Ignoring this sally, she handed him the newspaper. "Waddell has been murdered," she said. "Look."

He sighed heavily and took the paper from her. "I was afraid of something like this."

"You were?"

"I discovered a rather unsavory organization in existence at Oxford. I was afraid he might be tangled up with it."

"What kind of organization?"

"Brownshirts. Nazis. Students and professors. Their principal activity is terrorizing Jews. They also have a propaganda press."

"I have never heard of them."

"They are deep underground."

"How did you find out about them?"

"Purely by accident. It was Sunday night. I couldn't sleep. I was taking a walk down a back street when I caught a bunch of students breaking into a violin maker's studio. I shouted at them, and they ran. One of them tripped and fell. I grabbed him by the collar.

"Long story short, he talked to me rather than being taken to the police. He was having doubts. I gathered that he thought joining the group would give him some much-needed stature. But they don't make it easy for their members to quit.

"After telling me all the details, he said he was going to leave Oxford. He's a member of New College. I got his name."

Catherine sat horrified at his disclosures. "That's insane. You must call the police immediately to identify Dr. Waddell. Tell them what you suspect. Then the Oxford police need to know all about this awful gang."

"It's more a job for the Secret Intelligence Service, I think. I was going to go 'round to see them today while you are with Lady Margery."

"But you must go first thing this morning! This is terrible. I can't believe you're so *sang froid* about it!"

"I wasn't until yesterday morning when Dot phoned me about your break-in. Then it went completely out of my head. But Dr. Waddell's death puts another complexion on things."

Her tense stance softened at this evidence of concern for her. "I . . . I don't know what to say."

"Thank you?"

"Thank you. But in a case like this, I . . . I shouldn't come first. Not for you."

She picked up a piece of toast. "I'll fly and get dressed. Then let's both of us go to the SIS. If Waddell was murdered by this . . . this cult, it must be tied somehow to Dr. Chenowith. I found him in the women's dormitory doing *something* concerning the witnesses to her murder. And then he disappeared."

"All right," he said with a smile she read as indulgent. "Run and get dressed."

"Cherry!" she called.

* * *

The Secret Intelligence Service was almost hidden in the great sprawl of buildings known as Whitehall. By the time they found the correct direction for the office, it was half-past ten. A receptionist greeted them in a beige room without a touch of color. Behind her was a set of double oak doors, closed like a vault.

"How may I help you?"

Dr. Harry said, "I am Dr. Harold Bascombe from Christ Church College, Oxford. This is Miss Catherine Tregowyn, a graduate of Somerville College. We have information about the murder of the man who was found last night in the East End. We know who he was and believe his death may be tied to an underground group of Nazis operating at Oxford."

Stated baldly, Catherine thought the story sounded wildly improbable. Evidently, the receptionist agreed.

"Have you been to the police? Cases of this sort are normally passed along to us by the police if they think it concerns the Secret Intelligence Service."

Dr. Harry flushed deeply.

"We thought only to save time," Catherine said. "But of course we can go to the police."

Something of her reasonableness must have appeared to the woman, for she said, "If there is a connection to our concerns, you will be given immediate access to one of our people."

"Thank you," Catherine said. She took Dr. Harry's arm, and they left.

Taking a taxi, they went to New Scotland Yard where they asked for the detective handling the East End murder of the unknown man.

"He is known to us," said Dr. Harry. "And he is involved in another murder investigation in Oxford."

They had a short wait. When they were shown to the office of Detective Inspector Michael Underbridge, Catherine left the reporting to Dr. Harry.

"The dead man is known to us and to St. John's College, Oxford, where he was employed as Dr. Christopher Waddell. If you ring Detective Chief Inspector Marsh at Oxford Police Station, you will find that he was a suspect in the murder of a Somerville College don, Dr. Agatha Chenowith. Miss Tregowyn and I discovered her body and have been involved in the investigation. Dr. Waddell disappeared immediately after he was caught by Miss Tregowyn impersonating a police officer in the room of one of the suspects at Somerville College."

"Thank you, Dr. Bascombe. That is very clear."

Catherine guessed that Dr. Harry was a bit anxious about bringing up the Nazi connection, so she said, "Dr. Waddell was a known fascist. We don't know, of course, whether this had anything to do with his death or not. Just as we don't know what his connection was to Dr. Chenowith. However, you should be aware that there is an underground cult of Nazi students and professors at Oxford. Dr. Bascombe uncovered information about it on Sunday night."

Thus prompted, Dr. Harry told his story about the New College student he had collared. He finished his tale with, "The student was literally in fear for his life if he withdrew from the organization. Considering that Dr. Waddell was found murdered, we thought you should know about this organization . . ."

Chief Inspector Underbridge interrupted him. "We don't make it a habit of indulging amateur sleuths in our department. Please, facts only, and spare us your conclusions."

Dr. Harry stood. "Very well, then. Good day to you."

Catherine followed him out of the office. "What a gaggle of fools our government employs," she said. "You'll have to go back up to Oxford and see if Detective Chief Inspector Marsh will listen to your warning about that blasted cult."

"I feel like the Chicken Little crying that the 'sky is falling.' As soon as you mention Nazi, no one wants to listen. I wonder how many closet fascists there are in the government."

Catherine thought for a moment. "It's not so much that they're fascists as that no one wants another war. So many are still getting past the last war, they won't even consider the prospect of another. No one wants to pay the price of standing up to Hitler. Look at poor Winston Churchill. Everyone thinks he's a scaremonger, so they ridicule him."

"You're right, of course. My pride's hurt." He hailed a cab. "Let's get you back to your flat. I'll go see Marsh. Those kids were breaking the law if nothing else. And I need to check on my New College friend."

Catherine gave Dr. Harry credit for overcoming his wounded pride. She had learned in her life that it could be a very difficult thing for a man to do.

Chapter Twenty

Catherine's first impression of Margery was that her friend looked fragile. Her skin was practically transparent.

"Oh, Cat! It's so good to see you! It's been ages since I've been in your flat!"

"It's exactly the same," she said. "Here, let me take your case. Cherry has put you in the Rosebud Room—my old bedroom. It's the only feminine room in the place."

She set Margery's case just inside the doorway of the bedroom. "Take your time and freshen up. I always feel so grimy when I come down from the train. Cherry can unpack for you while we're out to lunch."

The Savoy was crowded, but Lady Margery was well-known there, and they were seated without a wait at a choice table a little way away from the string orchestra. They both paused on the way to their table to say hello to their many acquaintances. By the time they were seated, Catherine could tell that her friend was all nerves.

"Maybe this wasn't such a good idea," she said as they studied the heavy leather-backed menus they were given. "You seem overly fraught."

"I am all right, Cat. I promise. Just a little tired from the train ride."

Catherine knew better than to believe her friend but decided to let the matter rest for the time being.

They both ordered *Sole Meunier* with fried potatoes and French beans. When the waiter had departed, Margery said, "So when did Rafe appear? I understand he's been in Kenya. I read his stories in the Times."

"He's been back almost a week, but I've hardly seen him. He's been busy with his father doing business things. Evidently, his father has decided to hand over several companies up North to Rafe."

"I'm amazed!" said Margery. "I thought his father disparaged Rafe's business acumen."

"Well, Rafe will inherit everything, so I imagine his thinking is that it is better to have him set sail while Papa is still alive to keep his son from drowning."

"So," her friend said, leaning toward her with a confidential air, "How did it feel to see him?"

"Wonderful, of course. He's asked me to marry him again. I put him on a six-month trial."

"Darling, if you can't marry him after all these years, what difference is six months going to make?"

Catherine gave a gusty sigh. "He's just not stable, Marge. At least he hasn't been in the past. I hope every time we go through this that things are going to be different this time, but they never are. I need a certain level of reliability in my life."

"Then, your answer should be no."

The waiter brought their luncheon. Though not hungry, Catherine began to eat, as though it would stay the inevitable.

"I keep hoping that if I handle things differently, things will stay smooth and we will stay close," she said.

"His choices are not your fault. The same thing happens again and again. Do you honestly believe that you are in any way responsible?"

"He doesn't get violent or anything."

"Darling, you have to face the fact that he's not an adolescent anymore. And his choices are his responsibility, not yours."

Catherine felt a pain in her breast that was all too familiar. "I love him so. I want to smooth out the way for him. Maybe if we're married . . ."

"Marriage only magnifies problems, Cat. Take it from me. It doesn't solve anything."

Her friend's words were like the lash of a whip. Catherine put down her utensils.

"Marge! Whatever is wrong?"

To her surprise, her friend began to tear up. She raised her napkin to her eyes and carefully dabbed them so as not to smear her kohl makeup.

"I'm so dreadfully afraid," her friend said. "You were right, Cat. I am fraught."

"You're afraid of Sir Herbert?"

"No. He would never hurt me. But he had some kind of problem with Agatha Chenowith. He absolutely hated her. I'm terribly worried . . ."

"You're worried he might have killed her?" Catherine whispered.

Margery nodded sniffing.

Catherine was stunned. For her friend to cry in a public place like the Savoy meant her problem was real and immediate.

She signaled her waiter.

"Let me sign for luncheon," she said to him. "I'm afraid we must go."

"Very good, miss." He left her bill and then walked swiftly away.

Quickly scrawling her signature, she told Margery, "Pull yourself together, darling. We must get out of here and then you can have yourself a good cry."

Taking Margery's elbow, she led them around the outside of the dining room, out into the hotel lobby, and finally into the street where they got into a waiting cab.

Margery sobbed into her handkerchief.

"It's such a relief to tell someone. I don't know what to do."

"Wait until we get back to the flat. It'll only be a few minutes. Then you can spill the whole thing."

Once they arrived at Catherine's building, she paid the driver and helped her friend to alight. Hustling her into the building, she said, "Stairs. The lift operator is a bit of a ghoul."

They walked up two flights of stairs and, finally arriving at her flat, went into the sitting room where they collapsed on the sofa. She held her friend while she sobbed great heaving sobs.

"Oh, my," Margery said at last. "I've been holding it in so long. It's been so dreadful."

Catherine rang for her maid.

"Some hot, sweet tea, please, Cherry." When the maid had gone, she said, "Would it help you to talk about it? I've been finding out a lot about Chenowith since she died. She was not a nice person."

"She was horrid! I don't know what her hold was over Herbert, but he was paying her a great deal of money. I saw one of the cheques."

"Have you any idea why? Any idea at all?"

"He's very protective of me. I think it's all tied up with my poetry somehow." Margery blew her nose into her handkerchief. "I really think the woman hated me, and it had something to do with Herbert."

"Margery, why are you afraid he killed her?" Catherine felt a twinge of conscience even asking this question of her friend, but she told herself that if Sir Herbert was guilty, it was best that Margery knew.

Her friend was completely given over to tears. After a few moments, Cherry entered with her tea. Margery grasped the cup with both hands and drank it down as a drunk would a tot of whiskey.

Finally, she was able to speak. "Yes. I'm afraid. Desperately afraid."

"But what makes you think he did it?"

"When I called the Randolph after the sherry party, he wasn't there!" Sobs overtook her once again. After a moment, she continued, "I actually took a cab 'round to the hotel, in case he was in the dining room, but he wasn't there, either."

"Have you asked him where he was?"

"He won't tell me!"

Oh, dear. Catherine's heart began to thump with fear for her friend. Strangely, she found herself wishing that Dr. Harry were there.

"Oh, Margie, I'm so sorry."

"I don't know what to do! I lied under oath!"

She thought about Margery's testimony.

"You didn't really. You said you rang him, not that you talked to him."

"Well, *he* lied!"

"He did." And to save herself, Catherine couldn't think of an innocent explanation. But she also could never betray her friend by going to the police with this information. Was it possible that Dr. Waddell had nothing to do with the murder? That it had been Sir Herbert all along?

At that moment, the bell to her flat rang. She heard Cherry go to the door. Then she heard Rafe's deep voice.

"Miss Tregowyn is engaged, sir," Cherry said. "She has a guest."

"Never mind," he said. "I can handle her *guest*."

Cherry protested, "But you can't go in there!"

The door to the sitting room opened, and Rafe burst in.

Margery shrank from him, covering her face with her handkerchief. Rafe stood, apparently dumbfounded. Finally, he said, "Cat! What did you do to your head?"

Without thinking, Catherine had taken off her cloche, forgetting all about her wound, which was now uncovered.

"It doesn't matter at the moment, Rafe," she said. "You must go and return later."

"That's Lady Margery," he stated. "Whatever is the matter?"

"It's none of your affair, but she's very upset. You must go."

"Maybe I can help."

At this point, Margery wiped her eyes and looked up at Rafe. "I'm sorry, Rafe. There's nothing anyone can do. I'm just unloading on Cat."

He went to her and, bending down, took her hands in his. "May I speak to Sir Herbert for you? Does he know how miserable you are? It's plain he adores you, so I know it's not another woman."

"No. It's nothing like that," she said.

The situation was awkward in the extreme, and Catherine had no idea what to do to remedy it if Rafe wouldn't leave. Finally, she said, "Margie, would you feel better if you were to lie down for a bit? Cherry can bring you a cold compress for your head."

"That's a good idea," her friend said. Rafe helped her to her feet, and Catherine led her back to her bedroom.

"I'm so sorry about Rafe," she said. "He must have thought you were Dr. Harry. He's a bit jealous."

"It's all right. I actually think I might sleep after that good cry."

Catherine pulled closed the drapes and turned back the bed. "Here you are. Get some rest, and we can talk later."

Stopping by Cherry's quarters off the kitchen, Catherine asked her to prepare a cold compress for her friend. Only then did she go in to tackle Rafe.

"That was exceedingly rude to burst in on us like that!" she told him. "Poor Lady Margery is terribly embarrassed."

"I'm so sorry," he said. He wore a mulish expression which belied his words. "But a bit of a lie down will do her good. Now, will you tell me what happened to your head?"

"It happened days ago, and I have ceased to think about it. A professor called Stephenson went after me with a cricket bat. At night. On the Somerville Quad. He thought I could expose him for plagiarism."

He took her into his arms and gently placed her head against his chest. "My poor Kitty. He tried to kill you, didn't he?"

"Yes. But as William is always telling me, I have a thick skull."

"Have the police arrested him?"

Catherine's anger was melting, and she felt herself lean into Rafe. "Only just. But there's still a murderer out there. Dr. Stephenson has an alibi. I think the murderer may be whoever broke into my flat the other night."

"Let's sit down, and you can tell me all about this wretched murder. I'm done with the pater and ready to give you a hand." He led her to the sofa.

She gave him the full story, beginning with her discovery of Dr. Chenowith's body, and ending with Dr. Waddell's murder and her and Dr. Harry's abortive visit to the police that morning.

"It sounds like you might have been trying to force a connection when there wasn't one," he said of the police visit.

"Possibly. I'll be interested to hear what the Oxford police think. This business of Nazis at Oxford is more than a little unsettling. Waddell had to have known about them, and he was most likely in league with them."

"Does Lady Margery's distress have anything to do with the murder of Dr. Chenowith?"

"I can't betray her confidence."

"Even to this wretched Dr. Harry? And why do you refer to him in such a ridiculous manner?"

"It started by being facetious. He gave my poetry a bad review."

"Ah-ha! I knew he was a bounder!"

"You have no time for my poetry, either," she reminded him.

"But that's different. I have no time for anyone's poetry. I'm not made that way."

Her irritation with him resurfaced. "It's a big part of who I am, Rafe."

"Let's not get into that now. I'm sure if you are patient with me, I can be taught to appreciate it. But let's discuss this murder situation. Why are you so keen on solving it? Are you past seeing how dangerous it is? Are you only looking at it as some abstract puzzle?"

She felt herself deflate a bit. With the new information about Sir Herbert, she was now wondering the same thing. Was it worth betraying a friend to solve the puzzle? It *had* seemed abstract until she had witnessed Margery's tears. Now she couldn't bring herself to act.

But perhaps Dr. Waddell *was* the murderer, and he had in turn been murdered by his Nazi organization so he wouldn't bring attention to them. If that proved to be true, it would take Sir Herbert off the hook. How could she find out?

A bold and crazy plan occurred to her.

"I have my own reasons for continuing this, Rafe. Is your plane still at Croyden?"

"Now what are you up to? My plane?"

"I need to take a trip to the Isle of Man."

"That would be a nice little day jaunt. Why?"

"That's where Dr. Waddell was from. Perhaps I can discover something from his family or friends."

"Surely if he was an Oxford don, he has lived there for years."

"Dr. Harry...er...Bascombe has been investigating at Oxford. He did find out the man was a fascist, but nothing much beyond that. I'm sure he's reapplying himself to the task today. If he finds nothing more, the next logical step is to dig deeper. To go to his home."

"Well, of course, I'd be happy to take you there. I've been trying to get you to fly with me for years. I just bought a brand new de Havilland Dragon. It will come in handy to carry me and my associates back and forth to my new business in the North."

She rolled her eyes. Rafe would use any excuse to indulge his passion for flying.

"But now, we have something else to discuss. I want you to tell me about this Dr. Harry Bascombe."

Catherine was annoyed. "You don't own me, you know. We are not engaged. And you've been out of the country for a year."

"Is that how long this has been going on?"

"No. But you have to remember that when you left, we had completely broken things off."

"And yet my photo sits there on your desk."

She felt herself color but said nothing.

"I suppose Dot has been encouraging this?"

"She likes him, yes. More than I do, I'm beginning to suspect."

"Ah-ha!"

He sounded so triumphant that it galled her. "I've gone dancing with him," she said. "He's a beautiful dancer. He stayed with me in the hospital after my injury. I've been to his home. There. Now I've told you everything. Far more than you deserve to know."

"Shall he accompany us to the Isle of Man?"

"I would imagine so."

"When shall we go?"

"It will take only a day to go over and back? I have an engagement on Thursday evening," she told him.

"The flight shouldn't take long, but I don't know what you're planning to do there."

"Leave that to me."

"Then tell Dr. Bascombe to meet us at Croyden at ten o'clock. I'll pick you up here in my motor at nine."

"Thank you, Rafe. Now, I suppose you need to be fed?" she asked.

"Yes, please."

She rang for Cherry. When the maid appeared, she said, "Could you bring Mr. St. John some biscuits and cheese? And a bit of that chutney I bought yesterday? Thank you, Cherry."

While he ate, they discussed her new publishing contract and her job offer from Somerville and her problem with the dean.

"Do Somerville faculty have to remain celibate?" he asked.

"They rarely marry," she said. "But it's not unheard of."

"That's all right, then," said Rafe.

* * *

Margery woke around four o'clock and appeared in the sitting room dressed in a different frock, with her hair and makeup immaculate.

"Shall we go take tea somewhere?" she asked.

"I think I'll just amble along to my club," said Rafe. "I am glad you seem to be recovered, Lady Margery. Now you can keep Cat out of trouble."

"I wouldn't count on it," said Margery. "That job is more than I can take on."

Rafe laughed, kissed Catherine's forehead, and left.

Margery and Catherine had tea and hot cross buns at the bakery on the corner. She took the opportunity to tell her friend about the case against Dr. Waddell, his murder, and her plans to travel to his home on the Isle of Man.

"I hope you find something. Anything. Will you tell me if you do? I just don't know how long I can stand the strain of wondering if Herbert is guilty. If I know one way or the other, I shall know what to do, and I can adjust."

"I will see what we can find out," she promised. "And I will let you know."

This seemed to satisfy her friend for the time being.

* * *

Catherine rang Dr. Harry after dinner.

"Are you still Chicken Little?" she asked him. "Or did the Detective Chief Inspector buy your hunch about the Oxford Nazi group?"

"He knew of it, at least." She heard a sigh over the line. "He'd been notified of Waddell's death, but he didn't seem to buy my story of a connection between that and the Nazi group. I'm beginning to think maybe it was an illusion of mine brought about by too little sleep and an unconscious ingestion of opium."

She laughed. "Well, I've got a flight for us to the Isle of Man tomorrow if you want to take it. Rafe seems to think we could be back before Professor Williams's do on Thursday."

"Brilliant! Oxford certainly hasn't yielded many answers."

"You need to meet us at Croyden at 10:00. Can you make it?"

"Of course. You know, I don't have any recollection of how I intended to spend my Long Vacation before I got involved with you."

"Did you have plans to go somewhere?" she asked.

"I think I may have been planning the odd trip to the South of France."

"Oh," she felt suddenly guilty. "Well, if we wrap this up, there is still all of August."

"I'll see you at Croyden. Ten a.m."

Chapter Twenty-One

Catherine had never been in an airplane and was excited at the prospect. She had no worries about Rafe's capabilities as a pilot. He did everything well. It was all part of a natural inborn grace he seemed to apply to any task he undertook.

When he arrived at the flat, he looked at her clothing—she was wearing a white sailor blouse and navy blue trousers—and said, "That won't do. You'll freeze up there. I should have told you. The trousers are fine, but you must wear woolen socks and brogues. And put on a jumper and bring your thickest fur coat."

"I shall look ridiculous!" she said.

"Bring those shoes you are wearing. You can change when we put down on the Isle of Man. And you can shed the coat and jumper then, too. Do you have a stocking cap?"

Grumbling, she went to do as he said and to dig out her stocking cap.

* * *

Dr. Harry was better prepared than she had been. When they met him at the aerodrome, he was dressed warmly.

He greeted Rafe with a handshake and kissed Catherine on the cheek. She glowered at him.

Rafe's plane was shiny and new. A six-seater bi-plane with two engines, it had more than enough room for all of them.

He asked, "Ever been up, Bascombe?"

"Yes," replied Dr. Harry. "I enjoy flying."

"You can have the co-pilot's seat." Turning to Catherine, he said, "You shall sit behind. There's a blanket under the seat if you get cold. I had the factory install leather belts to help keep you in your seat. Be sure to fasten them." He passed out small balls of wax and instructed them to use them to plug their ears.

Catherine put on her extra gear and settled into her seat. Nerves and excitement fluttered in her stomach. "We should only be in the air about an hour and a half—a couple of hours at the most," he said. "We will be landing at an airstrip about six miles south of Douglas, the capital city."

With that, he signaled the ground crew, the engines started with a roar, and before Catherine knew it, they were moving toward the runway.

Am I ready for this? Golly! Did God really intend for man to fly? How will he get this thing in the air?

When Rafe reached the runway and began to push the airplane at ever greater speeds, she clutched at her seat, biting her lip. The engines were roaring, and the airstrip was far bumpier than it looked. Then, all at once, they were airborne, and she was looking out the window at the landscape below her.

It was an extremely queer sensation. Everything beneath began to look as though it were like William's minute railway set—tiny buildings, minute trees clustered around squares of green, and then a patchwork of farm fields. Catherine began to feel an exhilaration that conquered her fear. They were sailing on the air! Well, bouncing and sailing.

Dr. Harry and Rafe shouted at one another to be heard above the engine's roar. They both looked back to check on her, and she gave them a thumb's up. Rafe waggled the wings up and down and laughed when she grabbed her seat.

* * *

The landing was also quite bumpy, but at last, they came to a stop beside a small building that was the Ronaldsway airport according to the sign. Everything seemed strangely silent when the engines stopped.

Looking around her, Catherine saw that they were in the midst of nowhere. How were they to get to Douglas, the capital city where they were headed?

She had reckoned without Rafe, who had a taxi waiting. Stripping off her outer layers, she deplaned as best she could with numb feet.

"That was the most unusual and exciting thing I've ever done!" she exclaimed to both men. "Thank you, Rafe. Especially for not setting us down in the Irish Sea. I was worried for a minute."

He laughed, and she could tell that he was experiencing one of his extreme high moods. She could certainly understand why. In her exuberance, she threw her arms around him and gave him a great hug. He smiled down at her in a joy that lit his whole face. It was at moments like this that her love for him nearly carried her away.

Dr. Harry sat in the front of the taxi, while Catherine and Rafe took the back seat. They held hands and listened to the professor give the cab driver an address in Douglas. She realized that now that they had landed, she didn't even have a plan. Dr. Harry was better prepared.

"Where are we going?" she asked.

"St. John's had an address for him in Douglas. Apparently, he lives with his mother when he is here."

"Have the police been in touch with her? Does she know her son is dead?" asked Catherine.

"I have no idea. That would have been up to the Metropolitan Police at the Yard."

She began to feel a bit anxious. "I hope she knows. I wouldn't like to have to break it to her."

"Never mind," said Rafe. "I can be very reassuring when the situation calls for it."

She smiled at him as he looked down into her eyes.

Douglas caught her by surprise. It was a charming little city with a strip of pastel-colored Victorian flats rising five stories up from the strand along the beachfront. Mrs. Waddell lived in one of these flats.

"There's money somewhere in the family," remarked Dr. Harry. "I don't imagine these flats come cheap."

He paid the driver, and they set about finding the flat. It was in a pale pink block. The doorman inquired whom they were seeking. They mentioned Mrs. Waddell's name.

"We are from Oxford University," Dr. Harry told him.

The doorman rang up the Waddell flat on his telephone.

"She will see you," he said after a short conversation.

They took the lift to the fourth floor. Catherine squeezed Rafe's arm.

The flat was on the sea side of the building. Dr. Harry knocked, and a tall woman with iron-gray hair answered his summons.

"Yes?" she asked. "My, there are a lot of you. Are you all from Oxford?"

"Most of us," said Catherine, stepping forward. "I'm Miss Tregowyn." She held out her hand and shook the lady's. "Somerville College."

Dr. Harry offered his hand. "I'm Dr. Harry Bascombe, Christ Church."

Rafe thrust his large hand forward, "I'm Rafael St. John."

"Well, you had better come in," Mrs. Waddell said. She opened the door, and as they walked through, Catherine caught her breath at the beautiful sea vista. "This is breathtaking!"

"Yes, Christopher rents this for me. He loves the sea."

Catherine noted the present tense and cringed inside. *Best get it over with.*

"Have the police not been in touch with you?" she asked.

When the bewildered woman shook her head, Catherine said, "You had better sit down, Mrs. Waddell."

"What's happened to Christopher?" the lady asked, her voice sharp. "Tell me!"

Rafe spoke up, his voice deep and somber, "We're afraid he's dead, Mrs. Waddell."

"Dead?" Her face paled, and she looked from one of them to the other. "What is going on? Why are you here?"

Catherine seated herself next to the woman on the sofa. "I'm sorry to have to tell you this, ma'am, but he was murdered in London. We haven't heard why or how or by whom. It happened a few days ago."

The lady's face went blank with shock.

"I'm so very sorry. Would you like me to fix you a cup of tea?" Catherine offered.

The woman only nodded. Catherine got up and went to find the kitchen. It was tucked away at the back of the flat. Setting the kettle to boil, she searched the cupboards until she found the things she needed. The woman was extremely neat and organized, judging from her kitchen. She didn't appear to employ a servant.

There was a photo of Dr. Waddell sitting on the kitchen table. He was beachcombing.

When the kettle boiled, she poured the water over the tea ball into the teapot. Finding a tray, she set a cup on it along with the pot, sugar, milk, and a spoon.

Catherine carried the tray out into the front sitting room where she saw Rafe sitting on the sofa next to Mrs. Waddell as she wept silent tears. She held one of his handkerchiefs in her hand. Dr. Harry was down on one knee in front of her, speaking softly.

"Here, Mrs. Waddell. I have your tea," she said. "Do you take milk?"

The woman nodded, and Catherine poured milk into the cup and added four lumps of sugar. When the tea had steeped long enough, she poured it into the cup and stirred.

"Dr. Harry?" she asked. "Perhaps you can serve Mrs. Waddell her tea." She handed the professor the cup, her hands trembling.

For the next half hour, the three of them offered consolation and what little information they had.

When she judged the time was right, Catherine said, "Perhaps you would like to tell us about your son. None of us knew him, you see."

If the grieving mother thought the request bizarre, considering they had come all this way, she didn't say so. Instead, she seemed to find it a relief to talk.

"He was a lonely man. Quite unhappy, I always feared. The academic life suited him better than anything else, but just the same I think it was a disappointment to him. Too settled. He disliked theory and wanted action."

Mrs. Waddell blew her nose, beginning to calm as she talked.

"He was a happy boy, growing up here. He hadn't many friends, but he had a great imagination. I thought he might become a writer. He loved the old Viking legends and the German fairy tales. They abound here. He grew up to be deeply interested in the local culture and myth." She smiled a little. "He masqueraded as Wotan and Thor."

She held out her cup for more tea.

"Eventually the isle became too small for him. He wanted a broader canvas, I think. He was always a good student, and so he went on to Oxford, turning his love of legends into a career."

"Do you know why he was unhappy?" Catherine asked.

"No. I don't. It was more like a persistent melancholy. But lately, he was a bit different. He seemed to have found some direction. He never told me what it was, on the occasions when he visited me, but he did say in a letter that it was time Britain changed course. He said he was working with other men who felt the same way. Christopher felt the present government was weak and ineffectual, that Britain had lost its way. There was no one to lead the people."

"Did he mention the names of any of these men he was working with?" Dr. Harry asked.

She looked up sharply, suddenly seeming to come to herself. "Why exactly are you here?"

Catherine said, "We are trying to find out who murdered your son."

"Isn't that the job of the police?"

"We feel they are looking in the wrong direction. It doesn't speak too highly of them that they haven't even been in touch with his next of kin, does it?"

"But they wouldn't look on me as his next of kin, surely. That would be Agatha, even though they've been separated for a while."

Catherine's heart skipped and then began to pound.

"Agatha? Do you mean Agatha Chenowith? He was married to her?"

"You must not have known him well. But then, they kept it secret because of her position. As a female professor in an all-female university, she thought it best to keep it dark. She was ambitious. She hoped to be in the administration one day."

"I'm sorry to tell you this, Mrs. Waddell, but Dr. Chenowith was also murdered," said Catherine. "She was a professor of mine."

The lady just stared at Catherine, who couldn't do anything at the moment but stare back.

Agatha Chenowith was married? To Dr. Waddell? And no one knew? Even the dean? Or Miss Siddons? Or any of his peers at the college? What on earth did all this mean?

Catherine's head was spinning.

"Who killed Agatha?" asked Mrs. Waddell.

"That is another thing we are trying to find out," said Dr. Harry. "Perhaps the same person killed both of them."

Catherine pulled herself together and asked, "Do you know of any groups that your son was involved in at Oxford? Political or otherwise?"

"No," Mrs. Waddell answered. "He didn't talk to me much

about that sort of thing. Perhaps he did with his sister. She lives here on the island, as well. Sandra didn't like Agatha very much, I'm afraid. Until Christopher and Agatha separated, she and her brother were estranged, but lately they have become close again. She may know something."

Rafe asked, "Can you tell us where your daughter lives?"

"She has a shop on the strand and lives above it. It's a gift and snack shop called 'Sandy's Surprises.' She's run off her feet at this hour, but I think I'll call her in a bit and ask her to come and see me. She can leave the shop to her assistant. I want to tell her about Christopher myself. If you come by around five o'clock, you can talk to her and see if she has anything to tell you."

"That would certainly be best," said Catherine. "Thank you for the invitation. It doesn't seem right to drop such dire news on you and then leave you by yourself. Is there anyone we can call for you? Someone you'd like to be with you?"

"I think I'd rather be on my own, thank you. Sandra will come soon. I want to just go through Christopher's things and think about him. This is such a shock."

Catherine handed the woman one of her visiting cards with her phone number scrawled on it. "You might want to call Scotland Yard about your son's remains. A Detective Inspector Underbridge is handling the case."

She shook with sudden sobs and covered her face. "Thank you. He was still so young. So talented."

The three of them stood and took their leave, promising to call back at five o'clock.

Chapter Twenty-Two

The trio walked along the strand, passing Sandy's Surprises with its jaunty turquoise and white awning, looking for someplace to have a late luncheon. They settled on a fish and chips shop where they ordered the local dish—Manx fried kippers with chips and cheese.

"Well," said Dr. Harry. "Mrs. Waddell certainly set the cat among the pigeons. I don't know when I've been more surprised! Man-hater Augusta Chenowith married secretly to another professor! I think this fact links the two deaths for certain."

Catherine picked at her food. "I wouldn't be surprised if their separation had something to do with Dr. Waddell's new interest in changing the political direction of the country." She turned to Rafe, explaining, "We already know he was a fascist, but her friend, Miss Siddons, said Dr. Chenowith had no time for Hitler. Not a recipe for marital bliss."

"Try as I might, I can't see the woman married. And no one knew," said Dr. Harry.

"I know," said Catherine. "It does seem odd."

"And why is that? I never met the woman, remember," said Rafe.

"She was beyond prickly," said Catherine. "She carried grudges. There wasn't anything giving or soft about her. I just can't imagine her yielding her prerogatives to any man in a marriage relationship."

"Is that what you think marriage is?" asked Rafe. "Yielding? Giving in?"

He looked her straight in the eye, and she knew he was dead serious. "One must be prepared to go at least halfway to meet another person. Don't you think? Agatha Chenowith didn't ever give me the idea that she would be willing to consider a dissenting point of view. She was rigid and ruthless."

Catherine imagined Dr. Harry was almost squirming beside her at this discussion of marriage.

"You're right about being willing to compromise," said Rafe. "But one shouldn't have to give up one's basic self. In marrying a person, you accept them for who they are."

"But there are a million things that can change in the course of one's life," said Catherine. "A person isn't a static entity. He or she is always changing and adapting to new circumstances like parenthood, for example. One doesn't remain the person one is at the time one is married."

Rafe thought this over.

Catherine went on. "Again, I would be willing to wager that the evolution of Dr. Waddell's political beliefs is what caused their separation."

Dr. Harry picked up this thread of the specific. "I agree. But here is a question to which I don't have an answer. What was Waddell doing in the girl's dormitory?" he asked. "If it hadn't been for that little errand, we would never know a thing about him. He might very well be Chenowith's murderer and could have intended to plant evidence against someone else."

Rafe shot a sour look at Dr. Harry, which he appeared not to notice. "Or he might have been trying to solve the murder himself, as we are," said Catherine.

Rafe interrupted, "It's a good thing I don't live here. I could get used to these chips and cheese and lose my manly figure. Do you suppose they have a museum on this island?"

Catherine was annoyed at both men and their attempts to wrest the conversation. "I'm sure we could ask someone," she answered. "Why? Have you a desire to play tourist?"

"We have to fill the time somehow, and I was thinking—Mrs. Waddell talked about her son's childish pursuits and how they led to his scholastic career. You know—lecturing about myths and legends. Seems to me we ought to investigate that a little bit. What did those myths and legends signify to him? They must have been pretty powerful to have that much of an effect on him. A museum is what we're looking for."

She let go of her annoyance. "That's actually a good idea," admitted Catherine. "You know, I wonder if he was part of Dr. Williams's coterie. You haven't met him, Rafe, but he is the pundit of Teutonic legends and thought at Oxford. I've been invited to a soiree he's having on Thursday, which is why we have to get back."

"What kind of a soiree?" Rafe asked.

"Sherry and biscuits and a meeting of a group that just got back from Norway. Apparently, they found a people who have an oral tradition of old Teutonic legends passed down from ancient times. He's very excited about it."

Dr. Harry, finished with his luncheon, pulled out his pipe. "Williams is a proper old pagan. He subscribes to Carl Jung's theory of an Aryan collective consciousness. Wotan is the Nordic god who represents the idea. Sound familiar?"

"Strewth! Are we talking about Hitler and his 'master race' here?" asked Rafe.

"Yes. But Dr. Williams is an old sweetheart," said Catherine. "He works in Whitehall, for heaven's sake. He is interested in all this from a linguistic point of view. Legends common to speakers of Old English and the Teutonic Languages. I very much doubt he has much time for a thug like Hitler."

"This whole thing sounds increasingly rum," said Rafe. "Let's go see if they have a museum."

After questioning their waitress, they determined that there was a Manx Museum located at an old hospital inland from the harbor. The three of them took a cab and arrived at the unprepossessing old building that bore its name in faint lettering. It didn't look particularly promising.

When they entered and paid their fee, they began looking at the exhibits which featured an entire collection on the Manx Viking Heritage, including a hoard of Viking silver and gold.

"What did I tell you," said Rafe. "This would certainly catch a boy's attention."

Dr. Harry said, "But this museum was founded in 1922. That's only fourteen years ago. When Christopher Waddell was a boy this place didn't exist."

Catherine said, "I wonder if he had any part in establishing it?"

They walked through the exhibit which had a model Viking ship and paintings of Viking battles. A statue of a Viking dressed in full war kit was on display.

Catherine noticed a table with a stack of brochures. Paying the requested 50 pence, she picked one up and saw that it detailed the legend of the Vikings on the Isle of Man.

"Look," she said. "This thing was written by Dr. Waddell."

"Hmm," said Rafe. "I wonder how involved he was in setting up this exhibit."

It proved that Waddell was a primary benefactor of the Viking Heritage Exhibit, memorialized on a plaque fixed on the wall at the end. He was quoted as saying, "The spirit of the Viking hero is endemic to the consciousness of Manx citizens. We embody their appearance and values in our everyday lives. A study of the Viking culture is imperative if we are to understand ourselves."

"Sounds very like the Jungian creed of collective consciousness," said Dr. Harry.

"Agreed," said Catherine. "Kind of creepy, actually."

The rest of the museum was a less interesting history of politics on the island. They dutifully passed through it and then took their leave.

Because they had time, the three of them walked back down to the shore rather than taking a taxi. With her new knowledge of his improbable marriage and the obsession of Dr. Waddell with the Viking culture, Catherine had plenty to think about. Positioning herself to the rear of the two men who walked in single file down the winding streets, she looked at the sapphire sea without really seeing it. Since it had been hot in the museum, she relished the cool breeze on her face. She could have used either Dr. Harry or Rafe's arm but knew it would cause friction if she were to choose one over the other.

"I wonder how Aryan racism is born," she said once they reached the flats.

"I don't know that it starts out in any sinister way," said Dr. Harry. "For Christopher Waddell, it may just have meant embracing who he was. All young boys look for heroes. I think the idea just becomes pathological when it becomes exclusive. Today it targets Jews as the enemy, the corruptor of the purity of a superior race."

"I'm surprised a college like St. John's would tolerate such a rum philosophy," said Rafe.

"We don't know that it does. He may have preached it in a more diluted form. 'Roots of European Thought' or something like that," said Dr. Harry.

Rafe appeared to ponder this. "My Spanish great grandmother was Jewish," he said finally.

Catherine didn't know what he expected her to say. Finally, she settled on, "Best to stay clear of the Nazis then."

It was nearly five o'clock when they passed Sandy's Surprises. They made their way to Mrs. Waddell's flat.

A tall, red-haired woman with eyes that were obviously swollen answered the door.

"You are the people from Oxford?"

"Yes," answered Catherine. "We are so sorry for your loss. It must have been a terrible shock. I am Catherine Tregowyn. These men are Dr. Harold Bascombe and Mr. Rafael St. John."

"Sandra Christensen," she said abruptly, standing in the doorway with no apparent intention of letting them in. "I don't know what you expect to find out from us. What is your purpose here, anyway? You're not the police."

For once, Catherine didn't know what to say.

Dr. Harry smiled. "No. We're not the police. But as Oxford fellows, we've got hold of facts the police won't even look at. We're trying to see where they lead."

Catherine cringed at the lie. None of them were, in fact, fellows.

"My mother is still very upset, and I'm not doing too well, either." She eased out into the hallway and closed the door behind her. "We can talk out here. What are your questions?"

Catherine was surprised but decided to try to make the best of the situation. "It came as a complete surprise to us that your brother was married to Dr. Chenowith. Did your mother tell you that she was recently murdered, as well?"

"Yes, she did tell me. But Agatha and Christopher hadn't had anything to do with one another for the past year. They were legally separated."

Dr. Harry asked, "Could you tell us how long they had been married?"

"They married three years ago, but Agatha wanted it to be kept secret. She was like that. I really don't know why they married at all. They only saw each other at the weekend. They had a cottage in Bucks."

"Do you have any idea why they separated?" asked Dr. Harry.

"Why do you need to know that?" Mrs. Christensen asked, her voice hostile.

"It might have a bearing on the murders," said Catherine as gently as though she were treading on eggshells.

"Agatha could no longer tolerate my brother's political beliefs. They embarrassed her. You might as well know I had no time for the woman."

"What were his political beliefs?" asked Rafe, his voice only idly inquisitive.

"If you don't know, you're not much good as investigators. Now, I've got to get back to my mother. We're trying to figure out how we're going to afford to get Christopher's body back to the island."

"I'm so sorry, Mrs. Christensen," said Catherine. She handed her a calling card. "There is my telephone number in London. If you get any ideas about who was responsible for Dr. Waddell's death, I would appreciate your ringing me. You can reverse the charges."

"Thank you. I will keep it in mind," said the woman. Opening the door, she went inside and shut it behind her.

"Charming," said Rafe.

"I don't blame her," Catherine said. "We have no official standing, and we were the bringers of the worst kind of news. We must seem like vultures."

* * *

Rather than fly home that night, the little group elected to have a good seafood dinner, spend the night at a hotel and fly home the next morning.

Catherine felt she was probably the only one that was anxious to get home. The friction between Rafe and Dr. Harry was grating on her nerves. Either one of them alone was tolerable, but together they were too much. She couldn't take one's arm without the other bristling in silence. They seemed to bring out the worst in one another, as well. Dr. Harry was puffed up like a barnyard rooster while Rafe, though more conversant in matters outside of sport than she had ever known him to be, came across as a smooth matinee idol.

By dinnertime, she had had enough of both of them.

"I'm going to give dinner a miss," she said. "There is a nice little hotel I saw on the strand. I'm going to check in there and go to bed. I'll meet you at the airport in the morning. Ten o'clock?"

Both men looked surprised at her decision but finally agreed on ten o'clock. She parted ways with the two men in her life.

The Hotel Madeleine was pocket-sized and expensive, but her room had a view of the sea and a lovely private bath with a large Victorian bathtub. There was also a small dining room, so she didn't miss dinner, after all. After taking a bath and freshening her hair and makeup, she dined downstairs on lobster. It was lovely.

Catherine did not sleep well, however. She dreamed of brown-shirted gangs chasing her through the streets of the Isle. They had Viking beards and carried tridents for weapons. She was weighted down by the Viking gold and kept looking for places to hide it. Every time she thought she was safe; Dr. Waddell would discover her and call on his gang of brown shirts to come and get the gold. She would wake in a sweat, get a glass of water, and then return to bed where the dream resumed.

She woke in the morning exhausted and very glad she didn't have to go back to sleep.

CHAPTER TWENTY-THREE

When they met at the little make-shift airport, Rafe seemed elegant and rested as usual. Dr. Harry was fractious and didn't seem to have slept well, either. They all boarded the plane. Catherine swathed herself in layers of warmth, and soon they were airborne. This time, Dr. Harry sat next to her in the cabin of the plane.

"Well, I don't know that we're any forwarder," he said loudly to make himself heard after takeoff. "Except for the bombshell about the marriage."

"I wonder if he killed her," she shouted back. "Then who killed him? Were their deaths linked? Are politics important or irrelevant?"

They flew over the Irish Sea and then south over northern England. The flight was wracked with turbulent weather, and Catherine found herself instinctively holding on to Dr. Harry. Though she railed at herself for being a spineless female, she couldn't let go of his comforting arm.

When they finally set down safely at Croyden, she reluctantly let go of him.

"Thank you so much for taking us, Rafe," she said. "It was an unforgettable experience."

He scowled at her, and she knew he must have noted her clinging to Dr. Harry.

"Especially when I thought I was going to die," she added. Now she could grin about it.

Dr. Harry said, "I have my motor. Are you still going to Dr. Williams's soiree, Catherine?"

"Yes," she said.

"I'll be driving her up," said Rafe.

Catherine ground her teeth but didn't contradict him in front of Dr. Harry.

"Well, then. I guess I'll see you both there," the professor said, tipping his hat.

As soon as he was out of sight, she turned on Rafe. "I did *not* invite you!"

He just grinned. "Cat, I want to be part of your Oxford world. You're up to your pretty neck in this story, and you've intrigued me. Or don't you think I can hold my own at an Oxford sherry party?"

"You've never shown the least partiality for this part of my life. Is this Dr. Harry's doing?"

"Perhaps."

Since Catherine didn't know what to say to that, she just let him open the door to his Hispano Suiza motor and she took her seat in the luxurious automobile. He put the top down, making further conversation impossible.

She had to admit that her relationship with Rafe had always been lacking in the intellectual vein. The camaraderie she enjoyed with Dr. Harry had been refreshing that way. And until this little trip to the Isle, Rafe had never seen the intellectual side of her. Maybe it was time he did. *Certainly,* it was time he did.

* * *

He dropped her at her door with a stirring kiss, promising to return at five-thirty for the drive up to Oxford. Rattled by the kiss, she opened the door and greeted Cherry.

"Oh, miss I'm so glad you're in one piece. I didn't like to think of you in an airplane!"

"It was actually fun," said Catherine. "Any messages?"

"Yes. Someone called Jennie rang. She said to tell you she has something important for you. I told her you would be coming up to Oxford tonight. She's leaving it at the porter's desk for you. I hope that was all right."

Catherine's pulse quickened. *What could she have found?* "Yes. Thank you, Cherry." She handed the woman her fur coat. "Now I would love a bath!"

* * *

After her disturbing night, she decided to spend the two hours remaining to her napping. When she awoke from a heavy sleep, Catherine was startled to see that it was five o'clock. She had only half an hour to dress. Cherry entered her room.

Catherine said, "You choose something. My mind is entirely taken up with something else. I am not at all in the mood for a party."

"Oh, miss, what's wrong then?"

"It's just this mystery I am entangled in. It's turning out to be much more involved than I thought."

"I'm that sorry, miss. I hope you can see your way clear soon." Cherry opened the wardrobe and began flipping through "cock-tail" dresses. "I think this one will do," she said, pulling out an apricot silk frock with a fitted skirt that flared at the knees. "You have a scarf that will go with this that I can tie over your head with a bow over your ear. The hair is finally starting to grow in, but it looks awful."

Rafe arrived just as Cherry was putting the finishing touches to Catherine's make-up. She sprayed herself with gardenia scent as her maid went to answer the door.

"Darling, you look lovely," Rafe greeted her. "As always." He kissed her lightly on her powdered cheek.

He looked fabulous in a white dinner jacket. "I thought we might go to Carmichael's after the sherry party."

"I'm really tired, Rafe. And not looking forward to this. But I think it's important that I go."

"Any reason why it's more important than any other Oxford cocktail party?"

"The reason for it."

"Ah, yes. The Teutonic legends. You think it might have something to do with Waddell?"

He opened the door and they walked to the lift.

"It may. Jennie, my scout, called and she found something important in Dr. Chenowith's rooms. She's leaving it at the porter's desk. We can pick it up on the way to the party."

The lift arrived and they suspended conversation.

When they walked out into the lobby, Rafe said, "I wouldn't be surprised if Waddell made the leap from those old pagan philosophies to Hitler."

"Not much of a leap. We already knew he was a fascist and that he wanted a stronger government in England."

They reached the street. "But I don't understand why a woman like that would even marry Waddell," said Rafe.

He handed her into his car, and went around to let himself in. The top was now up, she was glad to see.

"She'd been badly burned by Margery's husband after an affair that lasted over a long period of time. I think the idea of marriage came along right as she was on the rebound from that disaster."

"Ah," said Rafe. "Poor woman."

"I am sorry she was murdered, but she wasn't a nice woman, Rafe," said Catherine.

"So, what are you hoping to find out tonight?"

"I'm just going to keep my ears open. It seems to me there must be some overlap between these ancient Teuton lovers and the modern-day Aryan worshippers."

"That makes sense. I'll keep an ear to the ground, also."

* * *

The Old Common Room at Balliol was a space used for a variety of purposes. At present, it was set up for a comfortable sherry party, with deep sofas and upholstered chairs brought in. There was a little stand with a microphone, and a couple of waiters moved around with trays full of sherry glasses and canapes.

The only person not drinking sherry seemed to be Dr. Williams, who held the much-beloved cup of tea he preferred to any other beverage. It was well known that he bought it from a Chinese import company in the City.

When Rafe and Catherine arrived, Dr. Harry welcomed them at the door. "The undergrads are going to take the stand at eight o'clock. I've noticed a few men I recognize from the Bird and the Baby who used to drink in the St. John's contingent with Waddell. Don't know all their names, but I'm going to try to find out."

"Good idea," said Catherine.

"I'll see if I can detect anyone else here who might have belonged to that Nazi cult. I might have to pose as someone in favor of the philosophy. Turning up here for this news about Teutonic legends might give me a little credibility. I'll see you two in a bit."

"Good," said Catherine, looking about her. A moment later, she said to Rafe, "I don't recognize anyone except Dr. Williams and the Somerville Dean. I imagine my tutor, Dr. Sargent, would have been here if she were not in the South of France."

A waiter came by with a tray of baby shrimp canapes and another of sherry. Rafe and Catherine helped themselves. She frowned.

As soon as the waiter walked away, she said, "Do you think that's wise, Rafe?" She put her hand on the arm holding the drink.

"It's only one sherry. I can handle it, Cat."

"All right." She forced her mind into the matter at hand. "I think Dr. Williams is such a popular professor that some people come to Balliol just to study under him," Catherine said. "He's enthusiastic and entertaining. I don't know how he's managing his job at Whitehall with his professorial duties."

"He works at Whitehall? You mentioned that before, but I didn't quite take it on board. What does he do there?"

"Something hush-hush, apparently. I have no idea. He did mention to me that he is going to Germany next month to look at some early Teutonic document. Perhaps he'll do a bit of spying while he's there," she said *sotto voce*. "Let's split up and make some friends."

Rafe agreed.

During the next half hour, she met scholars in Old English and Early Teutonic languages, German myth and legend, English myth and legend, but no one she could identify in any way as being a likely candidate for the "Nazi club," as she privately called it. She and the dean steered clear of one another.

Suddenly, the proceedings were disturbed by the horrible sound of someone falling to the floor, crockery crashing, and violent vomiting. Everyone stood back from the scene but began to gather on the fringes. Rafe found her. He could see over the crowd.

"It's a man with white hair and a goatee."

"That describes half the professors at Oxford," Catherine said, moving toward the commotion. She heard a shout.

"It's Dr. Williams! Someone fetch a medico!"

"Dr. Williams!"

"Dr. Williams!"

Catherine ran out of the room through its only inner doorway looking for a telephone. There was a small pantry filled with trays of food. It had a telephone. She rang 999. While she waited for an answer, she spotted the colorful box which held Professor William's tea.

"I need an ambulance at Balliol. Old Common Room. Someone is violently ill. It was very sudden."

Chapter Twenty-Four

Catherine made one more call.

"Sergeant, I'd like to speak to Detective Chief Inspector Marsh. This is Miss Tregowyn. I am in the Old Common Room at Balliol. I suspect there's been a poisoning."

When Marsh came on the line, Catherine said, "I think there's been another attempted murder. Another of the members of the sherry party at Somerville, Dr. Williams, has just collapsed at another sherry party here at Balliol in the Old Common Room. He vomited violently and fell to the floor. I suspect poisoning. I've rung for an ambulance. He was drinking tea. Is it alright if I impound the source of his tea before someone can make away with it?"

"I'll be right there," said the Detective Chief Inspector. Use a napkin or something to remove the tea, so as not to disturb finger-prints. I'll ring the ME. Don't let anyone clean up the scene. Why do you think there is a connection to Dr. Chenowith?" he asked, his voice brisk.

"I have further evidence in that case that links them. With Dr. Waddell also."

"More amateur sleuthing!"

"Please save the lecture for later and just come," she pleaded.

* * *

The professor, still alive, was carried away to the Radcliffe Infirmary by ambulance. Fortunately, the arrival of the police had preserved the detritus of his illness and the broken teacup.

Catherine told Marsh, "I know the tea seems odd at a sherry party, but it was his characteristic beverage." She handed him the tea box, shrouded in a linen napkin.

"It's time you told me what made you suspect poison," Marsh told her.

"It will take a while for me to explain," she said. "It's complicated."

"All right. But you *will* tell me later. Now. How many people left the room before we got here?" he asked.

"It's hard to tell. Most of them were anxious about the professor, and I think they stayed around to see what the ambulance crew said. He is very beloved. By the way, he also works at Whitehall. But I suspect you already know that."

"Does your theory embrace that fact?"

Catherine was slightly taken aback at the aggressive question. "I don't know. It might. I'm just not sure at the moment."

Dr. Harry found her moments later. "What do you think is going on?" he asked.

"I believe it's everything we've found out is connected. Dr. Williams must somehow be connected to that Nazi group. I must have been wrong to have put him above such things."

"But wouldn't the government know that? Wouldn't they have checked him over thoroughly before giving him a sensitive job?"

"Yes. It's very puzzling."

"I have it!" said Dr. Harry. "What if he's infiltrating the group on behalf of the government?"

"That makes sense," said Catherine. "That's brilliant!"

"I do try," he said.

"Try what?" asked Rafe as he came through the door. Catherine immediately registered the blank look on his face that came when he had been drinking too much.

"To make sense," said Dr. Harry.

"And he occasionally does," said Catherine. "He thinks Dr. Williams was infiltrating the clandestine Nazi group on behalf of the government."

"And this was attempted murder, of course," said Rafe with a little laugh.

Catherine felt her heart drop to her middle. She should have known better than to bring him to a party where any kind of alcohol was offered in abundance.

She explained her theory about the tea. "I'm not versed in poisons, but it would be easy to poison his tea with arsenic, I should think."

"That's what's in rat poison, right?" asked Dr. Harry.

"I think so," said Catherine. "The only problem is, it doesn't work immediately. The rats crawl away to die."

"The poison may have been in that box of tea for a while," said Dr. Harry. "He may have been being poisoned a bit at a time if it was in his tea. It may just be coincidence that he finally collapsed here tonight."

"Well, I suspect the evidence will tell," said Catherine, wrinkling her nose at the memory of Dr. Williams's being sick.

She saw Rafe grab another full glass of sherry from a tray on the table when he thought she wasn't looking. Quelling her uneasiness, she watched the guests who were standing about in groups talking or sitting on the furniture.

Detective Chief Inspector Marsh came up to her. "My men are interviewing the guests. Let me take you to the college office. I've arranged for a room there. It's just across the Garden Quad."

She set off with the policeman, leaving Dr. Harry and Rafe behind.

* * *

"So," she concluded, having told the Detective Chief Inspector about their trip to the Isle of Man, the Waddell-Chenowith marriage, and the things she had learned about the former's pro-Hitler leanings. She had also explained Waddell's passion for all things Aryan and his probable Teutonic studies connection to Dr. Williams.

"I must swallow my pride and thank you for this," the Detective Chief Inspector said. "Since Waddell's death is not being investigated by my office, there is no way I would have made the Chenowith-Waddell connection. Have you informed Scotland Yard?"

"We only returned this afternoon from the Isle of Man. Besides, Detective Inspector Underbridge informed us that he had no use for amateur sleuthing."

"I shall inform them, but you need to put your pride in *your* pocket in this instance, Miss Tregowyn. They shall probably be in touch with you."

She thought again of Jennie's message. No matter what the hour, she needed to retrieve whatever the scout had found from the porter's lodge.

* * *

When Catherine returned to find Rafe, she discovered him happily drinking yet another glass of sherry extolling the virtues of Africa to Dr. Harry. How many had he consumed? Fear and the old feeling of helplessness clutched at her.

"Dr. Harry, may I speak to you for a moment?"

"Of course," he said.

They moved off to the other side of the room. She felt the heat of Rafe's eyes following her.

"Rafe has no tolerance for alcohol," she said. "Just how much sherry has he had?"

"You think he could get drunk from *sherry?*"

"He can get drunk from anything alcoholic," she said.

"Well, he seems pretty merry to me. He had a couple of glasses while you were with Marsh. But then, so did I."

"I don't imagine it affects you the same way," she said. "I don't know if I trust him driving to London in this condition."

"Come now. You're too hard on the man."

Catherine felt her patience snap. "You don't know him like I do. Did he have anything to drink the night I left you together on the Island?"

"Now that you mention it, he didn't. I remember thinking it was odd."

"He's drinking another glass now. Can you help me get him to the Randolph?

"I'm sorry. Of course. I'll do anything I can."

But Rafe wasn't having any of it. In a loud voice, he threw off Dr. Harry's hand on his elbow, "What are you doing you insufferable little tick? Who gave you the right to touch me? I'm Rafael St. John! Of the Wiltshire St. John's!" He drew Catherine unwillingly to his side. She knew enough not to try to extricate herself. "You're poaching on my preserve, you louse. This bit of stuff is mine! She's been mine for eons. All I have to do is crook my finger and she comes running. Haven't you learned that by now? You count as nothing." He tried and failed to snap his fingers. "Nothing."

Rafe had never spoken this way in her presence. Her blood boiled. Is that what he really thought? His bit of stuff? All he had to do was crook his finger? In *vino veritas?*

All the guests that remained were looking at them. She yanked herself out of Rafe's arms and he reflexively cuffed her on the chin. Catherine only barely kept her balance.

"Keep your hands off her, you bounder!" cried Dr. Harry. Coming up behind the man, he grabbed Rafe's forearms and forced them behind him. He began to frog march him out of the Old Commons Room.

But Rafe was strong. Again, he pulled away, his face red with fury. "You think she cares about you," he said. "But I'm all she's ever cared about. She belongs to me." He socked Dr. Harry in his eye.

One of the burly police sergeants who had been questioning the remaining guests advanced on them. "Need some help, miss?"

"Yes, please," Catherine said, deeply ashamed of the situation. "Can you lock him up for the night? He's clearly a public nuisance."

"I saw him strike you," said the sergeant. "Do you want me to book him for assault?"

"I don't think that will be necessary. Just lock him up until he's sober."

"With pleasure," said the policeman, taking his handcuffs off his belt.

Once he was cuffed, the belligerence seemed to leave Rafe. Catherine and Dr. Harry watched him go, in between two policemen, out into the night.

Catherine sank onto the sofa, mortified and deeply hurt. For so many years, she had been protective of Rafe during his bouts of drinking. And so many times he had promised to quit. But his words of this evening painted an ugly picture. She writhed at the remembrance.

His drunkenness was a nightmare she had lived too many times, but he had never struck her. She swore to herself she would never put herself through this again. Yet, below her anger dwelt pain so deep she was afraid to feel it.

"Could you take me to the Randolph?" she asked Dr. Harry. "I don't think I'm up for a train ride to London tonight."

"Of course," he said. "Let's go."

They said nothing while riding in Dr. Harry's Morris motor. After arriving at the hotel, he parked in front and walked her inside to register.

Once she had her key, he asked, "Do you want to talk about it?"

"No," she said. "I only want to be alone."

"I'll call for you in the morning and take you back to the City."

A small ember of light burned in the darkness reigning inside her mind and heart. "You must have other things to do."

"Nothing as important as you," he said, walking her to the lift.

"You are so kind to me."

"You deserve nothing but kindness."

"Thank you," she said.

"Would eight a.m. be too early?" he asked.

"That would be perfect," she said. "Goodnight, Dr. Harry."

"Surely it should be Harry by now."

"I like Dr. Harry. Think of it as an endearment," Catherine said with half a smile.

After he left, she took the lift up, feeling an intense need to speak with Dot. But such matters as these shouldn't be discussed long-distance where the exchange might listen in. But how could she bear the fresh pain in her soul?

Close to tears, she unlocked her door and went straight to the bathroom, where she began running a bath.

Desolation fell upon her as she thought of how there was no going on with Rafe ever again. The ups and downs were at an end.

Rafe: larger than life, striding through her barriers, dampening down her memories of the "last time." Then, Rafe: reckless and seemingly carefree stumbling through life on a wave of self-destructive drunkenness. How long would his Hispano Suiza last before he crashed it beyond repair?

Her body felt leaden as she climbed out of the bath. Drying herself listlessly, she pulled her chemise on over her head and crawled into bed. Looking at the clock, she saw that it was eleven p.m. Dot had to work tomorrow. Though she wanted her friend desperately, she knew she couldn't wake her.

The tears came at last, and sobs wracked her as her sorrow and anger hollowed her out with the relentless blade of memory. And there were no answers. She couldn't keep waiting for Rafe to find his strength. Especially now that she knew what he really thought of her.

But how can I live without the hope of him?

Never again, she promised herself. Never again. He has no respect for me at all.

Chapter Twenty-Five

When she woke heavy-eyed in the morning, she washed and dressed in last night's gown, situating the scarf over her head to cover the bald spot. What would Rafe think when he woke up in jail? She was very glad she hadn't had to face him that morning but knew her reprieve was only temporary. Her heart was leaden with hurt and hopelessness. How was she going to go forward from here?

At ten minutes to eight, she went down, checked out of the hotel, and waited for Dr. Harry in the lobby. As she sat on the camel-backed sofa, she suddenly remembered poor Professor Williams. Had he died?

"I checked on St. John at the jail," Dr. Harry said after greeting her. "He's still asleep."

"He'll be fine. Don't worry about him. He always lands on his feet," she said bitterly. Poor Dr. Harry was sporting a black eye.

They walked out to his Morris. "Have you found out from anyone how Dr. Williams is this morning?" she asked.

"I rang the infirmary. He's stable and conscious. I imagine they're analyzing his stomach contents and his blood."

A tiny bit of her gloom lifted. "Well, that's good news anyway." She smacked her forehead. "I just remembered! Jennie left something for me at the porter's desk. She found it in Doctor

Chenowith's rooms. Can we retrieve it before we leave for London?"

"Of course. The resourceful Jennie."

* * *

Catherine retrieved a brown paper parcel from Hobbs. It was in the shape of a book.

Once she was back in Dr. Harry's Morris, she opened it, heart thumping.

It was a faded pink silk covered volume. Jennie had included a note.

I found this between the mattress and the springs in Dr. C's room. I thought it might be important.

"Oh, golly," said Catherine. "A journal! What a find!"

Opening it at random, she came upon a date some three years earlier. "This goes completely against the grain, to read another's private thoughts," she said. "But if we're lucky it will help us to find her murderer."

Paging forward, she came to the present year, but to her surprise, the words of the journal were replaced by squiggles, dots, and dashes. "This must be shorthand. It looks like it starts a few months ago."

"She obviously was afraid someone would come across it."

"She was scared. At a guess, I'd say this is what she didn't want to tell even Miss Siddons. It must be the bit that concerns Somerville. It continues clear through to the end."

"Do you know anyone who reads shorthand?"

"Yes. Fortunately, Dot does. She took a course when we left college because she thought she would only be able to get a job as a secretary. She learned typing and shorthand."

"Why don't you go back a bit? It can't hurt, and maybe we can put the shorthand in context that way."

"I saw a bit back here a few years about 'H.' I suppose that might mean Sir Herbert."

"Why don't you read it aloud to me," Sir Harry asked. "If you can read while I'm driving."

"All right. Let's see if I can find it again." She looked back for three years. Dr. Chenowith had not written terribly often. She found the entry written in peacock blue ink.

She began to read.

> *I have given my everything to H for more years than I'd like to count. He knows me better than anyone on this earth. And now he has become engaged to one of my Undergraduates! A mere girl! What does he see in her? She has no intellectual powers beyond the obvious! But aha! She has money and she has looks. I thought Herbert was a different sort of male. I didn't think him swayed by those obvious gambits. We have shared everything. If what we had wasn't love, then I should like to know what love is! I have years of letters I could show her. Worst of all, little Miss Ackerman thinks she is a poet! Not if I have anything to say about it.*

"It looks to have been written at the time of Margery's marriage. I almost feel sorry for her, but her jealously made her a bit short-sighted. Sir Herbert is truly in love with Margery and remains so to this day."

"How long after that did she marry Waddell?"

"I'm afraid we'll have to wait until we get to London. Reading this while riding in the car is making me a bit sick."

"I'm sorry. You must stop then. It won't be that long until we're in London."

She was silent during the rest of the drive, unwilling to burden her companion with her thoughts. Thinking of Agatha Chenowith's heartbreak made her dwell on her own. It hurt so terribly to know how Rafe thought of her. Trying unsuccessfully to get her mind off him, she watched the summer landscape go by without taking it in.

Dr. Harry had once called him "the idle rich," and she had protested. But that's exactly what Rafe was. And he had every intention of pulling her into that life with him. She cringed when she thought how willing she had been. But there was more to Rafe. Wasn't there?

Why had she put off ringing her brother? He would have reported on their life in Kenya. But she hadn't wanted to know. She must get in touch with him when they got to the flat. Putting it off wasn't going to change things.

As always happened on occasions such as this, she remembered childhood—back before Rafe had discovered alcohol. She and Rafe and William had spent their summer days on the beach below her Cornwall home. Fishing, sailing, swimming—they had been brown as berries, and her poor mother had despaired of Catherine's complexion. They had played Red Indians. Rafe and William had even constructed a teepee. Her mother didn't know, but she had even ridden bareback across the tops of the cliffs. When he was feeling particularly affectionate, Rafe still called her "Squaw."

But she must consign their childhood connection to the past. She was fully grown, and childhood memories were just that and nothing more. Rafe had grown into a man she didn't want to know anymore. She kept telling herself that. Over and over.

By the time they reached her flat, Catherine was steeped in melancholy. She greeted Cherry and asked if there was any food in the flat.

"Not much other than tinned soup, miss. But I can go down to the bakery and get some sandwiches to go with it."

"That would be spiffing. Thank you. Any messages?"

"Mr. St. John rang. He said he would try again later. Lady Margery also rang. No message."

Turning to Dr. Harry, she said, "Make yourself comfortable.

I am going to change out of this dress and ring my brother. Then we can dig into the journal."

"I can get started on the journal," he said. "If you don't mind."

"That's a good idea. Thank you."

* * *

She castigated her brother for not ringing her when he got home. "Darling, you're not in a funk, are you?"

"More or less," he said. "Thinking of going down to see the parents. For some reason, London doesn't hold much appeal for me right now."

"I'm sorry. You aren't missing Kenya, are you?"

"No. I'm glad to be back in England. But I may prefer country to city now. I've been racketing around since I got home—you know seeing all the friends. Doesn't particularly appeal anymore."

"Will you come 'round tonight? I'd love to see you, and I need to talk to you."

"About Rafe? What's he done now?"

"Only the usual."

"Well, I'm sorry, Old Lady. Matter of fact, I've got something on I can't get out of tonight."

"Just tell me, then. Was he drinking a lot in Africa?"

"You didn't think he'd give it up, did you?"

"He promised he'd changed," she said, her heart aching.

"Well, he sobered up a bit the last month before we sailed. But other than that, it was pretty much as usual. He's not good husband material, Cat."

"So I've decided. Thanks, Wills. Come 'round before you go down to Cornwall."

"I will. Promise."

They rang off. Since she had only the one telephone, Dr. Harry had overheard the conversation.

"The idea was that he was going to Kenya to sober up," she told him. "Apparently, he didn't until the last couple of months.

I'm worried about my brother. He's not himself. I've been so pre-occupied with Rafe and this murder I haven't given him a thought. I guess I had just expected him to call me. He usually does when he gets back from a trip."

"Are you close to your family?"

"Not really. But I'm closer to William than I am to my parents. We were boarding school kids."

Cherry entered and laid out luncheon.

"Is your brother not well?" he asked.

"His health is indifferent. He's going to go down to Cornwall. London doesn't agree with him."

"I'm sorry. St. John couldn't have been the best company in Kenya if he was anything like he was last night."

"You're right. But they used to be great friends. My brother brought him home for every Long Vacation from the time they were ten. Even when they were at Oxford. I'm sensing that Rafe has turned some kind of a corner. He has never talked about me or to me the way he did last night. And he has certainly never hit me."

"If he is an abusive drunk, I think it was bound to happen sometime. I don't understand how someone sensible like you could have spent so long thinking he would change."

Catherine sat down on the sofa and looked at the picture of Rafe that sat on her desk. Dr. Harry's words hurt.

"I don't expect you to understand, but you see, I was a very solitary child. For whatever reason, I never connected to my parents or my brother. I was separate. I lived in my own little world."

"I can see it," said Dr. Harry. "Were you a writer, even then?"

"I was. I scribbled stories, away in my room. I never showed them to anyone."

"Not even William?"

"No. But then Rafe came, I was smitten by his vitality. He was unlike anyone in my very strait-laced, vanilla-colored family. He had a smile that took in the whole world. Suddenly, I wasn't separate anymore. I connected with him. I shared my life and my stories with him. I lived for those summers when he was there."

"And you're still connected?"

She felt the raw place inside where she had cut Rafe out the night before. It still stung. "Not after last night. I tore him out last night, but no one will ever understand the cost to me. I still believed one day he would change. I guess that in that one way, I had never grown up. Now I am separate again. It hurts abominably."

Catherine couldn't believe she was confiding all of this to Dr. Harry, but Dot wasn't available, and she had to express it. Probably, if she had been alone today, she would have put it in a poem.

"I'm sorry." Dr. Harry reached for her hand. "I understand. I am honored that you would tell me. As wonderful as my parents are, they have each other. I have always felt separate, as well."

"For as long as I remember my childhood, Rafe will always be part of my life. Did you ever connect with anyone?"

"Tennyson. King Arthur. The Victorians. Prince Albert. I lived in my head," said Dr. Harry. "Give me a book, and I felt comforted and secure."

"Stories have amazing power. Look at how batty Dr. Williams is about Teutonic Legends."

"I think Hitler must have been, as well. And now he's using his pet theories to ensnare a nation, cultivating the Aryan myth."

She shivered. "It's diabolical, isn't it. I need to set my little tragedy to one side and call Dot to see if she has shorthand. Maybe she can meet us at the Spot again tonight after work."

"That was quite a jolly pub. I can't even imagine it on Friday night!"

"I know."

The telephone rang.

"Cat?" She heard a much sobered Rafe.

Dr. Harry stood, as though to leave the room, but Catherine knew there was nowhere for him to go. She motioned for him to be seated. "I have nothing to say to you, Rafe. Now or in future. Good-bye."

"But, Cat, it was just a few drinks! How on earth did you get them to lock me up?"

"It was their suggestion. You hit both me and Dr. Harry. A number of policemen witnessed it."

"I *hit you?*"

"Yes. After saying horrid things to me. I don't want to see you again, Rafe. Ever. Stay away from me, or I will swear out a complaint against you for assault. There were plenty of witnesses."

"I'm sure I didn't mean anything I said. But I'll stay away from liquor. Even wine," he said.

It took every bit of her will, but she managed to say, "No. You won't. Now leave me be." She rang off.

She couldn't finish her chicken sandwich or tomato soup. Instead, before she could think any more about Rafe, she called Dot at work.

"Darling, you know shorthand, don't you?"

"Yes. At least I did. I learned it in my secretarial course when I thought I should have to earn my living that way. Haven't used it in quite a while. Why?"

"Jennie found me Dr. Chenowith's journal. Toward the end, just where we are the most desperate to know what it says, she starts writing in shorthand, I think. Just a bunch of squiggles and some random letters I think must be abbreviations here and there. I was wondering if we could bring it to you tonight at the Spot after you get off work."

"Smashing! Who's 'we?' You and Rafe?"

"No. Dr. Harry."

"Perfect. I'll see you then, darling."

While Dr. Harry was finishing eating, they discussed what he had been able to read while she was changing clothes.

"You were right. I think Chenowith married Waddell on the rebound. They were married in a London registry office and honeymooned at Lake Como in Italy. She doesn't say a lot about him.

Most of what she writes is about her poetry and her students. I had just gotten to the part where 'C' starts to change when you came in."

"Suppose you read it aloud to me until we get to the pothooks and things."

"Pothooks?"

"Shorthand."

"Okay," Dr. Harry agreed.

The account he read was much as they had imagined, but there were no names. "C" had fallen under the influence of "B" whom, her husband claimed, had a brilliant mind and complete understanding of "what this country needs." "C" became so deeply involved in this that he soon had no time left for Agatha Chenowith. She asked him to choose between "B" and her, and he chose "B."

She decided to separate from Waddell, divorce not being an option for her unless she could prove adultery. From that time forward, the journal had been encrypted in shorthand, except for some abbreviations.

Catherine's heart still pained her, but she forced her mind to the task of trying to decrypt the abbreviations.

The first few pages were all about "C " and something called "ABH."

"C is still Christopher, of course," said Dr. Harry. "And based on what we found out on the Isle, would you say ABH might be the Aryan Brotherhood? It's just a stab in the dark."

"I think you very well could be right. Let's consider it until we find out more from Dot. This is so frustrating!"

"It could easily have been some ingenious cipher and then we wouldn't have had a chance to figure it out. Why do you suppose she switched to shorthand?" asked Dr. Harry.

"Obviously she didn't want her husband to read it. But if she were living at Somerville exclusively by then, I wouldn't think there was much chance of that. Maybe she didn't want someone at Somerville to get hold of it," Catherine speculated.

"That makes sense. It must be explosive stuff. Look, there's the letter 'B' repeated throughout. Do you think it's connected to the GBH?"

"This is futile. I suggest we do something else until Dot deciphers it. We're just wasting our time." And her thoughts, not fully engaged, kept drifting back to Rafe.

"You're right. And I'm uneasy. I keep thinking Rafe is going to show up here," he said.

"I know. Me, too." She went to the window and looked out. "It's not raining, nor likely to. Let's go to the Kew Gardens and take a walk."

They put the journal in a big string bag Catherine kept for shopping and rang for a cab to take them to the gardens. Once there, they sought out Windhurst where they were able to ramble through the woods as though they were in the country.

"You were right, you know," said Catherine. "Rafe is a member of the 'idle rich.' I just didn't want to admit it."

"He doesn't have a worthy avocation?"

"Sport, aviation . . . those are his interests."

"I can't see him being any kind of husband for a woman like you, Catherine. You've grown in different directions."

"Not unless he were to be sober. But I am giving up that dream. He would have to do it for himself and not for me. And, at bottom, he really doesn't want to do it. He's never grown up, I guess."

The realization hurt, but for the first time, she believed it was true. And she needed to hold on to that belief.

They strolled the gardens the rest of the afternoon hours, sometimes in silence and sometimes Dr. Harry would repeat stanzas of poetry from the Romantic poets about the glories of nature. Catherine appreciated the effort to keep her entertained instead of brooding. She enjoyed the scent of green growing things that she missed when she was in the city, but she grew progressively more anxious. She knew she hadn't seen the last of Rafe, and she worried about their next encounter.

At length, after several hours of rambling, they took the

Underground to Fleet Street. Friday night at the Spot was even busier than the last time they had met there. This time, Dot was not waiting at a table. She was engrossed in conversation with a man in a white shirt, loosened tie, and open jacket. Catherine took him to be a Fleet Street journalist like most of the patrons.

Dot was biting her lip, her eyes fixed on the man's face. Concerned, Catherine walked up to her. The moment her friend saw her, she signaled her conversant to stop speaking.

"Thank you," she said to him. Then taking Catherine's arm, she said, "We need to go somewhere quiet."

Dr. Harry had joined them. He noted Dot's demeanor. "What's going on?"

"I've got some rotten news. It just came across on the ticker. We need to go somewhere private. My office, I think. Everyone pours out of there at six."

Puzzled, Catherine followed her friend out of the pub into Fleet Street. It was mad with foot and road traffic. Dodging fellow pedestrians, she followed a resolute Dot as they walked against the flow of the crowd down to the corner where they turned into a quieter street. At the Simpson Building, they entered and walked up a flight of stairs to a pair of glass doors. Dot opened them. The Arrow Advertising Agency featured a large main area crammed with desks and telephones. Behind that was a row of offices. Dot took them into one of these and closed the door. She perched on the edge of the cluttered desk behind which was an Art Deco picture of an enormous ocean liner looking like it was sailing right into the room.

"Take that seat, Cat." Dot indicated the chair facing the desk. Dr. Harry took the seat next to her.

"I just heard. I'm sorry to tell you, darling, but according to my newspaperman, it just came across the ticker. Rafe crashed his plane into the Thames. A couple of fishermen saw it happen and were able to rescue him before it went down. But he's unconscious. He's in St. Thomas's."

The blow hit her in the chest, where her heart seemed to pause and then started pounding furiously. She felt the blood leave her head and the room shrank to a pin-dot. Then blackness.

When she came back to consciousness, she was stretched out on the floor of Dot's office, and she knew she was going to be sick. She choked out a warning, and Dr. Harry raced for the dust bin which he held next to her. Fortunately, the feeling subsided.

"Breathe," Dot said. "Take deep breaths."

"Oh, Rafe," she moaned. "What have you done?"

"The fishermen are enjoying their role as heroes of the hour," said Dot. "They're giving quite an account."

"Did he hurt anyone else?" Catherine asked.

"No. He missed the bridges," said Dot. "Rather a miracle."

"I imagine . . ." started Dr. Harry. He shook his head and stopped.

"No," said Catherine. "Continue."

"I just thought that he might be under arrest for 'reckless endangerment.'"

"He certainly should be," said Catherine firmly. "And I'm going to tell him so." A small sob escaped her. "If he wakes up."

She struggled to her elbows, thankful she was wearing trousers. "Please help me," she said to Dr. Harry. "I need to get up."

"I don't want to cause you unnecessary stress," said Dr. Harry. "But do you suppose this is some spectacular suicide attempt?"

Catherine was sitting now. Anger and outrage wouldn't even let her consider the suggestion. "I really doubt it. I'm sure it seemed like a tremendous lark. That is more typical."

"That sounds about right," said Dot.

It was time Dot knew about Rafe's fall from grace. "Last night. Dr. Williams gave a sherry party. He went with me. A person has to drink a lot of sherry to get drunk, but he did it. He made a dreadful scene." She looked at Dr. Harry. "He spent the night in jail. I wonder if that will come out."

"Cat, the man's dangerous. There's no getting around it. This isn't Kenya, where there are acres of open space. He could have killed a lot of people," said Dot.

"Do you feel you must see him?" asked Dr. Harry.

Catherine consulted her violently veering emotions. "I think I must. I'm so terribly afraid he might die," she said. Then as though it explained everything, she said, "I've never fainted before."

"Can you stand?" Dot asked.

Catherine gingerly got to her feet. She picked up the string bag containing the journal and handed it to Dot. "You two go on to the pub. I can take a cab to the hospital."

"Are you crazy, darling?" asked Dot. "You just fainted. I'm coming with you."

"I am, as well," said Dr. Harry.

* * *

St. Thomas's at Southwark was the largest teaching hospital in London, and Catherine was very glad that was where they had taken Rafe. When she inquired after him, she was told he was still unconscious.

"He is not able to have visitors in his condition," said the sister at the reception table.

"But, I'm his fiancé," said Catherine, lying without even a twinge of conscience.

The woman appeared to consider. Finally, she said, "Well, I suppose you might help rather than hinder, in that case. But your friends must stay here."

Catherine climbed the wide stairs to Rafe's ward with trepidation. Was he going to die? She asked herself for the umpteenth time.

Chapter Twenty-Six

The ward extended over the entire floor. There were perhaps twenty beds. Most of them were full.

Her first glimpse of Rafe's unconscious face rent her heart. He had a white bandage on his forehead and both his eyes had reddish bruises. His arm was in a complete cast from the shoulder to the hand.

She sat in the chair next to his bed, taking his good hand.

"Rafe, you foolish boy. Why would you do such a crazy thing?"

A nursing sister overheard her remark as she passed by. She said with some asperity, "He's not a boy. He's a man. And it is my understanding that he could have killed many people if he had hit one of the bridges. It was indeed a foolish, drunken stunt."

Catherine quailed at her words. "How do you know he was drunk?" she asked.

"He reeked of it. His blood-alcohol level was astronomical."

The sister's words smote Catherine's heart. Drunk. Again. She let go of Rafe's hand.

"Is he going to regain consciousness, do you think?" she asked.

"I would say so."

At that moment, Rafe blinked his eyes. Spotting Catherine, he smiled. "I knew you didn't mean it. I knew I'd get you back."

She took in his words, but it was a moment before she

understood. Anger soared through her body. "You did this because of me?" Catherine got to her feet. She spoke with barely controlled ire. It was an effort to keep from yelling. "Are you insane? You could have killed dozens of people. You were stinking drunk. You will never grow up. I don't think I will ever forgive you, and I can only thank God that I never, ever married you."

She knew she had to sever herself from him completely and for good. Standing, she walked off the ward, anxious to find her friends.

* * *

"How's Rafe?" asked Dot.

"Conscious. I found out he was drunk."

"Of course he was, darling," said Dot.

"I am absolutely finished with him. I hope he gets arrested and put in jail."

"That didn't do the trick last night," said Dr. Harry.

"Let's go somewhere and transcribe that journal. I don't want to give him one more second of my concern."

Exiting the hospital, they took the Underground to Piccadilly and went into Lyon's Corner House. There Catherine ordered Shepherd's Pie and ate heartily. Her attempt to forge ahead with her life was folly, however, as she was forced to race to the WC, where she lost everything in the toilet. It wasn't going to be easy to put Rafe behind her, but she was going to go on trying.

The others ate, unaware of her distress, and when they were finished, Dot had a go at the journal. From her briefcase, she extracted a tablet and began transcribing.

To begin with, Chenowith gave an account of her decision to separate from Waddell because of his association with the noxious Aryan Brotherhood which was spelled out in shorthand. Dr. Harry had been correct.

Chenowith especially abhorred his association with "B," who seemed to be a don at another Oxford College. Abhorring their secret meetings at anonymously rented digs in Woodstock, Chenowith went on to decry their blatant anti-Semitism, justified by the myths of Aryan strength and superiority.

Later in the journal, she recorded that to her great shock, she had discovered the affiliation of "SD" with the group. Up until that point, she had been gathering evidence with intent to expose the group, but now she never could because of the connection with "S."

"Oh, Crikey," said Dot. "What do you suppose "S" means?"

Catherine's thoughts flew back to what Miss Siddons had said. "Probably Somerville. Her friend said she was concerned about something at Somerville."

"And SD?" asked Dot.

"SD," repeated Catherine. Then everything became clear. Her encounters with Dean Andrews. "SD." Somerville Dean. "Of course. The Dean." And with that discovery, her brain switched almost fully from her preoccupation with private matters to the task at hand.

"We can never prove it, though," said Dot. "Not with just this journal."

"She was at Dr. Williams's soiree last night," said Dr. Harry.

At this point, they decided to take a break and adjourn to Catherine's flat for coffee. They settled their bill and took a cab. Cherry greeted them with the news that Lady Margery had rung again, as had the Oxford Detective Chief Inspector Marsh.

The policeman had left a number, and Catherine put a trunk call through to him.

"Miss Tregowyn, do you have any reason to suspect Dean Andrews of poisoning Dr. Williams?"

Catherine bit her lip. *Crikey*, as Dot would say.

"Uh, he was poisoned?"

"We found arsenic in his tea. Dr. Williams has regained consciousness and he claims his latest batch of tea was a gift from Dean Andrews. He can trace the beginning of his stomach ailments to the new batch of tea. Those ailments culminated in his terrible illness last night."

"Is that typical of arsenic poisoning?" she asked. "That it builds like that?"

"Yes. It can."

"Well, I do believe Dr. Andrews is guilty of something. You see, Jennie, my scout at Somerville, brought me Dr. Chenowith's journal. It's in shorthand. We are just trying to transcribe it. There is a reference to a person at Somerville she was protecting, and we think that person was Dean Andrews. But there's no proof or anything. She just says 'SD.'"

"What was she protecting her from?"

"The reason Chenowith separated from her husband was because of his involvement in that Nazi group Dr. Bascombe told you about. SD was another person involved. She was distressed because that SD was from S, which we took to mean Somerville. I have had some unfortunate encounters with the dean, ending in her banning me from the campus because I wouldn't give up my investigations."

"But that doesn't explain why she would poison Dr. Williams, even if what you surmise is true."

"I know. I don't know what she was up to."

"I think it sounds as though you had better bring that journal up to Oxford and turn it over to us. I read shorthand. It was part of my training when I was a sergeant."

Catherine sighed. She had been afraid of that. "We will bring it up to you tomorrow."

"How is Mr. St. John doing today?" he asked, obviously trying to sound casual.

"You haven't heard?"

"Heard what?"

She said, "It will be on the BBC tonight, I'm certain. He crashed his plane into the Thames."

"Crikey. Drunk again?" the policeman asked.

"I'm afraid so."

After a renewal of her promise to turn over the journal, she rang off.

"Well, people, we must make hay while the sun shines. He wants the journal tomorrow morning."

"What was that about the dean?" queried Dot.

"It appears she gave Dr. Williams the tea laced with arsenic. That's what caused his collapse last night. He's conscious now, and he told the police about the tea."

"That's truly weird," said Dr. Harry. "I wonder if it has anything to do with this Nazi business?"

"You ponder that. I must quickly ring Marge. This is the second time she's rung."

Catherine put through another trunk call, this one to Somerset.

"Darling!" Margery greeted her. "Rafe is all over the news!"

"Don't remind me," she said. "I'm trying to put him behind me. Is that why you rang?"

"No, as a matter of fact. I wanted to tell you that Herbert finally told me what he's been holding back."

"Did he? It's good news, I imagine."

"The best, although it didn't immediately seem that way. You see, Chenowith had been blackmailing him. Apparently, they had an affair once upon a time, and she was threatening to show me his letters. The silly man didn't want me to be hurt by them, even though it was eons before we were married."

"Men *are* so silly sometimes," said Catherine.

"The night she was murdered, Dr. C. wanted Herbert to meet her at the chapel with the latest payment. He thought she was being coy and wanted to renew their relations. He wanted to put an end to all her manipulations. But when he got there, she wasn't anywhere about."

Catherine thought of the corpse of 'Dr. C.' hidden under the bench. "I can understand why he didn't want to open up about that. The body was concealed. She was probably dead by then. Did he see anyone?"

"He saw the figure of a man, but he was hatted and coated and far away. He couldn't identify him."

"He might not be the murderer anyway," she said. "But I'm so glad that things are in the open between you. And thanks for telling me about it. I can cross him off the list."

"Yes, thank heavens. And thank you for listening. If you want to talk about Rafe again, I'm happy to listen."

"I'm determined to get over him for good this time but thank you anyway."

When she had rung off, she informed her colleagues about Sir Herbert's confession to his wife. "So, if he can be believed, the only person remaining on our official list is Dr. Waddell. Let's see if there's anything else interesting before we have to turn this journal over to the Detective Chief Inspector."

There followed in the journal accounts of various individuals identified only by initials who were affiliated with the Aryan Brotherhood. They hadn't the least hope of identifying them. However, it emerged that "B" was their leader. And finally, Dr. Chenowith revealed that she was convinced that "B" was employed by the Germans as a spy. She stated her intention of confronting him with her knowledge. It wasn't hard to see that she intended another spot of blackmail.

"Chicken Little, I may be," said Dr. Harry. "I am going to push for Marsh to turn this over to the SIS."

"That's where it belongs," said Catherine.

Dot seconded her.

They were finished with the journal. Cherry had long ago retired, so Catherine made coffee. Dr. Harry said that he would stay at the Christ Church Alumni Club, but Dot declared her intention of staying with Catherine, for which she was grateful.

She said goodnight to Dr. Harry with a surprising amount of regret. He promised to take the journal to the police in the morning.

Catherine kissed the tips of her fingers and placed them under his blackened eye. "Thank you for listening today," she said.

"Any time," he promised. Kissing his fingers, he placed them on the bruise on her chin.

* * *

Dot prescribed a long hot bath for her friend. "You've had a terrible day, darling. Go wash it down the drain."

"I scarcely know where I am," Catherine said. "Between Rafe and Chenowith."

"Not to mention dear Dr. Harry."

"Oh, please, Dot. Don't start with that. I'm far too drained."

During a long soak in her tub, she was no closer to understanding the mystery surrounding the two murders, Dean Andrews' actions, or the train wreck of her love life. She should have skipped the coffee. Her brain was on some kind of super drive.

Afterward, Dot administered her patented foot rub, and they had a little ceremony where they burned Rafe's photograph in one of her ashtrays. It was a sad business.

"I think in these last years, since Rafe first went away to Oxford, my connection to him has been rather a connection to the person I made up. He was my ideal, and I was regularly heartbroken when I was face to face with the real man. I loved a figment of my imagination. It's really not his fault that he didn't live up to it," Catherine said.

"I don't think anyone could have," said Dot.

"Probably not. He was my childhood hero. I guess it's time for me to grow up and quit expecting to meet my other half."

"Let's not draw cosmic conclusions from one broken romance," warned Dot. "It's time for you to get some sleep."

A tear escaped and rolled down Catherine's cheek as she went meekly to bed.

* * *

Cherry woke her in the morning. "You have a phone call, miss. I told her you were not taking calls yet, but she was most insistent."

"She? Who is it?"

"It's the dean of your college, miss. Dean Andrews."

"Oh, good heavens!" Catherine sat straight up in bed. "She's supposed to be in police custody."

"It's a trunk call from Oxford. You had best hurry."

Catherine threw on her dressing gown and went to the telephone in her sitting room.

"Hello?"

"Miss Tregowyn, this is Dean Andrews." The voice was clipped and harsh.

"Yes, Dean. How can I help you?"

"I have something important to discuss with you. It concerns the future of our country. It is far more serious than you know. I would like to meet with you in person. There will be many like-minded people there. We have formed a group. But you must not tell anyone about it."

Catherine's brain reeled.

Is the woman mad? She just tried to poison poor Dr. Williams, and she wants to talk to me about the future of our country? She must know she is wanted by the police!

Stalling, she asked, "Why do you want to talk to me, of all people?"

"Because you understand the damage that has been done. Two people have been killed. He must be stopped, and the work must go forward."

The dean's voice was familiar, but Catherine began to realize the woman was in the grip of some strange mania. She was raving mad. But it sounded as though she knew who the murderer was. Or was this all a clever trap?

"I would like to talk to you. Where shall we meet?"

"Have you something to write with?"

Catherine gripped the pencil next to her message tablet. "Yes."

"I'm at a flat on Kingston Road. Do you know where that is?"

"Past Somerville. On the way to Woodstock."

"Yes. It's Number Seventeen. Flat B."

"As you know, I'm in London. It will take some time for me to get there."

"I'll be waiting." The dean rang off.

Catherine sagged into her desk chair. Her brain raced. What should she do? First, she should inform the police and Dr. Harry. Then she should wake Dot.

Catherine picked up the telephone again and placed a trunk call to Detective Chief Inspector Marsh. When it finally went through, she was told he had left word that he wasn't to be disturbed. He was in an important meeting.

Frustrated, she told the sergeant, "This is Catherine Tregowyn. Tell him that Dean Andrews is at Number Seventeen Kingston Road, Flat B. I'm coming up from London and am going to meet her there. I want to speak to her before he arrests her. She knows who the murderer is."

"Yes, miss. I will give him the message as soon as he's available."

She rang off and then called Dr. Harry's club. He had already left.

Dot was already awake sitting in the kitchen reading the *News of the World*.

"Rafe's father has despatched him off to Kenya. Straight out of the hospital. I guess he was afraid he'd be charged with something," her friend announced.

Catherine refused the bait. "You'll never guess who called and wants to meet with me," she said.

"Who?"

"Dean Andrews. She's clearly off her head." Catherine repeated their conversation. "I called Marsh, but he is unavailable at the moment. I left a message."

"Call Harry. He can help you decide what to do, Cat. You can't just walk into a trap," said Dot.

"The dean is a little old crazy woman. She can't do me any harm," said Catherine.

"Sound like famous last words to me. Crikey! Who would believe the dean was ravers?"

Frustrated, she asked Dot, "Can you motor me up to Oxford?"

"Of course. I wouldn't dream of letting you go alone."

* * *

By the time Catherine and Dot had dressed and eaten their breakfast buns, it was already nearly ten o'clock. Feeling anxious, lest the dean should change her mind, she urged Dot to drive as fast as she could.

"You'll pay my fine if I get stopped by the traffic police?" Dot asked.

"Of course!"

Subsequently, they made good time to Oxford. Calling in at the police station first, they found that Marsh was still unavailable. Catherine left another message.

Dot drove her to Seventeen Kingston Road and promised she would find Dr. Harry if at all possible. Catherine was trying to quell the nervous fluttering in her stomach as she pressed the buzzer for Flat B. Was she doing the right thing?

She had to find out who the murderer was.

The dean answered, looking perfectly normal with her hair in its customary bun at the nape of her neck. She wore a serviceable navy blue skirt and a white blouse, her glasses held by a chain around her neck. She frowned at Catherine's trousers.

"Come in, Miss Tregowyn," she said. "We have much to discuss."

The flat's sitting room was queerly furnished with sofas and chairs all pushed against the walls, and a big space in the middle of the floor.

"Where are the others?" Catherine asked alarmed.

"They will be here shortly. I have called a meeting, but I wanted to speak with you first. Now, my dear," the dean began, her hands folded in her lap, "I am sure that you are very concerned as am I for the future of our country. Any thinking person must be alarmed at the harm the Labor Government is doing to Britain. Its policies are only weakening the people, not helping them! It is past time for action before the whole country languishes and dies."

Catherine decided a nod would be the best response. Her stomach was in knots.

"Socialism is completely the wrong platform for any kind of change. Our heritage dictates that we have a strong, virile government with a steady hand on the helm of our Empire. We have no shared history with Russia and the Communists, but we have a great and ancient history with Germany, the other great Aryan nation.

"As weak socialists, we would be in direct conflict with our brother country. There would be a hellish collision—a great war on our own soil which could totally destroy Britain.

"There are thousands of our class, Miss Tregowyn, who feel this way. Here at Oxford, some of us have established the Aryan Brotherhood."

"Pardon me, dean, but how do you fit into the Brotherhood, being a woman?" asked Catherine in genuine puzzlement.

"I am at the head of the movement. But, as you have so aptly pointed out, I am a woman. I have men who work for me.

"However, lately, there has been a great disturbance. Men have their uses, but they are far too hot-headed. As you know, only too well, two people have been murdered. Bill has clearly gone 'round the bend and must be stopped. He would destroy us before we gain our strength and begin to sway public opinion. He has the blind arrogance of a male—he thinks violence is the only solution."

Bill? Who is Bill? The "B" of Dr. Chenowith's journal?

"I guess I am a little confused about what you want me to do."

"I want you to see that Bill is arrested for murder and hanged.

That is the role you have cast yourself for, isn't it? I have invited him to meet us here before the others."

Her words took Catherine's breath away. The dean was executing a power play. If Bill was B, he was the head of the Brotherhood. How did she expect Catherine to arrest Bill without involving the police?

At that moment, she heard the front door open. At last, Detective Chief Inspector Marsh.

Instead, in strode Dr. Wesley Williams.

Chapter Twenty-Seven

"Hello, Charlotte. I see the police haven't picked you up yet. We need to expedite that, I suppose." He caught sight of Catherine. "Miss Tregowyn! What a lovely surprise. Have you decided to join the ranks?"

Wesley Williams. Something hush-hush in the government. Was he spying on the Brotherhood from the inside?

Catherine stood up. "Thank heavens you've recovered," she said, shaking his hand. "The dean was just familiarizing me with the tenets of the Brotherhood."

"She is going to see that you get arrested, Bill," the dean said to her astonishment. It was as though a kaleidoscope turned. The facts rearranged themselves in Catherine's head in an instant.

Bill? The Bill of Chenowith's journal? The head of the organization? The murderer?

"You may leave now, Miss Tregowan," said the dean. "You have your assignment."

Instead, Catherine blurted, "Is she right? Are you called Bill?"

"Since childhood, I'm afraid," the man admitted with a feral grin.

Catherine saw him suddenly as another madman. He wasn't the "sweetheart" of her thoughts, but a killer. In her hubris, she had dismissed him as harmless. He was anything but.

"I understand why you murdered Agatha Chenowith," she said. "She was going to blackmail you, wasn't she? But why Christopher Waddell? He was a proper Nazi."

"Ah, but he was a husband, first. He wanted to shop me for Agatha's murder and take over the Brotherhood. Just as Charlotte is attempting to do." He looked at the woman, who sat completely composed with her hands in her lap. "She's crazy as a loon, you know."

"Oh," Catherine said. "Are you certain you are quite well, yourself?"

"The arsenic has wreaked havoc with my stomach, but I shouldn't be getting any worse, at least. Now, what to do with the two of you?"

"I have always thought you were such a dear man," Catherine marveled. "I wouldn't expect you to fall for Hitler's line."

"He's the chosen vessel. A remarkable man. A true visionary. If we don't join with him now, he will take this country apart, brick by brick, and then he will rebuild it to suit the gods. Like he's remaking Germany."

"The gods?" she exclaimed. It was easier to believe that the man was deceived in Hitler than to swallow that he actually embraced the madness. "You truly believe that stuff?"

"I suppose you believe in the other myth."

Guessing he referred to Christianity, she said, "It's no myth. Don't deceive yourself."

"Now, let's not argue. It's so uncivilized."

"Whereas murder is not? What are you going to do now?" Catherine asked, trying to keep the quiver from her voice. "People know I'm here."

"How good of you to inform me of that fact. I guess we'll have to make 'here' disappear."

Catherine looked at the man. The madness was there in his eyes. They were darting madly about the room, looking for inspiration.

I'm five foot seven. He's five foot five if that. He's middle-aged. I'm young.

She began walking towards the door. She was almost there when he reached her and twisted her arm up behind her back. "You're not going anywhere, Miss Tregowyn."

The dean came up behind him, and Catherine watched over her shoulder as little Charlotte Andrews kicked the back of his knee. He collapsed. Catherine sat on the middle of his back, straddling him as he struggled. She was very glad she had worn trousers.

Opening her purse, the other woman removed a small bottle and her folded handkerchief. She opened the bottle and wet the cotton square with the liquid inside. Then she held the handkerchief to "Bill's" nose. Catherine felt him relax underneath her.

"Chloroform," the dean announced. "Help me move him to the hall cupboard."

The dean grasped the man's feet, and Catherine gripped him under his arms. Pulling him to the entry hall, they stuffed his body into the cupboard and locked the door. The dean put the key in her purse.

Wary of the hand holding the drug-sodden handkerchief, Catherine wondered what the old woman had in mind now. "Should we ring the police and tell him where they can find the murderer?" she suggested.

"At this point, he is in our power. I would rather dispose of him myself," said the dean. Going to the draperies, she began pulling them down off the windows. With the handkerchief securely looped in her belt, she heaped the drapes in the center of the carpet.

"Help me," she commanded.

Catherine didn't understand what the dean was doing but thought it best to follow her instructions at the moment. She pulled the drapes from the other window, bringing down the rod with them. She slid the draperies free. Unfortunately, she couldn't decide how she could best use the lengthy rod as a weapon. She was still considering this when she smelled the chloroform. By then, it was too late.

* * *

Smoke!

She woke up coughing. The dean was nowhere to be seen. She heard a thumping sound and realized it was Bill trying to get out of the hall closet.

Catherine knew she needed to escape but everything was black. Where was she?

Rolling over, she felt the floor beneath her. Linoleum. The WC? It must be. Her stomach rolled with nausea as she got to her hands and knees. She must find a way out. She had the answers she had sought. She must get to the police!

Crackle. Hiss. Smoke was coming through the bottom of the door.

The house is on fire!

Getting to her feet, she staggered to the right and encountered a wall. In the other direction was the toilet. She tried another way and found herself against the door. Panicked, she threw it open. A wall of flame faced her.

Adrenaline kicked in and she no longer felt drugged. But there was no way out.

"Cat! Where are you?" She heard Dot calling her from beyond the flames.

"Here!" she choked. "Don't open the cupboard! The murderer's in there!"

"Harry's here! He's coming for you!"

A shrouded shape appeared through the flame barrier. "Catherine?" She heard Dr. Harry's muffled voice.

"You're on fire!" she cried.

"It's just the blanket," he said, his voice calm as he threw it to the floor. Stamping on it, he said, "Thank God you're all right. We have to get you out of here."

"There's water in the WC behind me," she said. She found the light switch, and they threw the smoking blanket into the bathtub.

"Hurry!" the man urged. "The fire's spreading!"

She turned the bathwater on full strength and wet the blanket thoroughly. By that time, the fire was at the door of the WC.

"Here. Stand on the edge of the bathtub and wrap your legs around my waist and your arms around my shoulders. Duck. I'll put the blanket around both of us, and we'll dash it."

"Dot! Where are you?" she called.

"Here!"

Once she was in position, he wrapped them closely in the heavy, sodden blanket and ran through the flames toward the voice. She felt the searing heat through the blanket but clung to Dr. Harry for her life. When they came out the other side, Dr. Harry threw the blanket to the floor, and they both stomped out the flames.

At that moment, the firemen finally arrived, followed by the police. Catherine felt both singed and wet like the blanket on the floor. She ran into the vestibule. Marsh didn't even recognize her at first, as the firemen pulled hoses through the front door. She was in the way, but she stopped to tell Marsh, "Your murderer is in the hall cupboard. Dr. Wesley Williams. I heard him confess myself."

"Miss Tregowyn! Thank God you're all right! Who set the fire?"

"The dean," she said. "Did she get away?"

"Yes," he said. "It's my fault. I should have been available. That was unconscionable. I was transcribing the journal. You need to come outside now and get in my motor. I'll carry you all to the station."

"What about Williams? He's the 'Bill' of the journal."

"The fire seems to be under control. I'll let him sit in that cupboard until my detective constables get here."

* * *

Catherine, Dot, and Dr. Harry sat huddled under dry blankets in the police department, having given their statements. Dr. Williams was safely in custody, and the dean had been found in a tea shop around the corner from the burning flat having a cup of tea and a currant bun. She had raged against the police, telling them they would never stop "the work." Only the handcuffs subdued her.

"I'm very glad that's over," said Catherine, still shivering from shock. "I must have the worst character judgment in the world. First, Rafe, then Dr. Williams, then the dean. And we still don't know what Waddell was doing in the girls' dormitory!"

"I imagine he was trying to solve Chenowith's murder, just like we were. Only he had facts we didn't and stumbled to the truth faster."

"And the dean must have known about the journal. She was the one who burgled my flat."

"Your motorcar is outside, miss," said the constable who had been sent for Dot's motor which she'd been obliged to leave at the scene of the fire.

"Let's go then, troops," said Dot.

"Where to?" asked Catherine. "I won't be seen looking like this, but I'm starved."

"How about if I get cleaned up and grab something to tide us over?" suggested Dr. Harry. "Then I can follow you down to London."

"It's a plan," said Dot, the calmest of them all.

* * *

That evening, Catherine sat cuddled into Dr. Harry's side on her sofa. His arm was around her. Now that the adrenaline had gone, she kept nodding off, but she didn't want him to leave.

"So, what's keeping you from taking Dr. Sargent's place at Somerville?" he asked.

"I haven't thought it through, yet," she said with a huge yawn.

"Maybe this will help. I have a confession to make," he said.

252

She perked up. "And what is that?"

"I like and esteem your poetry. I admit I was a bit put out by the fact that you bested me with the Penwyth *Life* and didn't give you a fair review. I was pretty pathetic. But now that I've gotten to know you, I do feel that you can do even better. I don't think you've fully explored the depth of your talent."

A feeling like warm honey rose inside her, and she nodded against his shoulder. "You're right. I've been holding back. Cleaving to convention because I've been too afraid to expose myself completely. Afraid of Dr. Chenowith's censure, as a matter of fact."

"I suspected that. But now she and the dean are both gone from Somerville. You can settle in and make a place for yourself there. Set yourself up as an authority."

"You just want me to write good reviews of your stuff," she said with a chuckle.

"That, too," he said.

She laughed again, and he lowered his head to kiss her most thoroughly.

Umm. That's nice. Canoodling at its finest.

"I'll give it a year," she said. Then she went back to kissing Dr. Harry.

The End

Other Books by G. G. Vandagriff

Mysteries
Cankered Roots
Of Deadly Descent
Tangled Roots
Poisoned Pedigree
Hidden Branch
*

Romantic Suspense
Breaking News
Sleeping Secrets
Balkan Echo
*

Suspense
Arthurian Omen
Foggy With a Chance of Murder
*

Historical Fiction
The Last Waltz: A Novel of Love and War
Exile
Defiance
*

Regency Romances
The Duke's Undoing
The Taming of Lady Kate
Miss Braithwaite's Secret
Rescuing Rosalind
Lord Trowbridge's Angel
The Baron and the Bluestocking
Lord Grenville's Choice
Lord John's Dilemma

Lord Basingstoke's Downfall (novella)
Her Fateful Debut
His Mysterious Lady
Not an Ordinary Baronet
Love Unexpected
Miss Saunders Takes A Journey
The European Collection (anthology)
Spring in Hyde Park (anthology)
Much Ado About Lavender (novella)
*

Women's Fiction
Pieces of Paris
The Only Way to Paradise
*

Non-Fiction
Voices In Your Blood
Deliverance from Depression

ABOUT THE AUTHOR

G.G. VANDAGRIFF is a traditionally published author who has gone Indie. She loves the Regency period, having read Georgette Heyer over and over since she was a teen. Currently, she has thirteen Regency titles in print, but she writes other things, too. In 2010, she received the Whitney Award for Best Historical Novel for her epic, *The Last Waltz: A Novel of Love and War.* She has also written Romantic Suspense, and her mystery fans are always urging her to write another book featuring her wacky genealogical sleuths, Alex and Briggie. Her latest work is a 1930's Golden Age mystery series.

She studied writing at Stanford University and received her master's degree at George Washington University. Though she has lived in many places throughout the country, she now lives with her husband, David, a lawyer and a writer, on the bench of the Wasatch Mountains in Utah. From her office, she can see a beautiful valley, a lake, and another mountain range. She and David have three children and seven adventurous grandchildren.

Visit G.G. at her website http://ggvandagriff.com, where you can read her blog, keep track of all her books and her work in progress, and sign up to receive her newsletter. She has an author page on Facebook (G.G. Vandagriff-Author) and on Goodreads and Amazon. She loves to hear from her fans!

Made in the USA
Coppell, TX
17 January 2020